The Toasters Club

Dr. Ott and the Bots

by

Mark Fairbanks

First Edition

Copyright © 2018 by Mark C. Fairbanks Case #: 1-6895386191

September 2018

Artwork by Madison Bang

First Edition September 2024

Contents

CHAPTER ONE
Forward Into Battle

"It HANGS LIKE a thick dark cloud ostensibly alive as if it were a monstrous black bird hovering above the heads of a flock of humans, chasing them with the intent to single the weak one out and pounce. It's like a twisted braided dark grey cloud with sharp burrowing talons protruding downward, to satisfy its intent to wrap its claws around its distracted, stressed-out prey, and squeeze."

Nina gives these words as if they are her last. They are a warning to the world this Christmas Eve. The Toasters club have all gathered to film and document this historical resistance against Dr. Ott's advancing war-bot forces. This is a live coverage. Nina believes the power of affirmation can change the world, one person at a time. It is simple, we all expand by tapping into the Light. If we side with evil, we shrivel. It is her battle cry. She continues.

"It is fear, it is pure worry, and it collects from us by canceling our confidence, love, and rationality. It hunts down and crushes these things within anyone who foolishly invites it in. Not the same fear as found in wisdom, but the kind weaponized by evil, to manipulate the strong who do not know their strength, weakening them to become their prey. Fear is a lie, and a lie only has power if you believe it."

"Today it knocks on the door of every home existing, in, around, and about the neighborhood of Beachside Park, California. It places its foot in the doorway as it's seeking anyone who is foolish enough to open up and let it in. I see two ways to look at our situation. To fear, or to fight. I no longer fear evil. Today, I am here with my friends. We will fight to the end."

With cameras still rolling to capture Nina, her speech is disrupted by a loud explosive bang followed by a thunderous jet noise as the enemy rocket breaks the dark early morning silence with a blast of bright brilliant flames. Her film crew is there to broadcast what they are experiencing live, as the rocket jets upward above their head. Hamster and Matt drop their film gear and run toward their weapons. Nina drops everything and follows them while Annie tells Lizzy, Bolt, and Peter to continue shooting film. She wants to capture video footage of the rocket, as it quickly jets toward them streaming a white contrail behind it in the sky. Nina grabs her heavy automatic rifle and runs toward a boulder to brace her rifle for steady accuracy. Watching Nina, Annie yells out.

"Wait Nina. Wait… I sure hope that you know what you are doing."

With the missile incoming, Nina ignores Annie and quickly positions herself next to the rock, using it as a brace for her rifle. No one knows that she had practiced at the shooting range with her dad since she was 7 years old. She adjusts her high-power scope and waits. Hamster and Matt take their rifle, lock, load, and begin firing from the hip, in bursts toward the incoming rocket as it jets above in the dark sky. Their bursts of red flare 30 caliber tracer bullets cris-cross as both Hamster and Matt take aim by lining the tracer bullet flairs with the moving target, but they miss. Hamster and Matt pause for a moment to cool their barrels. The rocket continues to ascend higher above in full flame thrust, as it jets even higher in altitude towards its peak arch in its pre-determined configuration to maximize its incoming trajectory. Hamster and Matt take aim again, popping off more bursts of rapid-fire tracers up into the night sky toward the missile, in a last attempt to destroy the rocket or at least knock it off course.

Click, Click, Click. "Out." yells Hamster. "Me too." Matt reluctantly replies.

As the rocket continues to climb to reach its peak, Nina cooly waits. She is looking for it to reach its top speed and altitude prior to flaming out. It slows just before heading back down to earth. Now with the incoming rocket getting ready to glide to its target on our side of the barricade, the film crew keeps filming the rocket. Anny looks over to see Nina nonchalantly gazing at herself on her cell phone. She is calmly using it as a mirror while applying lipstick to her lips.

"What?" says Annie. Her voice quivers.

"There is no place to take cover.'"

"Don't worry, I got this," Nina replies.

Nina's cell phone illuminates her face, making it glow in the dark momentarily as she replies to Annie. She puts away her makeup and removes a large 50-caliber tracer bullet from the banana clip and kisses it. She then clips the bullet back in, loads the cartridge, locks the kissed round in the chamber and takes aim. She squeezes off a 3 series burst of rapid-fire tracer rounds with each blast echoing across the distance. It looks so effortless as she cuts the missile in half, knocking it out of the sky in pieces.

It immediately sparked a large uproar of applause from the Beachside Park troops who are only volunteer townspeople currently waiting in position for the fight along the barricade. They seem charged. Confidence is catchy.

Annie cries out. "You did it, you did it." Realizing the weight of what just happened. Lizzy, Peter and Bolt join in with Annie. "Oh man, Nina. That was so cool." Standing still, Matt and Hamster just dropped their hands and staired. It was hard for them to process what they had just witnessed happening with Nina. Nina quickly disassembles her rifle and puts it away. Hamster whispers to Matt. "Why did she kiss the bullet?" Matt remained speechless watching Nina as she walked away.

Nina heads toward the next filming position to continue her media coverage on the barricade. Nothing was going to bite her this time. She had finally had enough of the devil's tricks. Fear. This time she opted out. Everyone in the club saw something new in Nina. Adversity had sparked a growth in her, giving off a scent of relentless determination and confidence that inspired them all.

"Look alive guys. Let's finish." Said Nina.

The team quickly gathers as Annie adjusts her camera on Nina, saying, "ready in three, two, one. Go." Pointing her index finger toward Nina as a call for action.

"Yes, we have just witnessed the enemy's scare tactic disrupted once again. By us… ha, ha, ha! As the blue-grey sky signatures the morning, a beam of sunlight breaks the colors from dark shadows to bright rays. When I look down, it seems dark. But when I look up, the

Southern California skies give way to a light sky-blue color with puffy white clouds that line the sky in shiny silver. With darkness at my feet, can I keep my head up toward the light?"

"Cut."

"Let's take a break," says Annie.

Nina responds. "Hey guys, I am going to go up the hill to capture some intel from the other side. Rest up. I will report back in 30 minutes."

"Hey, I'm coming with you," says Annie.

"Look Annie, I need to do this alone."

"Alright then," says Annie. "Be safe."

Nina grabs her backpack. It holds a portable field studio so that she can capture some more film. In it is a High-Power HD Telephoto mobile device lens with a handle adapter that turns her cell phone camera into a monster video shoot. She also has a palm-size camera drone, additional lenses & filters, tripods, wireless connections, and battery packs.

Nina tosses her backpack over her shoulder and hops on her bike pointing it on the trail toward the hill. The smoke from all the campfires along the barricade is thick in the air. People are all gathered in circles around each campfire. Although the fire is warm, the morning air is also unusually warm for Christmas eve. It is supposed to warm up to 90 degrees today.

Nina rides past dozens and dozens of people. Some are gathered to make plans of attack. Many are startled as Nina rides by. A few stand up and motion her to turn her bike around and stay in camp along the barricade. Since she is riding out of town, her safety cannot be guaranteed. Janitor Ed stands up and yells out as she passes by.

"Come back Nina … that's not a good idea." Looking straight ahead with her eyes fixed forward she responds. "Don't worry, Janitor Ed. I'll be okay."

Nina rides her bike up the street to the neighborhood on the hill until she finds a good place to begin filming her news story addition. She narrates out loud.

"I am capturing a close-up view of a row of houses on the block. This is near my house, and I must say it is an eerie feeling to be here. It is so quiet. So evacuated. As I capture the scene on camera, I will begin my film hosting by describing what I see. There are deflated Christmas ornaments in the front yards. I see a plastic snowman as it takes a bow downward, completely limp on the lawn. The carrot nose on its squashed face, points across the street at a plastic Santa and his nine-goofy reindeer. They are completely deflated and collapsed in a pool of plastic across the front lawn."

Nina rolls her bike down the street straddling her feet on each side and kicking from the ground to propel the bike forward instead of pedaling, so that she can keep her film smooth. She continues to describe the scene as she goes.

"There is a real estate sign that hangs on a post in the front lawn of a house for sale. The sign clearly shows Greg and Nancy's photograph with two large mouthfuls of sparkling bleached white real estate teeth. It's hard to look at; however, it sure draws attention."

Nina focuses her camera on the buildings down the hill and films downtown. It takes a moment to process what she is seeing. It is so strange. Normally this is a season of joy. With initial thoughts gathered, she begins to unravel what she sees and feels in her next narration piece.

"Look over there; all you can see are neon-lit signs of the main street and the business district. It is completely closed and desolate, giving one a Twilight Zone "Stopover in a Quiet Town" moment, as Hanukkah, Christmas, and other holiday decorations are out, but nobody is around. It's a spooky scene. Just weeks before, shops were jammed full of this season's shoppers. There was absolutely no place to park in the entire town. People were everywhere, going here and there. Making plans and getting excited about the season of joy. But today no one is celebrating. Everyone in town is at the barricade, getting ready for war."

As Nina focuses her camera across the town, she catches a film of the business buildings in the square. The neon signs show Ace Karate, Pacific Coast Dance, Mount Zion's Korean Market and TacO's. Pausing her camera for a moment, she rests. She is completely without sleep, and now getting hungry. Her body is craving for energy. She ignores it and instead begins to improvise by speaking spontaneously.

"I see TacO's. I know it is closed, due to the impending battle, but man, I sure could kill a robot, or two, for one of those Cheesy Bean Burrito's at TacO's."

Nina comes upon the valley of the enemy. It's time for her to change lenses and spy. She is in an excellent position. As she looks across the distance, she can see the enemy movement along the battleline. Reaching into her bag, she takes out a high-powered lens and quickly fastens it to her camera. She captures film of the thousands and thousands of robots all aligned and ready to attack. She pauses and then turns her camera off. Saying.

"Man, I don't have the heart to share this intel that I am seeing with the team. We are totally outnumbered. The enemy robots look quite capable and ready. They make our troops look small. Like a band of ill-equipped shop owners, workers, and students in comparison. The one secret weapon that we do have is our grit for freedom, coupled with our thirst for a better life. They have no right to barge in and take this from us. Sure, they are well organized with access to the latest AI battle scenarios and the equipment to destroy all of us, as we stand in resistance."

Using her camera Lense, Nina takes another look at the battlefield. She sees robots lined up in a nice tidy row, ready to go.

"What an excellent target they have become. How revolutionary."

She looks over at the barricade. And begins filming. It is made up of a pile of tires, furniture, boxes, and other junk stacked high across the creek bed of Beachside Park. It's at the barricade across the town where everyone in town has gathered to form a large line and fight back against the evil robot forces.

Looking across the scene, Nina remembers when her dad once told her about the jets that they had used to fly range safety during live missile tests. They all had come from the Vietnam war and were facing decommissioning and retirement in the boneyard. Fortunately, these jet planes were salvaged and recommissioned to go to Edwards Air Force base, Flight Test Center. They were modified to carry instrumentation to be use as cruise missile chase birds. One of the F-4 C Jet's had an interesting story behind it. During a sortie over Vietnam, it was shot down by a single arrow that was slung by a bow as it jetted subsonic at a low altitude above the highlands of Vietnam. The arrow lodged into its aft horizonal stabilizer, limiting the controls, so the pilot had to carefully hightail it back to the base and make an emergency landing. Imagine that. An arrow brought down a fighter jet.

Nina speaks out loud. "Today, we are that arrow. "

Nina reaches into her backpack and takes out a small GPS guided palm-size camera drone. She fires it up. All engines hum at hovering speed as it positions itself 15 feet up and behind her bike, tracking her on camera as she points her bike downhill to ride towards the barricade for some excellent video footage.

Just before she rides, Nina gets a scent of fresh sea air as the ocean wind meets her. Pausing momentarily, with the drone camera still capturing aerial footage of her from above, she closes her eyes and lifts her arms out to greet the morning wind that blows inward from the ocean. With eyes still shut, the strong gust of wind feels as though it is picking her up. Like she is flying. Her hair lifts slightly across her face, as a gust of wind cuts in, presenting once again that scent of fresh sea air.

The smell takes her back to those careless times when Nina had spent all her sunny days at the beach, soaking up the sun, feeling the warm sand beneath her beach towel. The scent of coconut sunscreen lotion smeared all over the leather seats of her parents' car while driving home after a day at the beach. It smelled like wealth and certainty. These were much better days. A moment worth savoring. She allows it to take her a thousand miles away. Away from this persistent stochasticity of war.

Nina rides on and reaches the team near the barricade in no time. She lands her mini drone. She sits down with her laptop and takes a moment to collect all the raw film for edit.

"Okay, I got some excellent film to add to the broadcast. Says Nina.

"Excellent. Let's see what you got." Lizzy replies.

Lizzy, Hamster, Peter, Annie, Bolt, and Matt circle around Nina as she merges the film for editing. She begins to fumble a bit, so she overcompensates by focusing harder. Lack of sleep slows her down and she has become more self-aware as everyone is watching her make the final cut for the prerecorded broadcast loops that they have been pitching for the last 45 minutes. Nina adds some original music clips to the film. The songs are composed by Lizzy.

"There, we got it. Sending now." Says Nina.

"Wow, guys this is fantastic," says Annie.

Hamster helps. "I'll check online to see if our video has been published. Nothing. I'll give it a few more minutes. The internet feed has been very slow since the siege. I hope it is getting through." Says Hamster.

Nina remembers the impending odds that she just witnessed on the hill during her recon bike ride moments ago. "Never mind that Hamster." She begins to reflect in deep thought.

"From the day I decided to stand up and succeed in life, nothing has been easy for me. With the enormous success of the Toasters Club, I have also experienced envy, jealousy, and the distancing of friends and family. Annie, Lizzy and Hamster are experiencing the same as I. Nobody invites successful friends to their own backyard parties. Personally, I have been struck by a thousand adverse words, casting doubt on all my dreams. It's as if to dream of becoming a success in a business of creative performance is an irresponsible, unforgivable sin. I hear it over, and over again. Why should humans be creative? We have AI for that."

"In a true sense, this becomes like gravity that pulls down, and the ocean waves that toss around. Its resistance builds up energy and strength through pain. What was meant to crush me instead becomes resilience on my pathway toward living a life of substance. I now can dream at scale."

Suddenly a lot of commotion starts to happen on the barricade. Several enemy drones have come across the barricaded borderline carrying arial loudspeakers to voice more of Dr. Ott's propaganda, just like the bought-off television media. The drones start to hover over the heads of the troops, but in a swift motion, the Beachside Park troops shoot them down with their secret weapons.

"Guys, we have activity on the barricade." Says Peter,

Nina, knowing the situation full well, says. "It's time. Let's go."

The team gathers equipment and weapons. They swiftly run to the barricade. As Indie Film warriors, we are here to film and fight. They are completely unaware that their video uploads for live broadcast is indeed getting out. It has gained millions of viewers over the last few minutes, with more viewers subscribing and tuning in. It taxes media servers as it reaches the most actual live simultaneous hits on record. The followers this time are from all around the world. They are all watching with great concern. How did this part of California become so isolated?

Hundreds of content artists begin to repost the broadcast. Although it is being heavily censored in Canada and the U.S. in North America, it has been getting out elsewhere around the globe. In fact, the Toasters Club live battle scene is being rebroadcasted in city squares as it slowly reaches these places around the world on large screens in the streets of Tokyo, Bangkok, Nairobi, Singapore, Stockholm, Taipei, Paris, Phnom Penh, Sidney, Seoul, Mumbai, Manila, Lima, London, Dublin, Dubai, Hong Kong, Johannesburg, Milan, Mexico City, Jerusalem, Moscow, Shanghai, Sal Paulo, Tashkent, and Yakutsk.

The whole world is watching the battle unfold. They watch as the townspeople arise, lifting their weapons high, running toward the battleline crying out with a loud ROAR. The intense roar shakes the atmosphere over the enemy. As the man behind the curtain peers through his binoculars with beady eyes, Dr. Ott feels his knees weaken uncontrollably. He can feel the emotions of their absolute disgust for him and his shameful bot ambitions. It carries within it the sound of their thunderous roar. The sound pounds deeply against his chest in a burst of infrasonic vibrations, as they roar loudly in one united voice . . .

Charge!!!!

CHAPTER TWO
Earlier in the School Year

THIS MORNING IS BRIGHT and sunny in Beachside Park, California. It is September and School just began its fall semester a week ago. Bolt got up early to go surfing before school. He was supposed to meet Matt on the water, but Matt never showed up. Bolt is experiencing 2-to-3-foot swells at southside cove. The water is smooth and glassy, making it hard to tell the difference between water and early morning sky on the waves. Bolt had been wave slapped a few times in the face already this morning, as it is hard to tell the distance as it approaches. He will be heading over to Lizzies house soon to give her a tow to the Wangs house.

Lizzy lives in a cool-looking house, of course, her dad is an architect. Their home looks like something from a Frank Lloyd Wright collection. Annie and Peter are enjoying morning coffee with their parents. Mr. Wang is going over the highlights of the Angels vs. the Dodgers game. Hamster is in the living room with his dad. They are having coffee together. Nina had been up for 2 hours; however, she is still adjusting to the idea of having to get on a steady schedule again after such a nice long summer break. Her dad is off to work, and her mom is getting ready. She volunteers at the high school office. This morning, Nina will be heading next door to meet with Matt so that they can ride bikes together up the hill to Annie and Peter Wang's house as they do on speech club meeting days. There is always that one home on the block where everyone loves to hang out. It's the Wang's house. They have the most gorgeous house in town. Everyone admires the Wangs.

Nina and Matt live just down the hill. Living next door to each other, they have been friends since forever, way before kindergarten. They are both the same age and in the same grade as Júnior's in high school. Matt is beginning to look in shape. He is growing taller every year. A summer of surfing tones one up well. He has broad shoulders and wavy long hair that drops in his eyes. He is always wearing a big smile with big white teeth that stand out from his surfer tan face.

We get a glimpse of Matt as his alarm sounds off. It is an annoying alarm. Matt slams it off and lays still for a moment in bed looking up at the ceiling, allowing his brain to adjust.

"Dude. Um, where am I?"

"Dude. What day is it?"

"Whoa dude… No, I slept in and missed surfing with Bolt. I'm such a dweeb.

"Dude, I got to snap out of it, Nina will be here at any moment."

Matt lays in bed momentarily before he wakes up. With morning hair in his face, Matt catches the smell of curry as it permeates his room. Its scent is thick, leaving a residue in the air that will last for days. His mom cooks South India style curry to add to Matt's lunch box. In it she placed rice, and garlic naan bread. The posters in Matt's room reflect his love for sports, especially outdoor sports such as fishing, crossroad biking and surfing. He bought the used electric guitar that is hanging on his wall with the money that he earned cleaning swimming pools last summer. With it, he not only creates his own songs, but he has also taken up collecting and building electronic and software gadgets that bend his guitar sounds, making it grungy and unique. He also follows the New Zealand Rugby team. Since Matt is a typical California guy, he is a fully-fashioned surfer. Perhaps even a true Romeo of Beachside Park in his own head, as he pretends to compensate for his average academic ability.

Beachside Park high school students are very different in that they are highly engaged in their studies. Their parents are mostly from various cultures that are very competitive. Over the years, this brilliant influx has uplifted Beachside Park to become a highly desirable place to live. It attracts the best of the best from all around the world and this sets off an amazing success story for all the schools of Beach Side Park school district. It is on the list of top public schools of California. Parents, wanting their children to succeed, press hard to afford to live there and on their children to engage in their prep work studies toward college.

Beachside girls show no interest in Matt. This can also be because of Matt's rebellious outward appearance. His wardrobe reflects a deep

American heritage in its fully fashionable taste, consisting of three articles of refined beach cultured threads worn daily to school. Shorts, tee shirts, and sandals. Do you know what he is planning on wearing today? Hum, I wonder.

Matt gets up and jumps into his grey shorts, white surfer tee-shirt and sandals. He has a precise morning routine that allows him to sleep right up to the very last moment. He looks in the mirror, slaps his face with water from the sink, and gives himself a sign of approval. Ready. He then scurries down the stairs into the garage for his bike. Nina knocks on Matt's front door at the same time she hears Matt's garage door opening, she rides over and meets Matt on his driveway.

"Good morning, Matt."

"Morning Nina. Let's ride."

As they ride up the hill to the Wangs house, it becomes hard to petal. The ride can be steep in some places. Nina keeps her thoughts to herself. "These steep roads are very frightening once pointed downhill." As she finishes her thought, Matt speaks out loud. "This is my favorite part of the ride. Don't you think? Just let gravity take you. No effort." "Totally Matt. I can't wait to jet back." Matt catches Nina's uneasy expression from the corner of his eyes. Thinking, "I need to take it easy with her."

Nina and Matt get closer to the Wangs house. They can see Hamster riding his skateboard on the flat surface up ahead getting there first. He stops in front of the house just as a flock of birds flies over his head and descends into the tree in the front yard, chirping loudly. Hamster looks at the birds in the tree with absolute curiosity, he drops his skateboard and backpack on the grass strip between the street and the sidewalk in front of Wang's house where the club gathers. He lays down on the grass, face-up under the tree where the birds have flocked.

Matt looks at Nina and says, "what in the world is Hamster doing?"

"Not sure Matt" says Nina. "Perhaps he's looking at all those birds in the Wangs tree."

Hamster is sort of short with a Barry Manilow nose, and dirty brown wavy hair. He has a huge personality. His Jewish mom always

says. "My son, you are such a handsome man… and a huge genius." It is quite interesting how the children of whom are bombarded with such loving positive words, turn out exactly as the greatness so spoken over them. They are indeed professions of future success. We can see how Hamster's personality shines brightly. One may think it could be annoying, but instead it is uplifting and catchy to be around Hamster. He has a form of intelligence that lights up the brilliance in others.

Everyone likes Hamster, especially all of Nina's girlfriends at school including Annie and Lizzy. Nina really likes Hamster too and this drives Peter, Matt, and Bolt crazy. They can't figure it out. Nina once overheard Matt saying out loud to Peter and Bolt.

"Dude. I don't get it."

"What do girls see in him?"

I mean really, what does he got that I don't got?"

Although Matt uses a poor choice of words here, Nina understood what he was saying; however, she didn't have the heart to explain. Just as Nina and Matt arrive at the Wang's house, more of the club members begin to show up as well. Matt decides to peal out on his bike and peddles fast towards Hamster who is lying on the grass strip between the street and sidewalk. Matt rides right up to Hamster and then suddenly slams on the back brake. He skids past Hamster, wheels locked, making a loud screeching noise. Hamster and the birds completely ignore Matt's attempt as they are neither startled, nor phased. Neither is Hamster. The only evidence of Matt's act of envy is a thick black half-crescent skid mark that he placed across the pavement. It smells of burnt rubber. He looks back at Hamster.

"What are you doing Hamster?"

Hamster, still counting, ignores Matt. Nina rides up, takes off her helmet, and gives Matt a look of disgust. Matt ignores it. Instead, he comments.

"I think he's counting something."

Hamster finally gets back to Matts question. "I'm counting the birds."

Matt and Nina both speak in unison. "What?"

Hamster, laying still on the grass counting, says in an uninterested tone.

"Quiet please, you're making me lose my count."

Nina and Mat both look at each other as if they are facing a perfect opportunity to tease. Hamster, not taking his eyes off the birds as he is counting, begins to count quickly and out loud. "123-124-125-126-127-128-129." It is as if it were a formal invitation to tease. "Dude, this can be fun," whispers Matt to Nina. "Hahaha. Oh man, what an interesting situation," Nina replies.

They both start counting randomly in unison. It is designed to throw-off Hamster's count as they bark out random numbers, such as. "139, 16, 47, 119, 34." Laughing in the excitement. Just then Bolt rides up on his bike. He is towing Lizzy who is on her skateboard. Bolt is wearing jeans, a blue tee-shirt and leather loafers. He likes to surf too. He also likes to target practice and is a member of the local Karate Dojo branch where Annie and Peter's family all belong. He works out at the Dojo every day. Only Annie and Peter know what his Karate robe belt color is, as they are sworn to secrecy. It is a lower rank. A few levels below Annie and Peter. Bolt tries to look rugged, his tan face bearing a scar on his chin. Chuckling inside, Nina remembers when his mom once told her that he got that scar when he was 5 years old and fell off his bike.

Although he tries to look rough, he is well-mannered and is respectfully polite around others. His hair is strait blond and falls in his face. He is trying to grow a beard so that he can look like his favorite Marshal Art's legend, Mr. Chuck Norris. The beard on Bolts 16-year-old face needs to fill in a lot more.

Lizzy is good at skateboarding. She is also a music composer who has written some very good songs. She hopes one day to write music for a full-feature motion picture. Her favorite composers are John Williams and Peter Gabriel. With golden skin and long dark hair, Lizzy was born in China, so she looks average like most of the other girls her age who go to Beachside High School. What makes Lizzy stand out are her beautiful eyes. She is very friendly and down to earth like her adopted parents. They are a very interesting family. Her dad is a famous architect and built many homes and office buildings in Beachside Park. Her mom is Jewish, from New York City. Interesting thing Lizzy's mom had a powerful encounter with our Creator while studying art in college. She expresses this deep connection in her artwork, and in her life. Lizzy's parents both speak Mandarin fluently; however, Lizzy who came to California as a baby, only knows how to speak Californian English. Sometimes Lizzy looks like a flower child with her laid-back California personality. But when she sees something Chinese, like the Chow Ming restaurant downtown, or a Jackie Chan movie, she feels an unexplainable connection. As if something is missing. It sometimes keeps her awake at night.

"Who am I? What am I compensating for? Am I just a fake?"

Lizzy is a master at the violin and cello. She also plays piano extraordinarily well and has recently begun playing the tin whistle, which is a beautiful instrument much like a flute. She first heard it played in a Peter Gabriel song called Mercy Street.

Today Nina has ballet dance class. Like Lizzy, Annie and the others, her thin frame fits well for ballet. She is wearing beige color shorts over black tights, plus a white tank-top over a loosely colored black tee-shirt. She tied her long dark hair in a ballet bun. Lizzy, and Bolt walk over and stand next to Matt and Nina so that they can watch as Hamster struggles to count the birds. Lizzy begins to laugh hysterically at their attempt to derail Hamster's count.

We hear the front door as Annie slams it behind her and runs toward the gang, stomping loudly as she makes it over to where everyone is watching Hamster count. She is beginning to look more like her mom the older she gets. Today she is wearing bell-bottom jeans, a red top and tennis shoes. With her mom's bubbly personality, she stands next to the others who have now, circled around Hamster. Annie yells with a loud voice.

"HEY … HOW' ARE YOU GUYS DOING?" The flock of birds fly away.

"There they go." Says Hamster.

"Don't sweat it, Hamster; they'll be back tomorrow." Annie quickly responds.

Nothing ever phases Annie. Her upbeat personality is catchy like her mom and dad. It is hard to feel down, or sad when around Annie, as her demeanor is always so uplifting. On the other hand, Annie's brother Peter is a genius like his dad, but one would not know it at first glance. That is because Peter is also upbeat and smiling all the time. They call him the Smiling Whiz Kid! If you need help in math, Peter is the go-to guy. He's a true prodigy.

There is Annie and Peter's mom, Mrs. Wang. She comes out the door bearing trays of delicious and healthy goodies for breakfast. She begins talking as she walks toward the team with her trays. We all love how she speaks. It's a singsong tone.

"Hey kids, here are some healthy breakfast bars with berries and nuts you can eat before your meeting starts. I also have freshly squeezed orange/pineapple juice that I just made. It is so delicious guys, so eat up."

Mrs. Wang sets the trays out on the brick wall in front. She is very well-liked within the community. At first one would think that it is because she is always giving away food and snacks, but a closer look reveals more. Nina's parents always say the Wang's, are people of substance. In addition to teaching Sunday school, she also volunteers at the soup kitchen where a group of co-volunteer's welcome folks who are down on their luck. They even have a food pantry where they hand out a month's supply of food to help families in their time of need.

At the Wang's home there is always something good to eat. To be invited to the Wang's BBQ is something their friends all look forward to. It is absolutely something to live for. The Wang's are hardworking people and honest business owners. Their business manufactures and sells custom high-tech hardware, sub-systems, and complex power & signal cables for electric vehicles. Their latest invention is a complex cable and connection that is capable of safely handling the energy it takes to plug in one's electric car into an ultra-high-power charging station. It solves the biggest problem that electric cars have. Range. By reducing battery charge times, electric car owners now have the reality of driving cross-country, as electric vehicles can charge in minutes, rather than hours, now matching the same time it takes to fill-up a gasoline powered vehicle at the gas station. It is one of many cutting-edge product offerings the Wangs have that are purely innovative.

The front door slams again as Peter runs out to greet the team. It makes one chuckle at the sight of Peter running. His legs seem as though they are moving faster than this body causing him to appear a bit off-balanced as he runs toward us. He can't wait to show the club his latest breakthrough for the Action Club school project. It is a media system with technology that will allow unlimited hits of streaming media from their school. It's easy to upgrade so that it can meet a high simultaneous hit demand. That is because it runs on the Cloud which can be replicated and scaled as needed.

Peter Wang is the youngest member of the team. He skipped 4 grades ahead when he was 9 years old, from 5th grade to 9th grade because he had amazingly excelled in all forms of academics. Peter is also a critical thinker, a creative design thinker, a gadget maker, and an inventor just like his dad. He happens to be the best friend of Hamster. They just seem to speak the same language.

Off to School, it's almost time for the speech club to begin. It takes about 10 minutes to ride downhill to the High School. The meeting today is in Room 122. It's located right next to the music room. Everyone in the Club, scarfs down the Wang breakfast snack. They get on their bikes, their skateboards and push-off. Hamster gets up, shakes off the grass, and puts on his helmet and backpack. He lays his skateboard out on the sidewalk and jumps on it. Nina looks at her watch and yells.

"Let's go."

"Yes, it's time to rock and roll." Says Hamster.

The gang hops on their mountain bikes and on their skateboards. Strapping on helmets and protective gear they prepare for their downhill ride to school.

Meanwhile the scene switches over to the music room at the school as the jazz band begins practice. It's the first song of the day. They play a sweet rock-in-roll tune that Dr. Roy, the music teacher, had written for the school. The song is called; Ott-N-The-Bot. Dr. Roy snaps his fingers and motions the band to play.

"Alright … Now hit it."

At the same time up the hill from the school all seven, including Nina, Hamster, Matt, Annie, Peter, Lizzy, and Bolt are all on the road pointed downward on their bikes popping wheelies and on skateboards jumping the sidewalk curbs. They charge ahead descending downhill toward the school.

Switching over to the school music auditorium, the band continues to play. The bass guitarist and drummer pounce on their instruments, followed by the horns. It's an upbeat song with more rock-n-role than jazz, but who cares? It's fun, it's lively, and it rocks. We see students on campus run over to the music room to listen. It is an immediate hit as students begin to fill the empty stadium in the music room, clapping and acting wild as the band plays.

Meanwhile, the club members are coming at full speed on bikes and skateboards. Matt pops a wheelie and rides past Bolt while Lizzy performs tricks on her skateboard. She's quite good. Bolt cuts over to the curb on his bike and jumps the wall.

Back in the music room, one girl playing trombone has a small toy stuffed hamster attached to the horn of her trombone. She is a secret admirer of Hamster. The music continues and the students in the audience get more excited as they stand, clap and dance. Mr. Bryan, the history teacher, joins in the group dance along with more faculty and staff as the school band continues to jam in the music room. The band is in full swing. The once-empty stadium is completely full, and the audience is going wild. The students are all standing, clapping, dancing, and cheering as the band plays onward. The girl with the trombone stands up and gives her improvisational solo piece. As she blows a high pitch tone, she focuses on the toy hamster attached to her horn. Its face looks as if it is in a trance with eyes ready to pop out as it gets completely blasted by the trombone.

Switching to the downhill ride, Hamster, Peter, and Lizzy flip their skateboards up the curb, performing tricks, cutting through alleys and sidewalks, and sometimes catching and passing up the bikes. It's a visual circus of stunts and jumps. Getting near the steep part of the road, Nina can feel her heart pound.

"Alright, yah" Nina yells, but manages not to show an ounce of fear.

Matt's bike starts to slip, losing momentary control. "Whoa, whoa, yikes!"

He lets out an involuntary high pitch scream. Nina pretends not to hear it.

He gains control again. "Woah dude. I almost bit it this time."

"I mean Dude, that was really scarry. How about you, Nina?"

She looks over and smiles. "Let's do it again."

The steep road levels out as they all get closer to the school. Once on campus, they can hear the band and the crowd roaring as they fly by the administration office and head right toward the music room hall. The music gets louder as they approach. They ride past a crowd of students who are gathered, dancing outside the doorway of the music room and stop to see what is going on. The jazz band whines down and wraps up their song ending on the beat, followed by a slight pause, just before a loud spontaneous applause comes from out of nowhere in a deafening roar from the excited audience. Nina, and the speech club members join in the applause. The surprised band takes a bow. As the crowd exits the music room hall. Nina and the speech club members all walk over to the meeting room located next door to the music hall.

"Man, we missed it. That must have been good." Says Nina.

"Did you see that crowd go crazy?"

"Yes." Said Matt. "That was wild!"

They are all on time for the speech club team meeting. The club members begin their 7:15 a.m. meeting. Nina and all the other team members talk about their speech club, they all agree that their parents

had an impeccable foresight to have placed them all together in the same club at such an early age. It was as if their parents were looking ahead into their life and future as one will need to know how to speak well, so as to move the mountains in life. Nina sometimes ponders about her parents. In her 17-year-old mind she wonders.

"How did my parents become so smart?"

Aside from having the chance to practice speech in front of others, they all were forming a purpose in talking about the subjects that really mattered to them. As soon as they were growing older, they discussed deeper problems such as "why does our city have a dog pound?" Or why do animals and children live in countries of war where it is harmful? Or how come the school cafeteria serves up horse meat along with the Bill Gates specially lab-grown "go green approved" petri-dish meat that tastes like chicken?

I'm not sure if that petri-dish, or horse meat rumor is true, or not, but every school cafeteria across the nation has that same rumor. This rumor must have struck a chord because it came up many times as a subject of discussion in their speech club as they sat around the table and spoke about the world's problems during that time in their lives.

Meanwhile, flashing back to the Wang's house, which is beautifully located up the hill overlooking the deep blue Pacific Ocean. Mrs. Wang, AKA; the snack lady, is preparing a shopping list to resupply her snack pantry. As she completes her shopping list, the phone rings on their land-line business phone. It's an automatic voice message advertisement put out by real estate agents Greg and Nancy. "Hello, I am Greg …"

The high-pitched tone of Greg's voice squeaks over the phone line, just a bit before Mrs. Wang swiftly hangs-up the phone, saying. "Get a life, Helium Head."

Mrs. Wang enters the doorway to her garage and presses the automatic garage door opener. Every move is organized perfection … her tall thin-body posture is straight and precise, just like Mary Poppins. She gets into her white luxury SUV, drives down her long driveway toward the main gate and proceeds down the street towards Mount Zions grocery store.

Once she arrives, she parks her car in the front row of the parking lot with her radio blasting jazz as she stops and parks her car. She waits for a moment, humming along as she listens to the song until it ends. She then gets out and walks through the sliding front doors of the store. With her right hand she grabs a shopping cart from the line of carts stacked there. She rolls it forward and turns right pushing her cart toward produce, humming the jazzy song from the radio as she goes.

As soon as she turns the corner, her cart gets broadsided by another shopper who pops right out of nowhere and pushes his heavily loaded shopping cart down the aisle toward the checkout counter. He is a middle-aged man in a brown jacket. He utters no word and no apology. The man just continues to head forward toward the checkout counter with his loaded kamikaze shopping cart.

Mrs. Wang then continues toward produce and is stopped by a shopping cart that blocks her path. She dodges around it only to be stopped by another shopper with a full shopping cart. It's being pushed by a very tiny old lady who is carrying a large purple purse that hangs over her shoulder. The purse drags on the floor behind her, slowing her down even further.

Mrs. Wang offers to help with the dragging purple purse, but the old woman ignores her and keeps charging onward to checkout. She is then blocked again. This time by two middle-aged women, each with their own shopping cart. They are pushing their carts, side by side, leaving Mrs. Wang no room in the aisle. She waits behind the pickle jars for them to pass. Suddenly four more shoppers with carts come running in unison from behind.

Mrs. Wang manages to dodge these kamikaze shoppers with shopping carts that head right toward her. Just as they miss, her shopping cart gets broadsided again, this time from the other side. Then rapidly, her shopping cart is hit one at a time by different shopping carts coming from all three sides of her shopping cart. This takes her for a spin as she is tossed around in a maze of produce aisles and lines of attacking shopping carts.

Then one cart hits her in the back, directly from behind. The force causes her to lose grip on her shopping cart as she falls backward to the freshly waxed grocery store tiled floor, hitting the floor in a flat slam and sliding backward a few feet. The floor smells of freshly cut celery and cilantro, giving her a clue that she is laying face up on the floor in produce.

She immediately gets back up, walks over, grabs her empty cart, and starts rolling forward to escape out of produce, but she hesitates as she sees something very strange happening. The displays of apples, bananas, onions, potatoes, tomatoes, peaches, and other items all begin to oddly move away on their own, clearing the floor center. Mrs. Wang finds herself standing in the middle of produce on an empty floor with her shopping cart facing a wall.

Suddenly the lights go out. In the dark, a big sparkly mirrored disco ball drops down from the ceiling and music begins to play. It's the same jazzy song that she was listening to on the radio just moments ago in her car. The song plays in unison with an array of colored laser light displays. It's an upbeat song.

Twenty ballet dancing shoppers push their shopping carts out onto the floor of the room. They form a circle around Mrs. Wang and begin dancing around her with their shopping carts. She tries to avoid them with no luck and is whisked away in the rhythm of the song … the "Shopping Cart" song. With the rhythm of the music, all of the shopping cart ballet dancers dance around Mrs. Wang, from in and out, side to side and back to front with their shopping carts in hand.

The expression of Mrs. Wang is that of perplexity and curiosity. With her eyes wide open, the ballet dancing shoppers begin to form a circle around Mrs. Wang. She tries to find a way to escape, but the ballet dancers block all escape attempts.

As soon as the music ends, the dancers drive their shopping carts away. The laser lights go off, and the disco ball retrieves back into the ceiling as the produce displays of apples, bananas, onions, potatoes, tomatoes, peaches, and other items all move back in place on the produce floor center.

The store lights go back on, and Mrs. Wang is left standing alone with her shopping cart. Everyone and everything in the store is back to normal at the flick of a switch.

Mrs. Wang leaves bewildered thinking to herself. "Whoa, did you see that? Wait a minute. What was that? What just happened? I mean, did that just happen? Perhaps I'm experiencing a psychedelic sugar high."

Nah … No Way!

CHAPTER THREE
Forming of the Toasters Club

THE 7:15 A.M. CLUB meeting is about to begin. The team has been struggling with the idea of continuing as a speech club. They had been together in the speech club since elementary school and now they are growing up. They don't want to just talk about problems, they want to do something. As a team, they know that they can do more. But who do we want to be?

Hamster has been quite persuasive here. He would deliver his speech to the club and end it with this quote from Jean-Paul Sartre's by saying. "To be is to Act." Sure, looking back, the team was getting tired of just talking about problems. No solution. No action.

One day Nina was having breakfast with her mom and dad at Sam's, a popular outdoor café that serves the best breakfasts in town. They decided to eat on the outside sidewalk tables. Nina's dad had just finished giving thanks for breakfast at the table. He sat up from that posture and was about to dig in. On his plate were two eggs over easy, one sausage and a stack of pancakes. Nina looked up and noticed her dad staring down the street. He pushed his chair back and stood up saying. "Go ahead and eat, I'll be right back."

He then jumped the small fence rail that separated the café along the sidewalk. Nina watched her dad as he walked down the street where there was an old man with a cane, struggling to fix a flat tire on his car, which was parked at the curbside around 20 yards down the street from Sam's Cafe. She watched her dad get on his knees, jack up the car, replace the tire with the spare, tighten the lug-bolts and drop the car for a final tire check on the spare. It looked like the old man wanted to reward him, but Nina's dad held up his hands refusing to accept anything from him. He then motioned that he had to go. Then surprisingly, the old man gave him a hug. Nina watched her dad as he ran back into the café, disappeared for a few minutes and then reappeared after cleaning up. Changing tires is dirty work.

As Nina's dad approached the table. She and her mom were just finishing up breakfast. He didn't say a word about where he went, or what he just did. He just sat down and began eating his cold breakfast. Nina overheard her mom whisper to her dad as she tapped him on the shoulder. "Now that's my Hero!"

Nina thought about how often her dad did stuff like that. He was a doer, not a talker. Nina couldn't get it out of her head as she was searching for a problematic topic for her next speech. As her parents drove her over to her Saturday morning dance class after breakfast. She asked her parents.

"What is the number one problem in this town?"

"Misappropriation of school funds," said Mom. Nina's Dad had a different view.

"I say the lack of professional job opportunities."

"Why is that, Dad?"

"People thrive when given the opportunity to develop and earn a decent living."

"Right now, this town can only offer low pay jobs like flipping burgers. I don't know why people rely on working for someone else when, like no other time until now, small business entrepreneurs have a chance to earn on their own.

"Tell me more." Nina says with great interest.

"Well Nina, a friend of mine had recently visited the beautiful countryside somewhere in Southeast Asia. I forgot exactly where. Anyway, he was telling us that the place he was visiting was far from the crowded streets of the city, yet he was able to pick up very high internet speeds where he was. The thing is most people around were not using it for business. They were still setting up local businesses as house cleaners, and vendors depended on the town's local economy."

"In Beachside Park, we have access to a sea of customers and partners from all over the internet. We have software applications that have leveled the marketplace with huge opportunities to gain wealth remotely with our cell phone."

"They just need a little coaching to shift their mindset away from the industrial age thinking that holds us back and transform to modern ways of wealth generation."

Nina's dad owns a business consulting firm and is a volunteer for the Beachside Park Fire Department. Her mom volunteers at the high school administration office. In the Tanizaki family, it was so commonplace to help others. It is how they roll.

That night Nina thought about her speech club and how they were all growing up and wanting to do more about the world. She thought about Hamster and the others in her speech club. She also thought about her parents, the Wang's, and others like them who carved out their own jobs in business, and always had the time and money to give of themselves and invest in the community. She strongly believed that inspiration comes from those who live the talk. The next day Nina walked next door to Matt's house and pitched her idea to Matt.

"Hey Matt,"

"Nina. What's up?"

"I was thinking more about our speech club."

"Okay, what's on your mind Nina?"

"I was wondering. What if we were to morph it into an action club?"

"You mean do things such as solve problems to help our school and our community?"

"Well yes, but I was thinking that we can do much more as an action club."

"Like what Nina?"

Nina pauses for a moment to express her idea. "We can create things that people need and earn money. We can become business partners and entrepreneurs."

"Woah now, hold on Nina. Your big ideas are hurting my brain. Don't forget that we are only high school students. We are supposed to live off our parents, earn good grades, go to a good college, then graduate so that we can get a good job doing something that we typically do not like doing, working the rest of our lives making other people rich while we pay interest, insurance, mortgage, and income taxes. Being happy that we earn enough to hold good credit scores, so that we qualify to live out our lives in debt."

"Wait a minute, Nina. So, tell me more."

Later in the day Nina and Matt pitch it to the team. Hamster listened to what they had to say. Then he mentioned something very interesting.

"You know, in school we are taught to have an industrial age mindset. This means to work for the man. We will never learn anything about investments, or how to start a venture. One thing I do know. In business, action requires an operational framework."

Peter chimed in and suggested that the club could adopt Dr. Edward Deming's adaptive processing techniques. Hamster agreed. Leave it to Peter and Hamster to mention their brainiac heroes. Peter and Hamster continued to carry out an intellectual conversation while the others stood around, trying to grasp their conversation.

"It's called the Deming Cycle:" said Peter. "Plan – Do – Check – Act." It is continual improvement based on the scientific experimental thinking of the Empirical Process Control of Scrum. Transparency – Inspection – Adaption. "It is where we can have total quality." Hamster adds; "Dr. Deming's strategies still transform production to this day. It is the future of work."

Matt gets right to the point. "Sounds boring dudes. Where does the part about making a lot of money come in?"

"Stay with us Matt," says Hamster. "This framework that we are speaking of here is paramount to the operations of building great wealth. It is simple, yet so misunderstood. Please pay attention."

Nina adds to the conversation saying, "my Dad has been working on a disruptive business process with Annie and Peters Dad. They have taken the existing elements of Design Thinking and combined this with the elements of Growth. Market growth. The problem that they have is that Design thinking only takes them to the point of realizing a good product as prototype. Good ideas are a dime a dozen. No one wants to purchase a good idea."

Annie provides more insights saying, "Nothing is new under the sun. They don't want to reinvent the wheel. Perhaps we can solve this. We have Design Thinking, input. We then have Market Growth, output. What framework would work to build things?"

One can hear the wheels turning between the ears of everyone in the room, as the discussion quickly turns into a brainstorming session with everyone gathering their thoughts and putting their best foot forward.

After a moment Bolt speaks out. I know guys. "Project Management."

"That was already considered Bolt," says Annie, "but its age-old industrial mindset does not complement the user interaction of design thinking and the rapid growth of today. But you are absolutely on the right track."

Next, Matt chimes in. "Alright guys, help me out here. I'm wondering. What exactly does an action club do?"

"Well Matt, they solve problems and get things done," Peter replies.

Bolt speaks up. "Get things done? You must be thinking of very tiny problems."

"I was thinking the same," Lizzy adds.

Backing up her brother's statement, Annie says, "Not necessarily guys."

She continues. "Any large, complex, or critical issues can be broken down into smaller pieces. The proper way to build is to aim small and accomplish a smaller task until done."

Matt chimes in again. "Done as in deployed, packaged, delivered, sold and fulfilled?

"Exactly Matt," Annie confirms.

"OH MAN I GOT IT," Matt shouts. Lizzy, noticing how uncool that looked, puts her hand on Matts shoulder and whispers in his ear in her native California English accent. "Be cool Matt. Try and maintain."

"No, dudes. Sorry Lizzy, you're right. I didn't mean… I guess what I am trying to say here is that I got a little excited. But guys, please hear me out, as I see how this relates to surfing. Okay here it is."

"All projects that we set our sights on will be toasted."

Silence grips the room like a bad joke on stage. Everyone looks at Matt. Hamster sees an opportunity to have fun in return for Matts skid mark stunt the other day. Clapping his hands he says.

"Thanks for that Matt. Hey guys, let's hear an applause. we all should thank Matt."

Hamster stands clapping in a mean attempt to get others to join in, so that he can make his crushing point. Matt cuts him off.

"Bite it Hamster."

"No, you both cool it." Lizzy intervenes. "There is no way that we can form a viable team if we are storming at each other's throats. Besides, if we are going to be doing stuff together as a team, we have got to be good with each other."

"As for me, I plan to grow wealth by having fun, with or without you guys. Hopefully with. Think about it. We can each go solo and carve out our own future of success, or we can form a team and aim for the stars together, at least until we grow apart."

"The Beatles grew apart after 7 years as a top rock band. The Rolling Stones have been together as a rock band for a lifetime. The thing is the band members of both bands became set for the rest of their lives, creating stuff, and earning wealth long after forming. How totally fun! They all produced great creative works throughout their lifetime. I want this type of life too. Sure, success takes a strong framework; however, it also takes strong teamwork."

"Guys, think of it. Each of us has a superpower of various talents and experience. Together, we are a goldmine of value that can change the world. Harry Potter uses spells and witchcraft. We are a superpower that uses proven systems applied in business and industry today. What we have is a pathway to do great things that help others and at the same time, generate wealth as a young team. How cool is that?"

"That was an awesome speech Lizzy," says Nina. "Before Lizzy's excellent talk on teamwork, Matt was telling us that all projects that we set our sights on would be toasted. I think you are on to something here Matt. You were getting to the team's name. Right?"

"Exactly Nina," Matt replies. "For surfing we came up with the word toasted."

"Toasted?" Said Nina.

"Yes, toasted is a word that me and my surfer bros started using. Right Bolt?

"You got it bro," says Bolt.

"You see, when a surfer nails a skillful trick perfectly while riding a wave, we say toasted." "Righteous and well-done dude."

Nina stares at Matt and again says. "Toasted? That sounds like a line from a Sylvester Stallone movie after he burns his enemy to a crisp."

"Yah, um, I guess so." Matt replies.

Matt sits down momentarily and then gets right back up to clarify his thought further by saying, "Toasted means done." He walks up to the whiteboard in front of the room and writes "We Are Toasters" and repeats it. He then clarified his thoughts saying.

"Toasters is the perfect team's name. It doesn't have to be just surfing; we can say toasted for anything well done... Scratch that. I mean, anything done well. It's a word to complement a great performance, like dancing, riding skateboards, or even playing the guitar. All these require practice for improvement and to achieve a top performance. I see our club, our small action club, doing the same thing, achieving the same perfection as we build cool stuff and perform well to help others in our school and beyond. Places where solutions are needed."

Nina walks over to Matt who is in the front of the room.

"So, when a routine is well done and nailed with perfection, it is toasted. Hey, I get it."

"In essence what you are saying is that any act, event, or performance done well is toasted."

"Yep. We are the Toasters Club" Matt replies.

"We are about innovation, creative design, and action."

"We are about improving continually and perfecting our skills. We are the Toasters Club."

Matt obviously thought this through. Although apart from surfing, this term is not well known. Matt and many surfers use toasted as a play on words in their native California surfer speech; however, Matt applied it to its alternative meaning of the name. Still today, not many people have really heard of the name. The Toasters Club and their idea to help others by producing things that improve the world, will soon catch on to be well known and hopefully spark others to form their own teams, and do the same.

"The Toasters Club. Now, that is a really cool name," says Hamster.

"Especially being that it is a name that is not so well known."

"It's a perfect name for us," Lizzy adds.

"I mean like… This is casually expressing one's inner thoughts with radically cool words. I mean totally guys. It's the California way."

Peter gets out his PC and looks up the definition for Toaster. He then hooked to a projector and flashed its definition on the wall.

"Okay, here's what we got:

Toast·er (noun). An electrical device to make toast." Says Peter.

Hamster stands next to Peter. "Hey Peter. Let's make some additions to that."

"Guy's gather around" says Hamster. They all move closer to forever coin the word.

Peter types the outline and says, "I need definitions for Toaster, Toasted and Toasters"

Toast·er(s) Noun

1. Toaster: A device to make toast. Typically, electrical.

2. Toasted; A word California's surfers, or skateboarders, use to describe an exquisite surf technique, or routine, performed well. "Nailed it! … Toasted!"

3. Toasters, as in (The Toasters Club): An adaptive, action-oriented club with a teamwork mentality that applies proven systems to get things done quickly with quality. This includes:

    a. An imagination to originate ideas of value.

    b. The ability to finish production, solve problems, inspire others, and increase wealth.

When they were finished defining the Toasters Club, they began to see themselves as an action club to create, innovate, and produce things that help others and generates business wealth. Each of them caught a glimpse of the vision and they began to see the great potential this movement has. Annie clears her voice.

"Wow, Matt. Is that how you coin a word?"

"Not sure," said Matt.

Hamster inserts. "Well, to be official, coining a word needs a consensus of peer recognition. But in this case, who cares? I like the idea of our name being The Toasters Club because it is obscure."

"Exactly." Says Nina. "I like that too."

Peter replies: "Yes, I hope our name remains obscure."

"I just want to be part of something cool." Says Lizzy. "The Toasters Club. How cool is that?"

Next week is the annual Jr. speech competition at the High School. All speech clubs will be meeting. The Toasters Club voted on Nina's speech this year since she had prepared a strong message about how job loss distresses the Pet Rescue Center. It is one of her passions to see abandoned pets get help.

The Toasters all agreed that after this, they would not only speak, but act on the things that mattered the most at their school and in their community. Hamster and Peter were already coming up with a list of items, cool undertakings including things like a website for pet rescue awareness and an online video management application for their high school. They even brainstormed a few product ideas; however, Nina was focused on rescuing abandoned pets.

It all began a year ago when a Pet Rescue Center announced a large influx of pets that needed a home. These pets were mainly dogs and cats, but there were also rats, hamsters, birds, snakes, and other living creatures abandoned during that year when residents had moved out of town in search of jobs. Right now, the rescue center is over-whelmed with pets to the point that they can no longer take on any more pets, so Nina decided to research this issue further.

It was a bad economic year. Nina heard about the large numbers of abandoned pets from her dad, so she rode her bike down to the pet rescue center to find out for herself. It was unbelievable, people had abandoned their pets. Why? Who would do such a thing?

The folks at the rescue center explained that when people go through economic problems due to job loss, they find themselves in a bad place where they can no longer care for their pets. Perhaps they lost their home and need to move out and cannot find a place that allows pets. Most rentals do not allow pets, or they charge an incredible fee for owners of pets.

Under poor circumstances, people find that they can no longer afford their pets, so they take them to the Dog Pound instead of abandoning them on the streets. Trust me, said one of the volunteers, this is not an easy decision for them. Just the thought of abandoning a family pet is horrible, so I am glad that we can offer help through the pet center. Not saying it is a good thing, but many who come to our center are desperate and in absolute tears. We also see these people as morally abandoning themselves. Abandoned by an economic downturn.

Abandoned by their job. Abandoned and forgotten by a current government agenda to grow big and force everyone under its control.

Some people are so worried about their own careers, so focused on themselves rather than the true purpose of their work in service, that they fail to see the bigger picture. This is common for leaders in public office. So, often people remain limp and ineffective, instead of building great businesses that last. Morally abandoned? Perhaps. Nothing good happens for the people and nothing gets done when the same office-bearer remains in position, performing the same useless status quo politics, day after day. Bad politics is bad business for everyone, and equals poor job conditions; thus, more dogs are on the street. These are things that Nina never thought about before. Wow, we are all responsible to research topics around our votes and strive for the good of the community with integrity. That means holding news sources, and economic control mechanisms accountable. Nina spent hours researching, getting down to the source of how pets end up abandoned. She titled her speech; "Bad Economies Hurt Pets."

A few days had passed and now the annual high school speech night was about to take place. All the members of the Toasters Club were present as they showed support to Nina as she represented them. She was the last speaker to go. When she walked to the stage, she couldn't help but think that this was more than a speech, it had become a passion for her. She wanted to help animals. During her speech she spoke about how bad it was for pets. In Nina's speech she pointed out how It looked as though they were in a government FEMA prison camp. Unfortunately, during her speech she got choked up with her emotions and began to break down and cry. She ran off stage.

"Oh no!" Said Annie. The team immediately got up and followed Nina to the room at the back of the stage. It was a spontaneous show of team support. They believed in her. While together, no one spoke a word. Matt, Hamster, Peter, Annie, Bolt, and Lizzy all circled around Nina until she broke the silence.

"Guys, it's time to transform. I don't want to only talk about things anymore, instead I want to do something about it." Total silence gripped the air as the Toasters looked around at each other. Matt speaks up.

"Alright Dudes, I think it's time. We have been talking about transforming into an Action Club, but tonight was us, still as a speech club that was going for the prize in the speech competition. Nothing wrong with that; however, today for us, this all feels so empty."

Nina looks down. Her eyes focus on a chip in the floor tile as she thinks things through. She begins speaking softly. "There are so many broken things that we all end up talking about, yet not fixing. That's just it. We talked about becoming an action club. We have a name … The Toasters Club. But what I am struggling with now is how are we going to become this great action club? I know that we were mentioning the frameworks and processes of Design Thinking and Growth, but how do we transform from talk to action? How do we become an action club, not a theory club? What does it take to become the action club that we want to be? The thing that can really lift us up to become The Toasters Club?"

The team remained silent, everyone except Peter. Normally quiet, Peter began to make motions. His face gave off an unusual vibe, as if he was just about to explode. Hamster caught on right away. "Guys hold on … I think Peter has an idea. Hey Peter, what is it?" Just then Peter chimes in. His voice bursting with ideas.

"I know the missing framework piece between Design Thinking and Growth. Let's add Agile values and principles to our approach and apply the Scrum framework to our teamwork as the power to act on an idea, build and get things done, and then scale to promote it. Design Thinking to Ideate, Scrum to Sprint, and Marketing is Growth."

Ideate – Sprint – Growth

The Toasters Club is an Action Club who applies three proven industry frameworks as an Action Club, to counter problems with idealistic solutions, produce them, and make them known in the universe. Ideate, Sprint, and Growth.

Peter's older sister Annie jumps up immediately and yells. "That's a great idea Peter." Hamster, who was standing next to Annie, was caught completely by surprise and let out an involuntary "screech" startling Bolt so much that he fell backwards right out of his chair. Bolt quickly rolled his way up off the floor in one motion like he had practiced hundreds of times in Karate class. He then reflected on the occurrence quietly inside as he was a bit embarrassed for also being startled yet satisfied that he had covered up through instinct. Well, that is what it looked like to him. To others, it was funny to hear Hamster scream, and see Bolt fall backward and try to cover it up. They all remained silent not wanting to embarrass Bolt or Hamster as they were both trying to keep cool.

Nina speaks out. "Hey Annie and Peter, what is it? I have never seen you two act this way." Peter and Annie began to talk in pure excitement. Peter stands in the front of the room to talk more about the Agile team-oriented framework called Scrum. He explains. "Scrum fits perfectly between Design Thinking and Growth, as it is a proven team-oriented way to develop a product, a service, or an event ideated and validated as a product prototype, or iteration in Design Thinking, and then completed and delivered well as a final product, service, or event. Ready for Growth and Delivery. In fact, as the team works together and gains the cross-functional skills and experience necessary as a self-managed team, they become a highly performing Scrum team that delivers high- quality products, and services, each time through the practice of continual improvement."

Annie steps in. "It's called Kaizen, which is Japanese for Continual Improvement. Scrum is a way to get things done quickly as a team and with Kaizen quality measures." Peter adds to Annie's statement. "It came from software development. Our dad's company made a fortune by applying this framework in his business. He is teaching me and Annie this technique at home. It's simple, but powerful. In fact, it changed the way software is being developed. Today it is being used to get many types of industry productions done and out to the marketplace. Our dad says that a Scrum team can be applied to build almost any task or job, to get it done quickly with measures of perfection."

In her excitement, Annie interrupts Peter with no pause. She speaks rapidly without taking a breath saying. "Agile is for flexibility and quickness, but it also takes a set of values and principles to work properly. Scrum is teamwork producing iterative small tasks, built within incremental timeframes to the final product. The name Scrum came from Rugby, which is an English football game where the team would pass the ball at a scrimmage. In short, Agile and Scrum is an adaptive and actionable process to get things done as team members are empowered to self-manage and perform great things faster and better. It empowers team members to think, and reflect on what they do, so that they can improve and perfect their team to win."

Annie reaches the end of her breath. Without air, she feels dizzy and starts to wobble a bit, and her face loses color as she becomes flush and hypoxic. Reaching for the chair she inhales a fresh breath of air as she steadies herself.

Peter steps in. "Catch a breath sister. Anyway, as Annie was just saying, it worked so well in software development that other industries took note. You see, we use the Scrum process to manage our chores, schoolwork, and family events at home. It's a way to tackle any job."

Just then Matt jumps in. "Whoa, wait a minute . . . Dude, you said that you use Scrum for homework? You both are straight "A" students. Is this your secret? Do tell." Annie steps-in after catching her breath. "Well Matt, we do study hard, but with homework you have got to be strategic to complete it well. What I mean is this. Homework is also about organizing your time, knowing where you stand, getting it done and then reflecting on what you can do to improve your approach to learning it. These things are the essentials of the Deming cycle of Scrum: "Plan – Do – Check – Act."

Matt's eyes brighten up as he begins to speak. "Whoa. Guys. You are blowing me away." Nina speaks out. "What do we need to do? "Just pay attention to Peter." He then runs up to the whiteboard and draws three swim lane sections: Backlog – Work in Process – Done. "Here is how we are going to design and build the Pet Rescue Center. Introducing the Scrum Board." He takes the yellow sticky note pads, passes them around the room and starts to speak. "Take three sticky notes and write each project feature as a story. Okay. Here is the story format that we use for each user story, so that we can capture three things: What it is that we are building, what are the benefits, and who is it for."

Peter shows a sample of a high-level epic, and its first user story. Here is how the story would go: As a Pet Rescue Center administrator, I need a website, so that I can make people in my community aware of the need to adopt a pet. Next, Peter talks about the steps to build our Pet Rescue Scrum Board. He then writes down the Epic. Here is the EPIC, the big story: To get support and to inform the public of the need for Pet Adoption in their community. Peter explains. "Okay, take your yellow sticky notes and write down three stories that you think will best serve to help support the pet store and to inform the public. Don't worry about the estimates or priority. We will vote on these later. For now, just write down the story title, and the story."

As the team was writing down their stories, Peter went over to the whiteboard and placed the Epic story on the board. Peter explains. "Next, we add user stories underneath these epics, describing what features a Web-App needs to have, so it can function well. We refine the product backlog by splitting these user stories into bite-size product features and then ballpark the story estimates by using a relative size technique that involves all team members to discuss, and to understand what it would take to build the story. We prioritize each user story by placing what we must have on top of the list, and what is nice to have at the bottom. Our Product Owner then helps us determine the overall Minimal Viable Product, or MVP of what is needed to develop first within a short increment of time. Scrum works so well because it's an iterative-based approach to building things." Peter completes the description of Scrum. Here are the steps. Peter goes through each of the elements of Scrum.

"Wow. I see how this works. I'm in." Says Nina. "Me too." Says Hamster. Matt looks at Nina and Hamster as if they are both out of their minds. Looking perplexed, Matt speaks out, "Really? You guys get this stuff? Wait a minute. You mean to tell me that we can establish a non-profit, create a bank account, and build a web site in less than four weeks?" Peter responds. "Yes. That is correct Matt." "No, that is insane, Peter. I got surfing, guitar lessons, surfing, tons of homework, and surfing. No way. I am way too busy." Annie steps in. This time with her normal cool, calm, and collective voice she says. "Matt, remember this is teamwork." Annie continues. "Here Agile & Scrum considers your time and my time in capacity planning. It also considers team skillsets. For instance, Peter, Hamster, and I are programmers and developers. Nina is a leader and loves to organize and write. Lizzy and Bolt have multiple talents including UX/UI, Web Development, graphics, and testing. You Matt, are good with people, processes, and tools."

"One thing that Peter and I forgot to tell you is that it takes an Agile Scrum team. That team consists of three roles. Developer, Product Owner, and Scrum Master.

1. Developers build, test, and do the work.

2. Product Owner's owns the product and accepts the work.

3. Scrum Master's facilitates the team and keeps them moving forward.

Annie continues. "Guy's … We are a TEAM. Our parents own a technical business. I can get the business license established and my dad will show me how to set up the merchant account. We got this." Annie adds. "If it takes more than two sprints, or 4 weeks, we will know once we begin assessing and planning. We will first build the minimal value add as a prototype to adjust and tweak what is necessary. We can add another 2 weeks sprint to enhance and develop more if necessary."

Matt says. "Well, okay Annie, but please explain to me how you and Peter use Scrum to do your homework. I don't see a team fit here." "Oh, that's not necessarily true," said Annie. "As the student, I take on the Developer role. My dad takes the Product Owner role and checks my work. My mom takes the Scrum Master role and keeps me on track with a quick daily standup. If mom and dad are busy, you just discipline yourself to take on all three roles as a scrum of one.

"Anyway, when I do my homework, I first breakdown and evaluate my teacher's homework assignments for the week through ideation. I write them down as user stories and place them in priority order on the Scrum Board under the backlog column. I take each story of homework requirements and move them on the board from left to right, beginning with the Backlog column, to the Work-In-Progress column, and finally, once homework is checked, the story goes to the Done column. The board is visual in my room, so it helps me to see what I need to do each day to complete it well."

Matt looks at Annie and Peter. "Dude … Are you telling me that you have a Scrum Board in your home?" "Yes, absolutely," says Annie. "We thought about going with an online Scrum Board app, but we like the physical white board best because it is so quick and visual. Besides, I like the action of moving stories from In-Progress to Done." "Alright, you convinced me," said Matt. "I'm in. Team, we can do this!" "Yes, we can do this." Said Nina. Matt blurts out. "Yes. All in favor, give a thumbs up."

Looking around the room, everyone on the team had their thumbs up. This is the beginning of the Toasters Club, and everyone is onboard. They pause in silence realizing that this is the start of something very big. They are on to something that will be quite meaningful for them to do with their life. They join in a warm spontaneous group hug. "Toasted!"

In the last few weeks The Toasters Club had completed the initial web site for the pet rescue center. This website prototype raised $3,500 resulting in 153 dogs, cats, turtles and rat adoptions. They worked out all the website defects and then deployed its final iteration. Once approved. They turned the pet rescue website over to the local pet rescue center. As of today, the Toasters Club has taken on many new projects, both for their High School and for the community; however, they continue to volunteer at the Pet Center.

It's 7:10 in the Morning. The Toasters Club daily scrum meeting begins in 5 minutes in room 122, which is a typical school classroom at the high school. It is located next to the music class auditorium and is open every morning, as Janitor Ed opens it ahead of time specifically for the Toasters Club meetings. Jumping off their bikes and skateboards the Toasters come running through the door just in time. The Toasters Club meets every morning between 7:15 am and 8:40 am. School begins at 8:45 so there is time to meet and hold a quick discussion before class.

The team begins with their Scrum meeting. They are presented with an Epic story to accomplish release planning for a new school project to enhance the school's streaming media servers so that it does not crash or slow down under heavy load. The team kicks into place to complete the meeting in 15 minutes. Nina stands up and chooses Hamster to go first. She goes over the items for Hamster to speak about. Hamster begins with his typical Hamster humor. "Yesterday was Sunday, so I did nothing." Everyone laughs as Hamster continues. "Today, I am going to review the requirements to increase the capacity of the school media server. No blockers." The same questions go around the room. Peter, Matt, Annie, and Nina completed the meeting. Each Toaster Club member gives their Scrum account, and they begin their meeting to announce what the Epic story is all about and to accomplish release planning.

Nina stands up and goes over the media server project with the team and says, "we all know that nobody likes our school's online media system because it always freezes. It can only handle so many simultaneous hits and then it crashes. No one can watch reruns, or live stream media footage of Beachside Park High School football games, music concerts, theater, and dance performances. This totally sucks, so we are going to do something about it. Here is the plan. Keep the existing streaming media App server and connect it through a hosting service. This will take the streaming media from our server and replicate it with hosted cloud servers. We leverage the cloud servers so that we can gain more capacity. Hamster and Peter have already investigated it. We may need to raise a little money; however, I checked with the school PTA treasurer, and she said the cost won't be a problem. Hamster and Peter will be making sure the schools internet security remains intact."

As the school bell rings. Nina yells, "Meeting adjourned." Lizzy darts out first and the club members follow out the door. Nina walks with Hamster as they are both in the next class. Together they walk past the music auditorium. Lizzy had walked ahead and had propped opened the music room door. Looking in, they see Lizzy placing her violin case on the floor. She is there with Dr. Roy in music class. Nina stops at the door and waves at Lizzy. Lizzy looks back and sees Nina and Hamster. She waves back. Hamster nods. They continue walking together to science class.

Onward!

CHAPTER FOUR
The Single-Sided View of Science

LIZZY BEGINS HER music practice by playing minor platonic blues scales on the violin. The music auditorium is where she will be auditioning. This is a chance not only for her to perform with an orchestra but also to enter her original music score in the annual music competition in December. The concert is to be held at the Amphitheater and will take place in front of thousands.

Lizzy sits down with her violin. She has been composing songs since she was 7 years old. She had composed this piece that she would be playing this morning for Dr. Roy, the high school music teacher. She begins with a pause of silence. Dr. Roy sits across from Lizzy. He stares at his notepad so not to make her nervous. Dr. Roy always looks relaxed. Sitting laid back and wearing his Hawaiian shirt, Blue Jeans, and glasses halfway down his nose.

Dr. Roy learned to play piano from the music director at the Waialua Church in Hawaii, where he spent his summers visiting his uncle, aunt, and cousins from all the way out in Tennessee. They lived near the sugarcane processing factory in Waialua, Hawaii, before it was torn down. They said he was a natural at piano and learned to play quickly. He loves music, he loves people, and he loves God. To Dr. Roy, music is a joyous occasion of adulation for our creator. He received his PhD from Julliard, but at first meet, you would never know the complexity and magnitude of this man from his southern accent and relaxed manner. Hawaii being the southernmost state, he would pick up Pigeon English over the summer and spread this southern accent too. To Dr. Roy, it was fun to play with words and speech as he often joked about the differences. But in writing and speech, articulation was nowhere to be lacking as he holds a strong command of the English language. He would always state this quote: "Malevolent music is of transience, while transcendent music is of congenial light. It's notes and vibrations have wings."

With such a mouthful for man to ponder, no one in class knows what Dr. Roy is talking about. No one except Lizzy. She has a lot of respect for Dr. Roy. She trusts what he says and believes his criticism to be fuel for her future. Lizzy hands over her music score to Dr. Roy. She then adjusts her violin stance and begins her song. It's a perfect tone. Slow and moody, hitting the deeper notes on her alto-violin. Then, after a few bars, she breaks into a rapid stance. As she burns up her violin strings with a multifaceted array of notes. Dr. Roy stops her, grabs her score,

"hold on, Lizzy, your songs are excellent; however, people like simple songs."

"Are you sure, Dr. Roy? People are going to think that it's boring.

"I wish that I could compose like the great composer John Williams."

"I wish that I could transition my song into something more exciting."

"Really? You think so, Lizzy?" Says Dr. Roy.

"I don't know. It sure could be better, Dr. Roy?" Says Lizzy.

"Don't try to be someone else, Lizzy."

"There is only one you, and you have a story to tell."

"Your song sets a very good tone and mood. Now play your story."

"What is your story?"

Meanwhile, in science class some students had taken their seats. As the bell rings, more students arrive including Nina and Hamster. They quickly run to their seats as the final bell rings. Ah, just in time! Immediately, Nina looks toward the front of the class. There is Mr. Dunn, the science teacher, standing with the school principal, Principal Spinner. She is wearing a bright blue pantsuit. The principal is a true bureaucrat. As opposed to Mr. Dunn's long, wiry scientific hairstyle, Principal Spinner has short blond hair. Her head is completely shaved on one side; however, on the other side, she grows it out long enough to flip it over to cover the shaved side. It goes down to the bottom of her earlobe.

Principal Spinner sits on the edge of Mr. Dunn's desk in front of the class. Between them is a man. A new teacher? No one recognizes this person. He is well dressed, well-groomed, and likely in his early 20s with perfect skin and perfect hair. He is standing up straight and well-postured. His upper torso is straight as a board, yet his legs are slightly bent; they are forward of his body and looks a little funny when he walks because his walking posture looks just like a puppet. It's as if he was walking on strings, and the puppet legs dangle in front like a balancing act. Well, perhaps that is an exaggeration, but his eyes. Now, that's the strange part. They are soulless, moving about class as if he is recording and calculating every angle. One senses something strange with this person. The atmosphere around him feels quite different. Unhuman.

Nina looks over at Hamster. He sits in the same row, but he is on the left side of the class. From the corner of her eye, she sees his profile as he looks intently toward the front of the class. The entire class looks stunned. How interesting.

Mr. Dunn is our regular science teacher. Nina likes the class, but she doesn't buy in blindly with everything that is taught in science. She was brought up with a strong sense of research and debate, as there are various views and at least two sides to consider when evidence is lacking, and both sides take faith. Mr. Dunn is a Darwin fanatic and strongly discredits opposing views, especially those that challenge any idea of random chance, as this is so profound in his view. At this point, opposing research is mistakenly considered forbidden expressions while on public school property, although the U.S. Constitution still precedes it at this time.

Nina holds her tongue in class, but Hamster is fascinated with and influenced by his Jewish heritage. Mr. Dunn begins his class by making the "Leave your Judeo-Christian beliefs outside class with your backpack" statement for science. Mr. Dunn says the same thing each day in class to drive the point. At first, it used to intimidate Nina, but now she has grown accustomed. Most students have no issue with it; however, I know that some are taken aback.

Hamster is proud of his Jewish heritage and family values. Sunday school goer, Bar Mitzvah at age 13, and conservative to the core. He is against Mr. Dunn's attempt to shut down any opposing view. Hamster says that the Torah, which is the first five books of the bible, Genesis through Deuteronomy, is full of science. Hamster always says that even the very first verse of the Bible, Genesis 1.1, is a perfect example of Time, Space, and Matter!

It declares. In the beginning (Time), God created the heavens (Space) and the earth (Matter). Does this verse complement science, or does science complement itself? Hamster often gets in trouble for speaking his mind. He says things like. "Mr. Dunn, this is totally Meshuggah. Evolution is not a proven fact. It is just a theory. How can anyone toss out their core value and beliefs of who they are over a theory?"

Meshuggah is a Yiddish word for crazy or senseless. To Hamster, it is more about the principle of scientific consideration. That means taking in and examining all the facts. Of course, Mr. Dunn is thinking quite inversely.

Hamster is different than the average bear. We often discuss our common beliefs in a living God. He actually studies the scriptures. It is frustrating for really smart people to just roll over and allow someone to crush their beliefs in return for a better grade. One would think that a strong education means studying and appreciating valid opposing views. The strength of truth comes from the test of time. But one can also see Mr. Dunn's point. It casts doubt on the theory and opens up too much diversity that can also get off-subject. Science is science, faith is faith . . . But wait, does it take the same sort of faith to believe in science?

Mr. Dunn looks at Principal Spinner as she gestures for him to proceed with the class. Alright, class! You know what I am about to say, so repeat after me. . .

"LEAVE YOUR OLD JUDEO-CHRISTIAN BELIEFS OUTSIDE THE DOOR; THIS IS SCIENCE."

Most of the class recites this, some with enthusiasm, others remain in silent protest. Principal Spinner chuckles and looks at the class with a big, fake smile. She then turns to look at Mr. Dunn as he continues his speech. "Okay, class. I need to make this announcement." One can see Mr. Dunn's face change. The class is completely silent as he finds the words. "Okay, class, um, here it is . . . Today, the school made a decision and . . . "

Mr. Dunn pauses again. His voice begins to quiver as he speaks. What is it? The entire class is now sitting on the edge of their chairs. Mr. Dunn clears his voice and says, "After today, I will be RA-RA-RA retiring. Nearly barfing up his breakfast bagel as he utters the word retire. The school gave me an excellent pension plan, and I decided to take it.

"I will no longer be your teacher." Mr. Dunn breaks for a moment as he gains his composure. The entire class is shocked. You can hear a pin drop in the classroom. No one moves. Mr. Dunn continues. "I guess you will no longer have to put up with my opening statement." He looks over at Hamster, who is intensely staring at him, as he says. "Now, Hamster, don't look so happy about that." The class chuckles.

Hamster does not respond. Instead, he keeps staring at Mr. Dunn, wondering why people of non-conviction so disparately need the approval of others. Why is that? The room gets quiet. No words. It's a nervous time.

On the other hand, Principal Spinner breaks out into a loud, short laugh. It sounds like a rickety, raspy, deep evil-sounding utterance. Like this . . . Ah-ah-ah-ah. The new teacher looks up, pauses then laughs in queue with Principal Spinner. His laugh is in short sprints, like a digital rapid-fire sound. "Augh-augh-ah-uh-ah- Ugg."

Very annoying! Principal Spinner shuts up and quickly looks down at her notes. She always uses speech notes, speech cards, and teleprompters. In fact, no one has ever heard her speak from the heart. She has others write her speech for her. She begins her speech to the class in a highly banal manner, while Nina's mind immediately begins to wander.

Nina can hear Principal Spinner speaking in a monotone voice, mesmerizing her as she fades away. With eyes heavy, she falls asleep. Her subconscious state picks up the time last week when Principal

Spinner held the school assembly in the auditorium. During the assembly, Principal Spinner told a story while reading from her teleprompter. The story was about the time when President Ronald Regan visited her college back in 1984. She told them all how she could not stand the sight of President Regan, so she protested his visit. Nina thought, how could someone possibly dislike the most likable president in the USA? She remembers how during her speech and in front of everyone at the school assembly, Principal Spinner stood. Reading from a teleprompter, she proceeds.

"There I was, two rows back from Nancy and Ronald Reagan. Two people whom I absolutely loathe. I then realized that I was directly in front of Ronald as he stood with his wife, Nancy." Loudly, Principal Spinner blurts out the word SIGH.

The auditorium remained silent for the moment just after. Then, the students began to react. One student yelled out.

"What did she say?"

Another from the auditorium yelled back, "Oh, how funny."

"Whoops Spinner. Where did your fake sigh go?"

"Pay more attention to your teleprompter."

"Oh man, ha, ha-ha-ha-ha."

The students laughed hysterically as Principal Spinner just stood there staring down at them in a condescending manner. She waited for the noisy students to subside while she closed her mouth, using her tongue to adjust her dentures back and forth. A short pause of silence quieted the auditorium, so Principal Spinner started to speak again, but more students in the auditorium realized what had just happened, giving way to a loud disruption as the entire student body broke out in laughter.

Nina starts to laugh in her daydream. No one notices as it is silent laughter. Still in a dream, the memory of the Principal Spinner incident, saying the word "Sigh." This daydream causes Nina to irrepressibly exhale every particle of air from her lungs, and then inhale loudly with the sound of rushing air as it is forced back into her lungs. Then she slumps down in her chair with uncontrollable laughter, catching herself in twilight as she wakes from her daydream. She clears her throat to cover up, looking around to see if anyone has seen it. A few classmates look over at her with a blank stare. She sinks back down into her chair, but no one seems to care. Nina thinks to herself, "Wow, nobody caught me dosing off. How cool."

Principal Spinner continues talking… Wah-Wah-Wah. Wah-Wah-Wah. It's been 5 minutes since she began her speech, but that 5 minutes felt like a lifetime of boredom. Just then, Hamster begins to lose his concentration on what Principal Spinner is talking about. He thinks to himself, "I have always opposed Mr. Dunn's opening statement. Being with the people group that is on the outside of a fallen society. Mr. Dunn's statement is so politically correct, but at the same time it is insensitive. It targets only two groups that are not under any politically correct protection."

Hamster continues to think to himself: "Whoa, wait a minute. Could society have changed its politically correct stance? Hum. Could it be that Mr. Dunn is getting fired over his daily class statement? No! But wait, wait, wait a minute. If Mr. Dunn is getting fired for it, why would he have made this statement in front of the class just now? Furthermore, in front of Principal Spinner? If he is getting fired for saying; LEAVE YOUR OLD JUDEO-CHRISTIAN BELIEF'S OUTSIDE THE DOOR, THIS IS SCIENCE, then Principal Spinner would not have broken out into her obnoxious laughter. Right?"

Hamster, holding this inside conversation with himself, goes on hold as Mr. Dunn breaks in. This is just after Principal Spinner finishes, so to save his class from her tremendously banal speech, and to continue his announcement. Mr. Dunn says. "Thank you, Principal Spinner."

A few people in the audience clap as Principal Spinner turns off her teleprompter. Mr. Dunn walks over to his desk and leans on it as he says. "Again, thank you, Principal Spinner. Class, today I will be with you to launch our 16-week study of evolution before I leave. Here with me is Principal Spinner to introduce my wonderful replacement who will take over from here."

Principal Spinner turns on her teleprompter, flips through her electric notes, and begins a new speech. She fumbles a bit and then takes her posture. It looks presidential. Then, looking down at her notes, she begins to read. "Class, it gives me great sadness to announce that we are losing Mr. Dunn today. He had requested a transfer to Maple Valley High School. I proudly granted permission for that transfer."

Students in the classroom immediately begin to mumble. Hamster raised his hand while Principal Spinner shifted her eyes away from looking at the students in class as she was obviously distracted. Looking nervously through all her teleprompt notes, she suddenly pauses. She found it. She continues.

"Until his transfer today to Maple, he had served this school well. In fact, he had been with us over the years. Actually … He had been with us for 26 years, 2 months, and 16 days. We are going to miss him." According to her teleprompt notes. Wait a minute. Did Principal Spinner just say transfer? The whole class caught the mix-up. Nina thought that her teleprompt speechwriter had messed up again. Just then, Hamster spoke up with his hand still raised in the air.

"Principal Spinner."

"Not now, Hamster!"

"But Principal Spinner!"

"NOT NOW HAMSTER!"

Principal Spinner tries to shut Hamster up, but it is too late. He stands to his feet.

"Wait. Principal Spinner."

"which is it?"

"Which is what Hamster?"

"You just told us that Mr. Dunn is transferring."

Principal Spinner leans forward to Hamster and gives him an ugly stare. She shakes her head from side to side as she responds to Hamster while adjusting her dentures.

"Yeah, Hamster. And what's your point?"

"I'm not trying to make a point, Principal Spinner."

"Well, you are interrupting me, so PLEASE SIT DOWN AND BE QUIET!"

Hamster is not one to contend with if one wishes to crash a debate. If one thing they can just put a lid on Hamster by stating an ugly comment, that person is in for Hamster's cool reply. He speaks well and has won multiple debates and awards. Nina refers to Hamster as the best speaker that she knows. Principal Spinner does not have a chance, as Hamster will not leave her discrepancy alone. Hamster sits down and then says.

"I'm so sorry, Principal Spinner."

Principal Spinner responds in a sulky manner with a stare. She looks at her notes as she uses her tongue to play with her dentures. The bulge behind her closed lips is obviously her tongue running across her dentures from jaw to jaw, cheek to cheek. Hamster might as well be wearing an Inspector Colombo jacket and carrying a cigar as he stood back up to his feet, perfectly emulating Inspector Colombo as he says. "No, Principal Spinner. What I meant to say is this … I'm so sorry, but earlier, did I not hear Mr. Dunn announce his retirement?" Annoyed and startled, Principal Spinner quickly jerks as she yells.

"WHAT? WHAT IS IT HAMSTER?"

Hamster replies. "So, which is it, Principal Spinner?" The class becomes real quiet as everyone stares at Principal Spinner. Just then, something happened that no one had expected. Mr. Dunn yells out. "Transfer," at the same time, Principal Spinner says, "Retirement."

The entire class broke their silence. Student voices in the classroom become thunderous as they all speak among each other. What in the world? Okay, now, what is the real reason why Mr. Dunn is leaving? Principal Spinner became obviously agitated at Hamster and the class. She faced the class and then ripped into Mr. Dunn for the discrepancy and confusion. She needs no teleprompter when yelling commands, screaming, controlling, putting others down, blaming Mr. Dunn and others for shortcomings that she herself holds. A moment goes by, and Principal Spinner, looking even more frazzled and fatigued, realizes her predicament. She decides to spin her whole ordeal.

"CLASS! CLASS! If Mr. Dunn is confused of his reasons for leaving, being retirement, transfer, or whatever … WHAT DIFFERENCE DOES IT MAKE?"

The class swings back to complete silence. Mr. Dunn stands to his feet and motions to calm the class down. He then introduces our new teacher.

"Class, I want to introduce you to Mr. Rob Ottkin. He will be your new teacher beginning tomorrow as he is replacing me so that I can re … retire (he stumbles over his words) and so … so also to dab …dabble in adjunct teaching at Maple Valley High … on occasion."

"Good recovery," mumbles Hamster under his breath. Nina chuckles along with other students who overheard Hamster. Everyone knows that this is not the truth. Mr. Dunn exists only for his Darwin section on Evolution in science. It is highly out of place that he would be leaving at this time. Especially to be leaving for good. Mr. Dunn proceeds. "Mr. Ottkin, why don't you tell us a little about yourself?"

Mr. Ottkin smiles and looks at the class. There is silence for 4 seconds. Then Mr. Ottkin gives his profound words in reply.

"Hello Class!"

There is a pause as the new teacher scans the room, looking face-to-face at the students. Its head veers from left to right, followed by its eyes veering from left to right. The class is expecting him to say more. Then Mr. Dunn motions to the class to say hello. A few students responded.

"Um, Hello … Hello, Mr. Ottkin." Mr. Ottkin replies. "Hello students, my name is Mr. Ottkin. I am your new science teacher." As if no one knew. This is an awkward moment. Silence falls in the room. We all know it is true that not all science teachers have social skills, but this is sort of weird. Mr. Dunn steps in. "Okay, well, we have a lot to cover today, so Principal Spinner, with your permission, Mr. Ottkin and I would like to get started with the Evolution Series lecture."

Principal Spinner looks at Mr. Dunn, then looks at the class, and without a word, she proceeds toward the door. She then turns to the class and says. "I expect you all to make this a smooth transition for Mr.

Ottkin." She looks down at Hamster with a stern stare and then walks out the door. Slam! Mr. Ottkin, the new science teacher, continues to stand in the front of the classroom while Mr. Dunn goes to the board and begins his lecture on evolution.

"Class, this is a pivotal section in our science studies. We have a lot to cover, but first, I need to make sure that I strip you of your mid-evil beliefs and replace them with wonders and hard modern facts. Darwin's theory is proven science."

"Those of you who have a belief in a god, or some sort of creator, supreme being, need to know this un-debatable fact . . . The god, or gods, of your small-minded parents, are not found in science."

"Faith is chance, and science is real. I see no debate. You know this, and I know this. Only small thinkers need a god to make up for their own ignorance."

"I implore you all to join humanism and become a Humanist of modern social science by turning from your puny traditional beliefs as a Realists would do. Modern man has no need for that stuff, as many of you all know, and many of you will soon discover in life. Hopefully, starting today in science. Today, we begin our journey through the hard facts of evolution."

Mr. Dunn goes to the whiteboard and writes in big letters the header; Fact One Origin. He underlines Fact One while continuing his lecture. "Fact One Origin: The earth is billions, billions, and billions of years old. Man has an extremely tiny part of this level, where the earth and life on earth just happened by chance."

"From stars and planets exploding by chance to where we have Earth, and it depends on other planets. Yes, we will be studying the planets, our earth, and the Big Bang theory where all things began from the goo of plasma to you and me, who are of our monkey ancestors. Who had evolved over time to become the mankind we see today. Here, the basis of man is no higher than any other creature on the planet."

"Man has no special value. In light of the entire scope of evolution, man has no special significance except for social responsibility and the responsibility to care for her life support – Mother Earth."

"Science is fact. Here, no one was born with a destiny or a purpose. Those who think that there is a God and that God gave their insignificant life a purpose are experiencing pure delusions of grandeur. Hope is no more than a pipedream that belongs separated from fact, from science. It is not fact; it is a religious wish, and those who believe this stuff will be plucked out by Natural Selection."

Mr. Dunn goes to the whiteboard and writes in big letters the header; Fact Two Natural Selection. He now underlines Fact Two. "Fact Two Natural Selection: Our destiny is not rooted in a wish to become something great."

"Class, what I teach in science is for your very survival! We must learn facts, not faith. Natural Selection is case hardened fact, for with it, we reveal a law to survive. Survival of the fittest will take over and crush the weaker man. We will study the law of survival and how animals had fought to survive, which is a fight from becoming extinct over billions of years."

"To meet this law, we must know that our puny ethics will only take on an interesting twist. You see, with the law of survival, it is for every man, woman, or genetic X mutation to itself. Yes, even the very genetic mutations or the number of gender identifications we have today, as there are many that one can identify with today. And for those with ears to hear. Listen up folks, transhumanism is just around the corner, making its mark with the help of Artificial Intelligence and Machine Learning, AI/ML. It's time to evolve people."

"This idea is a pure evolutional fact because technology is there, and genetic mutations are a necessary reality due to our environmental pressures. To survive, you must toss out your faith and learn the facts. It's about survival, not turning the other cheek to meekness. How pathetic, weak, and ignorant one becomes when they allow faith to rule over their intelligence, as they think it pleases some sort of god in heaven. Mark my words, god's kingdom is lost in space. Ah, ha, ha, ha, ha."

"Class, on this earth, you need to survive. Use your brain! Church people turn their brains off. Don't do that. You see, in this world, it's highly acceptable to win and to survive at any cost. Each one of you is

here on this planet for one thing, and one thing only, and that is to fulfill your bucket list. Follow your instincts as in the sacred words of modern commercialism: "If it feels good … Do it. Or might I add, "he with the most toys wins. Oooo, such wisdom comes off the sophisticated realms of a proud, self-made man like me. I need no introduction to a deity. Ha, ha, ha. Amen."

Mr. Ottkin, the new teacher, suddenly breaks out in applause. Some in the class follow in a slight low-energy golf clap-type applause. Nina just rolls her eyes. As a deep believer, she is very familiar with this sort of putdown. Hamster raises his hand. Mr. Dunn looks around the room, and when he sees Hamster, he clearly becomes agitated. "Yes, Hamster."

Hamster continues with his question, "Mr. Dunn, is evolution indeed a fact, or is it a theory?" "Here we go again, class." Mr. Dunn replies. The class laughs. Mr. Dunn really wants to crush this sort of question and challenge all who oppose Darwinism with such stupid questions. He steps back and pauses for a moment. The fact is, he is not quite ready to answer this question. If the truth is known, he does not know how to answer it, so he does what any intelligent teacher would do to save face when unable to answer a tough student question while in front of the class. He throws the question back at the class.

"Class, what do you think?"

Just then, the bell rings. Everyone jumps up and heads for the door. Mr. Dunn thinks to himself. "Whew, that was close." He then speaks out loud to the class, "I wish you all the best. Take care." The class responds.

"You too, Mr. Dunn."

"Later-on Dunn."

Nina and Hamster meet up outside of class and walk together again. Nina's next class is History. Hamster has calculus. Nina says. "What did you think, Hamster, wasn't that the craziest thing? "Wow, our new Science teacher is strange." Said Hamster. "Yah . . . What about Mr. Dunn leaving our school?" "Something very strange and inconspicuous is happening, and our principal is behind it. I think she is totally crooked." Nina replies: "You really think so, Hamster?" Hamster stops and says. "I know so."

Just then, Matt shows up. He is in Nina's History class. They usually hook up and walk over to class together. There is only 6 minutes between classes, but it's located in the next building. It's a short walk, so they have a little time.

Matt blurts out. "Hey guys."

"Hey Matt, you will not believe what just happened." Says Nina.

The math lab is on the other side of the school, so Hamster must bug out of there to make it on time. He says. "Got to go, I'll catch up with you guys in Music." "Okay, Hamster – catch you later." Says Matt. "Bye, Hamster." Says Nina. Hamster runs to his next class as Matt and Nina walk slowly to History class.

"Hey Matt, check this out," Nina tells Matt all that just happened in science class. Matt is not much for conspiracy theories, so Nina was very surprised at his next statement. Matt responds. "Do you think they will replace all our teachers?" "No, Mr. Dunn is retiring. That's all." Says Nina.

What Matt did not tell Nina was that he had recently been seeing some strange meetings going on in Principal Spinner's office. They look like a group of consultants meeting with her. Matt volunteers in the school administration office. He's been volunteering at school since he became a member of the Toasters Club. He said it gives him a better edge so that he can book our Toasters Club room and rub shoulders with school administrators in case he needs to pull strings to get things done for the Toasters Club. Matt is not the only one to see these meetings. He overhears office workers talk about it all the time. According to office rumors, people are saying that the school ran out of money, and to keep things rolling, it will be replacing all the teachers and all the workers with younger and less expensive workers from overseas per the new organization, The Transpacific Partnership (TTP).

Matt is not one to spread rumors, so he holds this to himself. He chooses not to tell Nina. It's this quality that she likes about him. "Of course, that makes sense," says Matt. Nina and Matt walk to class. Mr.

Bryan, the History teacher, greets them with a big smile and says. "Hi, guys." "Hi, Mr. Bryan," says Nina and Matt.

The bell rings as Nina and Matt scurry to their seats. Mr. Bryan is one of Nina's favorite teachers. She never had a history teacher quite like Mr. Bryan. She learns so much from him, as he is very knowledgeable and pro-American, which is highly unusual for a high school history teacher these days. She is not certain of which side Mr. Bryan agrees with. He seems to hold that to himself, as a respectful teacher would do; however, he does attempt to balance right and left ideas as he discusses polarization and the need to value both sides. In fact, he often paraphrases a quote from Dr. Ben Carson's famous 2013 National Prayer Breakfast speech; "An Eagle will never fly high and properly on one wing. It takes two wings."

One thing that Mr. Bryan is strict about is research. Although Nina finds research to be very painful, she can sure see why research is highly important. Research and balance are how one keeps from getting duped into believing in a false idea. Mr. Bryan teaches world history; however, he ties American history events with modern periods. It is interesting.

Nina was a little worried that Mr. Bryan would be leaving too, just like Mr. Dunn did; however, the class wrapped up with no sign of Principal Spinner and no introductions of a new teacher. Hopefully, the case of Mr. Dunn quitting science was just a one-off.

With history class over in no time, it is now time for Dr. Roy's Music Class. Hamster caught up with Nina and Matt in music class. Lizzy and Annie are also in this class. Peter is a grade younger, and Bolt has P.E., so he and Bolt are the only ones not in class, but most of the Toaster club members are in music class together. Dr. Roy is a real fun teacher. His speech and his unique personality indeed complements this. He starts class.

"Okay class. Turn in your textbooks."

He pauses and looks down at his notes while the class gets out their textbook and passes them forward to the students in the row in front. With Dr. Roy pretending to be focused on the notes in his hand, the front row collects the final textbook and piles them in the front of the room. Nina passes her textbook to Matt, who is sitting in front of her. Dr. Roy continues to pause. He waits until everyone has passed in their textbooks, and then he says.

"Turn in your textbook to page 248." Dr. Roy looks up at the class. "What?"

"Now, what are y'all passing in your textbooks for?"

"Lizzy, did I tell the class to pass in their books?"

"I just said for y'all to turn in your textbooks… to page 248. I did not say to hand in your textbooks. Class, y'all got to make some personal improvements here. Please take note of this issue that y'all have." Once they catch on to what is happening, the class begins to laugh loudly.

Dr. Roy continues. "Now pass them all back and then turn to, or open, to page 248."

He walks back and forth in front of a class, holding back his chuckle. This was on purpose. Dr. Roy does that sort of thing. He loves to joke around with the class. Silliness and laughter open people to the creativity and inspiration that so often gets knocked out of students during their early industrial-age school environments. He works all year to regenerate the Creator's likeness in them. It is absolutely amusing. The class loves his jokes once they catch on.

"Man! And here I was thinking y'all were top students in my class."

"Well, that's what they all told me."

"Beachside High … Blue Ribbon Californian School. Hum… really?"

"I reckon that I'm gun-a need to have a word with y'all about that."

The class laughs as the students pass their textbooks back to the rows. Dr. Roy, with his perfect southern accent and his PhD from Julliard, was contagiously filled with joy and laughter. Julliard happens to be the most prestigious Music school in America. They say, don't judge a book by its cover. Well, we are indeed lucky. Lucky to have Dr.

Roy as a music teacher. He is a real treasure for the school's music program. Just as Lizzy always says …

We're Lucky!

CHAPTER FIVE
A Word About Dr. Ott

DR. OTT, THE MAD scientist in town, is hard at work deep in his underground laboratory. He is in his late 30's with thick, coarse wiry black hair that is not well kept. His beady black eyes are covered behind thick metallic wire glasses that went out of fashion ten years ago. They are the ones that darken and convert to sunglasses while in the sun.

Dr. Ott lives with his mom, a very gentle old woman who is completely oblivious to the fact that her son is a mad scientist with ambitions to control the world, beginning with Beachside Park. She is also somewhat absentminded, still thinking that her son, whom she calls "Otty," is 10 years old. Otty is Dr. Ott's childhood name.

When Otty, DR. Ott, was 4 years old, his dad disappeared in a freak accident. His dad was highly intelligent. In fact, he invented a fuel system that converted water into hydrogen fuel. It only took a small modification of a conventional engine and worked with both piston and jet turbine engines. The system uses a catalyst that is fed with a high electric charge pulsed to convert water, which is H2O, to hydrogen at the point of combustion. Dr. Ott's dad was also an accomplished test pilot.

They say he disappeared during a flight test while he was FAA certifying his H2O to hydrogen fuel converter. His invention was easily modified from piston-driven aircraft to turbo engines for jets. Although flight testing is a dangerous profession, his dad's death was a mystery because the experimental jet exploded in mid-air. The thing is, the fuel tanks were full of antifreeze-treated water, not hydrogen fuel. H2O was converted to hydrogen within the engine's fuel system just prior to ignition. No hydrogen needed to be stored in tanks. It was completely safe from any Hindenburg-type incident.

Incidentally, during that time, there was a high mortality rate among alternative energy scientists and inventors. Big oil companies hate people like Dr. Ott's dad. Yes, there were many scientists who strangely died prematurely for inventing energy that was more powerful and cleaner than conventional oil-based fossil fuels. It was a mystery. They never found the body of Dr. Ott's dad.

With the disappearance of Otty's dad, Otty's mom did what any mom would do; she poured herself into Otty's life and his education. She also pushed Otty to grow up fast. She used all her financial resources for Otty's education. As a result, Otty had no life. With having no normal childhood life growing up, Otty became highly intelligent but socially disabled due to gaining no social skills at all. His school schedule allowed for no time, no friends, and no social activities as it was highly suppressed from the intended fullness of life. To Otty, in his young years, life was only Math.

Otty graduated high school at an early age of 14. He was top of the class. He went on to earn his undergraduate degree from MIT, where he also graduated top of the class. Within 3 years, he had earned a Bachelor of Science degree in chemistry with a minor in bio-computing. With honors.

It was just before his 18th birthday when he was invited to study in graduate school at Stanford University on a full scholarship. He spent the next 4 years at Stanford's School of Engineering, where he studied things like artificial intelligence, biophysics, robotics, and more. It was a dream come true.

When he received his PhD, he changed his name from Otty to Dr. Ott. Changing his name was a goal that Otty really wanted to achieve. He thought Mom would ditch the name Otty and now call him Dr. Ott. Well, it didn't work out that way.

Dr. Ott held several jobs; however, he was indeed socially challenged. Colleagues would talk about sports teams and the latest T.V. shows. Dr. Ott knew nothing about those things. Early in his career, he knew he would have to someday make it on his own and not rely on employment. He was not cut out to be an employee. One would think that this sort of thing would pan out during school years, as schools teach students to be good industrial-age era job munching employees, contributing as fiat currency income tax feeders. For Dr. Ott, this was not the case. He was highly respected at school; however, as an employee? Well, he never fit in. At one company his manager took advantage and treated him poorly. Dr. Ott was amazed at how little his manager knew, yet he was the top boss, earning the top salary. How could one be so lacking and keep his job through longevity during all the ups and downs and end up gravitating to the top? How could one go through life and not learn a single thing except for the soul-hardening survival skills of corporate politics? Dr. Ott learned that, in some cases, it's not what you know but who you know. These managers are leeches who grow fat by riding on the backs of workers. When the manager was done with a worker, all he had to do was badmouth the worker in front of the right people, and that worker was gone on to the next worker.

With the economic downturn, worker intelligence went out the door. Highly skilled leaders were replaced by highly skilled politicians who knew how to spin things so as to look good for themselves. It was many middle managers who had no practical skillsets. These managers would, in turn, hire brainless employees, thus proving the mediocre manager theory.

If you have never heard of the Mediocre Manager Theory, here it goes: Top A-quality leaders hire top A-quality thinkers and performers. But B-quality manager's fire those top A-quality professionals to hire, promote, and keep C-quality workers so that they can dominate and control. The mediocre manager blocks any action to make things great in order to keep the status quo. Ask any political expert. The mediocre manager's greatest fear is those who show true leadership acumen. The thing is, there is a certain guarantee that "A-Level" managers are indeed leaders of professionals as they are motivators and cultivators of highly performing teams of top-quality workers. They are true leaders who make hard decisions first, and others tend to follow them. That is because they are driven by a keen imagination where they always find a way to work things out and are more interested in building and progressing and are horrible and disinterested in corporate management, let alone the politics it takes to toss others under the bus, claw one's way to the so-called "Top.". They find this sort of positioning uninspiring and toxic.

The A-level managers make excellent Agile Leaders because they know how to empower, lift others up, and build up a team. They drive toward perfecting their craft, the work process, and the quality product.

They also know the power of praise and how to recognize and attract excellent talent. This is because they are highly skilled in mentorship, motivation, team cultivation, and encouraging workers to also do their best. They are focused on getting things done and making it great.

On the other hand, "B-level" managers are not leaders at all. This is because they have no imagination. No one will follow them; therefore, they are not open to what it takes to achieve Agile Leadership; thus, they resort to trivial tracking, reporting, and micro-management. They manage people via command and control. Here, they must hire C-level workers. This is because C-level workers are the ones who make the B-level managers look better, as they never challenge direction with ideas toward continual improvement. They just take orders thoughtlessly. Well, that theory continued to remain proven throughout Dr. Ott's career as an employee. The Mediocre Manager Theory!

After a decade of working for harsh managers and going through up and down employment, Dr. Ott became fed up with the corporate employment lifestyle where a certain lack of intelligence remained at the workplace while a majority of highly intelligent workers were standing in line at unemployment. Before long, Dr. Ott was looking for ways to get out of the corporate rat race. He developed a large distaste for the working world and dreamed of replacing every mediocre manager and every mediocre employee with a robot.

They say that this is what drove him to come out with his first great achievement; the invention of a realistic techno-charged plastic polymer that looks and feels just like warm human skin. This is what Dr. Ott uses to cover the human-like computerized frames of each robot. It makes each bot-teacher, humanoid worker bot, or robot seem alive.

With Dr. Ott's invention, he knew his time had come to begin his robot business. At first, his eyes were set on taking over the hundreds of thousands of minimum-wage jobs through AI and automation. As Dr. Ott always said to himself. "As minimum wage goes higher and higher, corporations will come running to me." You see, Big Government steps in and demands top salaries just for flipping burgers. With this, Dr. Ott is right … Forget human labor; let's talk robots … let's automate!

Dr. Ott calculated how if the burger flipper earns a high $ dollar minimum wage per hour, the government will also earn a hefty rate per hour per worker on top of that minimum wage. It is the additional regulatory fees, compliance classes, and the time business owners spend filling out endlessly growing government forms just for the privilege of having this forced partnership with the government. Most of the cost is through labor regulations, licenses, law, insurance, and taxation. The government also earns a heavy inflow of cash through taxing those poor employees. It costs the company at least 30 percent more per hour on top of the minimum wadge they business owners pay their employees. Who wins? It's the government machine who wins, not the people. With the government getting more wealthy, they can impose more government regulations, more insurance, and more state-run programs to help the jobless, the homeless, the student loan recipients, and so forth. What was once a high schooler job flipping burgers now becomes a main source of focus, as underemployment becomes the new norm. This elite "Hunter Games utopia" ends up pinching more profits as it punches talented professionals in the stomach until it implodes prosperity, and the skilled talent goes elsewhere to more business-friendly locations.

In the end, voting to put big government in charge of labor and business makes the government fat and wealthy, and citizens broke, out of work, and dependent on the impoverished nowhere life that big government has to offer. Beachside Park has high unemployment. Of course, with every crisis, there is always an opportunity. More robots, Dr. Ott, thinks to himself as he gives a big grin.

"How absurd."

"How utterly and wonderfully absurd."

"How enormously, yet wonderfully brilliant."

"Ah-ha, ha. Ugg. Ah-ha, ha. Ugg. Ah-ha, ha, ha, ha."

Dr Ott's raspy laugh sounds habituated. He continues. "I will introduce my lifelike humanoid robots to governments, schools, corporations, and other organizations in industry. My robots will work, and I will collect the paychecks. My robots will take over your puny, worthless jobs as they pay me for digital hours used. Today, AI and singularity will replace the jobs of people. "I will make humans the servants of my robots. Ah-ha, ha! Ah-ha, ha! Ah-ha, ha, ha, ha, ha!"

Dr. Ott is on to something. His ignorance of various skills deludes his view. In his mind, certain types of work are bottom of the caste, so robots are prime candidates. He severely discredits the importance of human workers. What does it take to flip-burgers, take orders, teach children, drive a truck, perform minor surgeries, administer medicine, engineer software, research law, fly a plane, or manage other people? In other words, what would it take to do your job? Is your job safe? Is it safe from Artificial Intelligence? Look around. Is your job safe from being taken over by robots and total automation? Dr. Ott stands up and cries like a super-mad scientist.

"People, your job is nothing. I am going to build lifelike robots that manage people, mentor people, educate people, inform people, transport people, entertain people, administer health treatments, manage bank accounts, help people with household chores, and become their best friends. Since AI relies on copying from a database of created originals, having no ability for original creation, it is the true creator, with human inspiration, innovation, and creation, that I fear. Creators are my only enemy, as they have the true ability to tap into the creator as their source. They are a threat to me, so I must crush them. "Yes. Crush the Creators." With my lifelike robot invention of imitators, I must keep people in the dark so that they never know real life from machines." Again, Dr. Ott lets out his evil laugh. It's a high-pitched, scar-throaty, raspy, whiney cry. Ah-ha, ha. Ah-ha, ha. Ah-ha, ha, ha, ha, ha!"

Ugh, such an evil smirk on Dr. Ott's face. There is one thing Dr. Ott had always done right, when he worked for other companies as lead Robot scientist. If you are an inventor, you may want to pay attention here. Whenever Dr. Ott was hired as an employee, he would make a deal where he was able to keep all his royalties. It was easy to do. You see, every time he was hired at a new job, he would amend his employment agreement so that he could get credit for his intellectual property. He would never sign up and allow the company that he worked for to receive credit for any of his inventions. Never!

Most employees do not pay attention to their employee contracts, but just about every company has a section where it demands its employees to turn over their ideas, their dreams, and their inventions. It's in the employee contract.

The thing is, most companies do not really believe in their employees beyond their view of them fulfilling the job title and description. It is evident that most companies, not all, view their workers as a commodity and not a value asset; thus, in most cases, these agreements to give away intellectual capital are just a formality. Most corporate managers don't think of their people as potential assets with valuable ideas and inventions. Managers who lack leadership skills believe workers will not amount to anything, and in many cases, their miscalculations of human ingenuity cost companies a huge loss in potential. As is true with many workers in America, there is no longer such thing as the employer employee loyalty once enjoyed by professionals in our grandparent's generation.

You see, once cultivated in the right environment, employees are worth much more than traditional management realizes. The key is to hire leaders and managers who know how to cultivate and empower workers. In other words, servant leaders not command and control managers. The worst sort of managers are ones with no imagination no people skills. I'm not sure why this is never screened out. Dr. Ott, his ideas are worth Billions of dollars today. Dr. Ott always listed the ideas that he was working on before joining the company; thus, his ideas were exempt. He was able to escape this horrible intellectual capital agreement contract as long as he kept the ideas he was working on listed prior to joining.

Dr. Ott invented the lifelike polymer by accident when he was fooling around with creating a rubber-plastic blue ball during college spring break. The plastic was wrapped with a thin conductive electronic mesh that created a charge. He was trying to get the ball to bounce up 100 feet into the atmosphere on one bounce as it was highly charged. His color additive gave off a chemical reaction that reached the perfect temperature of 98.6 degrees, and the material felt just like touching a human. The ball was a total failure … It never bounced more than 9 feet, 8.6 inches.

He was ready to give up when his college roommate needed a blue avatar outfit for a lead role in the school theater play. Otty created the costume outfit through body casting. It was so lifelike that the university theater commissioned him to create the entire set. Otty repurposed the lifelike polymer to replace human skin when he read about the orphanage home for boys in Ventura County, California, where so many boys working there were severely burnt, and some were killed in an orange fruit storage shed fire. The boys were using gasoline to clean out the black tar residue of oranges that stained the floors and walls during storage. The gasoline violently ignited when it came in contact with the pilot flame of the natural gas water heater. It caught fire and trapped so many boys in the orange fruit storage shed, burning them.

That same year, Otty introduced the idea of using lifelike polymer as a replacement for skin for burn victims in a speech at the university medical device conference, but his idea went nowhere. It was not until he began working for his first medical device company that his idea caught on. This is where he struck his first deal for the invention.

It gained such a high profile in the industries journal that the manager who he worked for learned of the deal and reported it to the company, suspecting that he used company time. His company took him to court; however, with his amended list of inventions already in play, he was cleared, so he won full credit and full royalties.

Dr. Ott made a fortune from his lifelike polymer invention. He used the money to build his secret underground laboratory. It is located underneath his childhood house on the hill in Beachside Park. It is interesting to note how Dr. Ott once wanted to help people. What went wrong? How did he end up a mad robot scientist?

Dr. Ott takes the elevator down to the first level of the lab. The lab is dark, with walls of LED lights and electronics. One can hear the assembly line in the background. The assembly line is on the bottom floor. The first and second levels circle around the lab.

Dr. Ott peers over the ledge of the first floor. He poses as he stares forward, looking over the laboratory. His glasses reflect the electronic lights that line the walls of laboratory systems. With eyes wide open he turns his head from one side to the other in a glimpse of total command. And then . . . A loudspeaker screeches over the intercom!!!!

"Screech!" It's mom ….

"Otty, Otty."

Dr. Ott's mom tries to whistle, like an old WWII Navy ship whistles before sounding a message. She continues speaking over the intercom. "Breaker one-nine. Breaker one-nine." Ham Radio speaks. Her voice echoes throughout the chamber as Dr. Ott collapses in humility as he replies.

"Yes, Mom."

"Otty, I've made milk and cookies. Come and get them while they're still hot."

Dr. Ott crouches down behind his laboratory chair and pauses. Then forgetting that the microphone is still on. He says, "Why me? I'm so Humiliated."

"What was that, Otty?" Says Mom.

"Oh … Um. I said I'll be right up, Mom."

Back with the Toasters Club, their school product idea was about to be story-mapped during their design thinking sprint, but first, the 15-minute scrum meeting. Matt positions the scrum board on the wall: Backlog – Work in Process – Done. The Toasters Club signed up to help their school share its streaming videos that inform students of events and allow students to post their video projects. They will be applying their actionable Agile Scrum energy to build a new web post and play the video application. The application is called "Talking Wolfs." The Talking Wolf's video application will have both online PC and Mobile capability. Talking Wolfs is named after the school mascot which is the Beachside Park High School Wolfs.

There are many hidden talents noted every day within the Toasters Club. It is amazing to see these talents come out when proper leadership techniques are applied. Agile and Scrum have been highly profitable for corporations that understood the need to scale winning teamwork and profit from this operational replication of professional self-managed teamwork. It's not popular with industrial-age management roles, but those who are natural leaders and business owners know the art of delegation and replication. Man. Agile rockets their ability and profits into orbit. It yields things like highly traceable team production scores where process improvement is consistently realized at greater than 300 percent within 6 weeks. Such empowerment has many benefits.

One of those benefits is the ability to bring out the best in workers. This is accomplished through its communications and its high emphasis on improvement; however, its greatest benefit is its leadership technique. Here, trust is valued and earned as leadership is framed with a laissez-faire "Hands-Off" approach, resulting in leadership that provides a high-value atmosphere where hyper-team production thrives. This style of leadership is not for sidekick career managers. Instead, it's for leaders. True leaders who are interested in making something great! For those leaders, Agile Scrum is sought after by organizations from around the world.

There are few teams that really know how to cooperate. Cooperation is the secret sauce of the Toaster's Club. Here, team members don't talk about problems. Instead, The Toaster's Club members act, speak, and solve problems. Although the action is calculated and assessed well for feasibility and value, it is never prolonged, regurgitated, or delayed. Flexible action is king. If the problem is complex, critical, or the first of its kind, then these factors are considered split into smaller, accomplishable sizes, and wisdom is warranted from outside experts. But if it is a matter the team can handle, then the team goes for it. It absolutely places empowerment in the hands of the team. Improvement, Cooperation, and Empowerment. It is here where team member talents explode.

Cooperation is where individuals come together and become team members. Although they have individual talents, they do not overpower the team, nor do they try and stick out above the team. Instead, they cooperate just like they would in a baton race where the runner holding the baton must become less aware of their own race and more aware of how they will successfully pass off the baton. This is actionable teamwork. In Agile Scrum organizations, workers find themselves involved in creativity, technology, and research. They find themselves continually improving the way they work.

It is amazing how work becomes satisfying and workers become more productive and profitable. Toasters find themselves in a total habit-changing atmosphere. They interchange roles so that they can gain new skill sets and become mentors rather than the student and vice versa. Toasters regularly change leadership roles; although some are better at leadership than others, it doesn't matter. The team members always cooperate and help each other out when necessary.

Today, Matt has taken on the role of Scrum Master. Nina is the Product Owner. Matt stands up and quickly addresses the Toasters Club. It's our stand-up Scrum meeting, and we all agreed that during this meeting, we would all stand to our feet and keep the Scrum meeting time at less than 15 minutes. Keeping the meetings within 15 minutes is not an easy thing to do, particularly for a complex project consisting of multiple challenges, from the User Interface (UI) to expanding the capacity of the infrastructure to take on multiple simultaneous hits.

Video is memory intensive, and so to keep it streaming at ultrahigh speeds and to also make the video stream a quality picture for everyone who clicks on the website, our system must have the ability to scale up to the video demand. Matt completes the Scrum meeting on time and hands the sprint planning session over to Nina.

Nina quickly goes to the board to assess progress. She addresses the team. "Okay, here is our approach for building Talking Wolfs. I built the product backlog, so we all can now go over it as a team."

"The Epic Stories are:

1) Design a simple user process flow to post and play videos on Video Wolf

2) Build the web framework

3) Create the architecture with capacity"

Nina then takes her Product Backlog full of yellow sticky notes and, places it on the screen in front of the team, and continues. "Matt, Hamster, and Peter helped me to create each Epic, Feature, and Story.

We also have a good start with detailing each of the stories. Today, we need the team to help decide which stories we will work on during Sprint One, so the first step is to assign estimate story points. We need you all to quickly help us determine the size of the story and to determine how many sprints we need to build the Talking Wolfs application."

The team goes through each story methodically. Most are easy to determine, and others are more complex; therefore, they get a large number, which means that the story needs to be broken down more. Each story has the statement:

"As a; <role>, I need to have; <the requirement thing of what I need>, so that; <I can provide the benefit and purpose>"

Hamster takes the first story. It reads: As a student and Talking Wolfs user, I need to quickly post my video documentaries so that I can have my message immediately available to the High School community. This is called an epic "feature" story because there are many tasks behind creating this one feature for the Talking Wolf application.

The requirements for Talking Wolfs are simple. There are three feature scenarios to consider. Two of the three features are for the user. They are to: 1) Post a Video. 2) Watch a Video. The third feature is for the Talking Wolf's administrator. It is here where a systems administrator would be able to set up security, develop the user list, and assess the system to maintain proper video content. This last feature will require a school standard of content and conduct to protect users from improper content. Hamster, being keen on ideas that can turn profits says,

"Hey guys, we will build this system as volunteers, which will help our school; however, thinking as a business, I see this as a proof of concept that we can grow into a major stream of income. I'm talking a major cash box."

Matt responds to Hamster grinning ear to ear. With a new sense of respect that shines through the open heart that Matt wears on his sleeve he says, "Whoa, I'm totally stoked Sir Hamster. Dude, you are well armed with a Toaster mentality.".

Continuing with the vision for the media product value, the team also captures a huge creative aspect that is paramount for their media product. This resonates with the Toasters Club, as they seek to converge art with science. This creative design applies with User Experience, UX, as it is necessary for both PC and mobile devices, along with a framework that maintains the speed of posting and speed of watching. Peter and Hamster's demo shows a working mock-up of the Talking Wolf's website. The team plays with it to see how it works. For improvement, they provide feedback on the product. This is also directed toward its functionality and features.

The Toasters club quickly produced the Sprint plan, and with it, they began building the Talking Wolfs' site. Each sprint is two weeks long, and they expect to have it completed within 8 two-week sprints or 4 months. The meeting adjourns. Hamster and Peter remain behind to review the Scrum board. Matt and Nina leave together. As they walk out the door together, Nina comments. "That was a good meeting." "Yah says, Matt. I think we have a good handle on this product. Talking Wolfs is really going to help the school, as communication is key to good organization. Video Content Management is perfect for that."

The Toasters Club has really taken off since they have become an action club. Although the Talking Wolf's website is one of the larger products they have taken on, there are many smaller items awaiting them.

Some products are web applications. Other items are action items to organize and take action on things like the pet rescue center and raising money for the school theater, the school choir, and the school band. Having an action club is like having a band of brothers and sisters.

With the Agile Scrum process it works very well for them as they go forth and makes their community a better place. The idea is to build up a community and resist those who attempt to derail the idea of making things great. Nina gets home in time for dinner. Her dad is sitting at the table reading email on his Mobile Phone. Still focused on his phone, he says, "Hi Nina, how was your day?" "Great Dad. How about you?" Nina replies. "Excellent!" Nina tosses her backpack on the floor and sits at the table. Her mom is adding the finishing touches for dinner.

She sees Nina and says. "Hi, Nina … Oh, get your backpack off the floor, and please help me set up the table. Dinner is ready." "Okay, mom."

Nina jumps up and gets the table ready; however, she forgets to pick-her backpack up off the floor. Her Dad nudges her. "Backpack?" "Oh yah." Nina quickly runs over, grabs her backpack, and sets it near the couch. She runs back just in time for Mom to lay out the plates. Tonight, we're having teriyaki chicken and rice. It smells so good. Dad begins by giving thanks. "Dear heavenly father, we are grateful for the many blessings that you provide throughout our day, including the meal we are about to eat. Please bless it to nourish our bodies. Amen."

Let's eat!

CHAPTER SIX
Dr. Ott's Bot Laboratory

D R. OTT'S LABORATORY is incredible. His mom thinks that it is a play area; however, it is filled with robotic assembly lines, test equipment, experimental prototypes, laboratory clean rooms, designs, video equipment, raw materials, and parts for final robot assembly.

The shop floor is the size of a football field. And all this is underneath the ground. There are robotic arms in the assembly room working constantly 24 hours a day to put out new robots. Robots building Robots … imagine that! An unmarked supply truck arrives every 24 hours to drop off supplies of circuit cards, rack assemblies, connectors, poly-fiber, high-grade aluminum, servos, and more. Several unmarked white buses come lined up in a row every week to pick up the finished robots. Supply trucks and robot transport buses park inconspicuously at night on the street outside the laboratory hill. Transactions are made through the floor doors that open to the heavy metal street-level door to the underground lab. The lab has three levels housing the control room, test room, offices, conference rooms, research rooms and the shop floor assembly room with a warehousing staging area and parts bins with highly modern RFID tracking and Supply Chain Management (SCM) for procurement and logistical matters.

Most of the work is performed by robots and machines. Perfect for getting around those wonderful "robot-friendly" Californian labor laws. Thanks to the government and its mandate to raise the minimum wage for humans, we see now today, more than ever businesses are encouraged to replace human labor with robots. Business is booming for Dr. Ott. Sure, he has a small, dedicated team of humans to help him with quality assurance and to help build and maintain his empire.

There are three ways to get into Dr. Ott's Laboratory. One way is through his house, where the elevator is located in the closet of his bedroom. The next way is through an inconspicuous utility panel box located just off the sidewalk at the base of the hill. There is a hidden button located on a large metal utility facade. Push the button, and the elevator aligns at street level; the doors open, you step in, and the ride takes you to the hallway at the bottom of the laboratory floor. This elevator drops fast, so hang on! The third access is through the large street on the outside. This access is located at the base of the hill on a main street. The facade is two large, heavy rectangular iron doors that are level and aligned with the street. The doors are made of the same material as those cast iron sewer manhole covers. Drive an 18-wheeler over the metal doors and hit the code; the bay doors drop down as the elevator moves up and locks into place. It is for sending and receiving from the Dr. Ott Laboratory Warehouse.

This is a highly sophisticated supply chain staging center to supply Dr. Ott's manufacturing center. Have you ever seen a large truck parked near the street where you live? It's common. Dr. Ott's delivery trucks pull up during the night, park and through the bottom of the truck, they go to work delivering robot parts, plastic raw stock, and electrical components. The trucks owned by Dr. Ott's Lab are unmarked. They also have full size white buses with darken windows to transport and deliver the finished Robot Products. One more thing. The elevator takes you to the bottom of the laboratory floor, in the open warehouse space opposite the manufacturing wing across the hallway.

The Laboratory is enormous. One would never know such a place existed in the neighborhood. It is truly a "high-tech" underground factory that is built underneath his house. It hollows out the entire hill. How did they do that? Just in panning the clean rooms and rows of modern electrical test equipment organized in system bay racks, lights flickering. It is a sight to see. Robotic parts and assembly equipment are all lined up in rows. Hundreds of robotic humanoid figures lay on the assembly line as they go through final assembly. The final step is to test the robots and make sure their human interface technology is perfected.

Each robot is built with a lightweight aluminum frame-shaped skeletal structure; it is housed in a composite covering with snap-in circuit boards that are comprised of actuators, servos, sub-processors, and controllers, all feeding the central processor located in the brain. Its eyes are powerful color mini cameras based on an ultra-miniaturized version of the Hubble space telescope and other spy surveillance lenses

patented with precise auto-focusable iris lens's that can focus close-up, and wide out as these robotic eyes can read the date of a dime from an orbit of 320 miles up in space. Yes, these are far more advanced components of a spybot. Its ears are sophisticated recording devices that can pick up and recognize a large frequency range beyond the 20 to 20,000 Hz human range. Its voice and sounds resonate via advanced speaker technology that emulates human voice yet can project sound through advanced synthesized technology and amplification. Its skin from head to toe and from right to left are sensing devices used for obstruction avoidance, balance, pressure, and navigation.

These devices can sense movement and gauge the distance of oncoming traffic with collision avoidance. Its body motion comes from its direct Artificial Intelligence (AI) learning human body motion, not from the body motion suits that graphic animators use, but from Dr. Ott's patented AI and Singularity found nowhere else in the industry. It is a highly sophisticated robot system covered with life-like polymer skin and holding a skin temperature of 37 C, or 98.6 degrees Fahrenheit. This temperature is kept constant no matter the outside temperature within a specification of between -55- and +130 degrees Fahrenheit at sea level. The skin and face cosmetics are a byproduct as they look so real and feel very lifelike. Even the introduction of air into the robots is done in rhythm. Instead of a constant fan, air comes in and goes out through an applicator that breathes in to cool down the computer machinery and exhales to replace the warm air with fresh, cool ambient air. With the look, feel, and rhythmic sounds emulating human presence. The distinction between what is human and what is machine is very hard to tell. Dr. Ott came out with this motto: "Is it real, or robot?"

Dr. Ott arrives in the lab. He surveys the underground assembly room and begins to hum a tune as he stares straight ahead. His face is intense, in a stance that is majestically intimidating. His manner posed as a world-dominating dictator. He stands in the robot assembly room. The machines make a rhythm as they fasten the robot together. Dr. Ott begins to hum a song as the music begins. Dr. Ott raises his hands in a tap dance stance to the music. He slides across the shop floor and across the assembly line as he tap-dances and sings in a crazy looney manner to "Big Head," which is a song about assembling robots. He tippy toes as he performs his dance on the factory floor, right where his robots are assembled. He twirls and dances to the rhythm. His face is fixed forward in a serious, deep trance as he dances across the room.

Dr. Ott takes a double look at the robot's head in contrast to the size of its body. He speaks spontaneously during the song. "Wow. What a big head you have. It's like my big head… I like that." Says Dr. Ott as he breaks into a chorus. "Ba-Ba-Baba." He hums, then looks down at the robot assembly schematic and continues to hum. He then breaks into a dance to the tune of the Big Head song. "It is jazzy!" Says Dr. Ott. "I think I can create an assembly procedure around this. Let me see."

"Dr. Ott sounds out the lyrics for the first time through. It's an improvisational song about the instruction to construct a robot. He calls it Big Head because the inside, the body if his robots are rather thin and empty compared to the head. The robot head is the most complex housing unit, packed full of electric circuitry, and cooling units. Dr. Ott begins singing. The Big Head song goes like this:

"Now … First take a housing core and fasten both the arms and legs."

"Attach to the hips, on the right and the left."

"Run wire through the core, snap to both feet and hands."

"Connecting servos straight through to the head."

Dr. Ott freezes in place. He thinks to himself. "Hum, not bad." His eyes forward, staring straight-ahead, face intense and in a stance. It is both majestic and intimidating, so he thinks. Humming to himself, his voice slightly cracks; however, he still holds his intense stance and stares. It is truly a Dr. Ott moment, as he takes his majestic pose. Arms to his side, he shifts his body to the left. Again, his head remains in one place with face and eyes straight forward still holding his grandiose stance. Loudly, he sings out his tune with no restraint. It echoes throughout the chambers of his underground laboratory.

Meanwhile, Dr. Ott's gang of evil-doers show up in the lab just in time to catch his act. They are early for the afternoon lab meeting. Dr. Ott did not see them come in. Quietly, they peak around the edge of the north assembly wall. They can't help but be curious as they watch Dr.

Ott dancing around the lab. Some people have reached a certain success in life where they feel free to express their eccentric behavior. The evil gang feels that Dr. Ott has achieved that level in his life. Or perhaps, he has reached his edge and is finally flipping out.

Dr. Ott completes his song and remains holding his stance. It's a world dominating pose. Then, out of nowhere, he is abruptly interrupted by Mom, as she turns on her shop floor intercom loudspeaker. ScreechHHHH . . . Feedback! Mom, in a playful voice, says.

"Otty?"

"Hello Otty?"

"Testing 1, 2, 3, 4, 5, 6 . . ." Screech.

Her loud, sharp feedback sounds off and reverbs throughout the lab while Dr. Ott completely collapses in humility. He gains his composure. This time, humbly deflated.

"Yes. Um, yes, Mom."

"It's Lunch Time, Otty. I made your favorite peanut butter sandwich."

Dr. Ott hangs his head down for a moment. He rubs his forehead while answering.

"OK, Mom, I'll be right there."

"Roger Will-Co. Over and out." Says mom.

Dr. Ott's mom is completely oblivious to what just happened, as it is one of many times she has deflated her son's ego today. His evil gang watches as Dr. Ott takes the elevator up to meet his mom for lunch. After lunch, Dr. Ott takes the elevator down to the lab. He meets with his evil gang in the 2nd-floor conference room. He takes command of the scene and says. "Now is the time to test our newly formed batch of masterpieces."

Dr. Ott's eyes stare intensely through his large wire glasses as he picks up the remote device control panel. He turns on the flat-screen monitors in the control room. He then activates the servo control panel for all the robots. Each robot comes equipped with active camera lenses for eyes, so he can see what they see. They also have GPS, so he can trace every motion live and real-time, while he remains in the war room.

This is the moment that Dr. Ott has been waiting for. He is ready for the slam dunk. His wild hair contrasts against the dark background like an exact emulation of that scene from the movie Frankenstein. He stares ahead standing profusely intense as if he is about to jump out of his skin. His gang watches from the conference room monitors as he stands with a fixed gaze, ready to charge.

Dr. Ott now commands his gain of evil workers to take to the control rooms as they move to the last phase of testing his last lot of robots. They engage the robots in everyday scenarios, such as making purchases at the mall. Tests are conducted remotely from the underground lab.

Dr. Ott has a labor recruiting office named Cambridge Cyber-Orders (CCO). It's located in a strip mall at the bottom of the hill, close to his laboratory. Instead of placing real humans, the CCO office places robots in the workforce. The goal is to replace twice as many humans in the workforce in half the time. CCO's latest robot models are bot-teachers programmed to teach all subjects and all grade levels. His employees at CCO are your typical recruiter-type people. They are good on the phone, talk alike and dress alike. Fetch and Nate are two of Dr. Ott's labor sales recruiters who are strictly assigned to place Dr. Ott's bot-teachers in all schools around town. These teachers are so lifelike that no one suspects they are robots.

All models are equipped with Advanced Artificial Intelligence (AAI) where they can trade stock, learn, and perform all forms of office work, play video games, and become your best friend. These robotic models also have sophisticated motion processors that allow them to have human-like motion. They can also speak, calculate, and access data on the internet; however, Bot-Teachers are different in that they come with a downloadable library of K through 12 course materials. They can pass the teacher's credential exam in no time, and they are cheap. This is perfect timing as the Beachside Park School District (BPSD) is once again burdened with misappropriation of funding. Dr. Ott says, "The smell of budget cuts is once again in the air."

Today, poor broke districts are commonplace and a reoccurring thing ever since career politicians have plagued the government offices of Beachside Park. This leaves Dr. Ott's labor robot business in an excellent position for growth. The school board is now actively cutting teachers and replacing them with bot-teachers, for half the price of a single schoolteacher. This sort of twisted staff-augmented thinking reduces professional workers into no more than a replaceable resource, an inhuman commodity. Dr. Ott collects the weekly paycheck from each of his bot-teachers. It is a win-win!

As for Fetch and Nate, these guys are complete clowns. Both are as dumb as they come. Today, they are going to first meet at the recruiting office, then later in the day they are going to be meeting with their clients at Beachside Park High School. Dr. Ott is still at the lab finishing the robot-human interface tests.

Fetch is slouching in his office chair, watching an old rerun of that famous reality TV show "Husbands of Rich & Famous Wives." You know, as in any low-class drama… when the cats are away, the mice will play. The reality show cuts over to a local daytime T.V. commercial. It is a Greg and Nancy Bloom commercial ad. Greg and Nancy are a husband-and-wife real-estate team who promote their real-estate agency and its properties for-sale in the area. Their commercials come on constantly during daytime or night. It rolls on all cable and internet streams, such as TV, video streams, social media clips, and free movie commercial streams in the Beachside Park area. Fetch is on the couch with the TV blasting in the back office. Greg and Nancy's commercial begins with the announcer saying. "It's Greg & Nancy and their dog Wolfy."

Everyone loves their dog Wolfy. Poor Wolfy … He always tries to get away from Greg and Nancy during the commercial. With the look on Wolfy's face, he is totally disgusted with them. Fetch yells to Nate.

"Hey, Nate. It's on."

"What?" Says Nate.

"It's that commercial with the dog I was telling you about."

"You got to see this … It's a total crackup."

"Hurry, Nate. You got to see this."

The commercial announcer continues, "Greg & Nancy's commercial is brought to you by G&N Bloom Real Estates." Greg comes on to introduce himself. He has an ultrahigh-pitched voice; in fact, he was nicked named Helium Boy as far back as kindergarten school. He readies himself for the camera and says. "Hello, I am Greg." His voice carries a high-pitched tone that gives off a helium-head vibe. Nancy immediately follows with a very rich, deep, and low earth-shaking voice. "And I'm Nancy."

The following moment, after Nancy speaks, gives off a low resonance frequency. The room shakes, rumbles, and rolls to the ultra-low seismic occurrence. The look on their dog Wolfy's face says it all ... "Psycho-Freaks." The commercial continues in the background with Greg's used car salesman style high pitch, in contrast to Nancy's low-hanging voice. This cheap homemade video is an absolute classic! Greg continues. "Yes, we are the Bloom's, and this is our dog Wolfy." Nancy walks over to Wolfy as he tries to get away.

"Wolfy, Wolfy. Come here, Wolfy!"

"Hey Greg, get Wolfy and bring him over here."

Greg walks over to Wolfy and bends down to catch him, but Wolfy backs up, moving just out of reach. The commercial continues with Greg in the background, trying to catch Wolfy. Again, Fetch yells to Nate. "Hey, Nate. You're missing it!" Nate looks out the front window to see Dr. Ott pulling up to the parking lot in his motor car. Nate yells to Fetch.

"Hey, Fetch."

"Turn the TV off. NOW."

"Fetch ... Hurry. Turn it off now the boss is here."

Nate can still hear the TV blasting in the background as Fetch is obviously not responding to his warning. He yells even louder.

"FETCH ... TURN THE TV OFF NOW."

"BOSS IS HERE!!!!"

Still, no response from Fetch. With the TV still blasting, Nate decides to take matters into his own hands; he runs down the hall to the back office, opens the door, and yells. "FETCH!" As he busts open the door, he sees Dr. Ott standing next to Fetch. Dr. Ott came in through the back way. Nate stands at the door, slides down to the door threshold, and sits on the floor as Dr. Ott and Fetch, completely unphased, stand and watch the commercial.

It continues with Greg walking past a long wall. There are pictures of homes taped to the wall as they are filming, just as if these homes were used cars. Each home has price tags and tagged messages with short, cheap slap-stick marketing slogans. Greg & Nancy's home sales commercial continues to emulate that of a used car salesman on a TV commercial. As he walks by each home picture, Greg spouts off hackneyed descriptions as slogans of each home: "This 1995 home has new paint, new plumbing, low popcorn textured ceiling, and a crystal chandelier. Priced in the low $ four million. This is a 1972 flat roof, single-story, two-bedroom beauty. With a carport, it's a real treasure. A steal at only $1.399 million. Well, what can I say? It's the California Coast. A perpetual sellers' market. And here we have a new home with no front yard, no backyard, built in very close proximity to the home next door, which is a true benefit. Want to borrow a cup of sugar? Simply open your window, reach out, and knock on your neighbor's window. Where else can one have a neighbor who is only an arm's length away. As for price, if you must ask, you cannot afford it."

Greg finishes and then darts after their dog. The camera focuses on Greg trying to catch up to their dog Wolfy, who is in the background running as fast as he can. Away in the opposite direction. Wolfy is getting away. The camera catches him as he is running further and further away. In the backdrop one can see Wolfy running toward the beach, successfully escaping Greg and Nancy Bloom as he runs down the street in the distance. Nancy butts in to wrap up the commercial. "Well, that's all for today." Dr. Ott, staring at the T.V., speaks out. "I wonder where Wolfy is going?" The final clip of the commercial finishes with Greg & Nancy Bloom's Jingle Song. It goes like this:

"If you need a home by noon – go see Bloom."

"If you need some extra room – go see Bloom."

"You can keep up with the Jones."

"Cause we have expensive homes."

"And our banks give sub-prime loans."

"Go See Bloom."

"We are located on Bandini and the 710 freeway, in beautiful downtown Vernon. I'm Greg (squeak) . . . "And I'm Nancy.: (DEEPLY DARK LOW FREQUENCY VIBE) "We are the Bloom's … and we'll see you soon's." Again, the T.V. vibrates for a few seconds, caused from the low frequency of Nancy's voice. Dr. Ott looks intense, like he is about to say something profound. He says:

"Awe Wolfy. I really like Wolfy."

"Yes, Wolfy totally makes the commercial." Says Fetch.

Nate just shakes his head. Nate is serious. He is serious about his career as an evil gang member and about the RR, Robotic Resources recruiting business. He provides Dr. Ott with the latest robot placement report. Nate says: "Good news, Dr. Ott, our numbers are off the charts. We now have 337 Bot Teachers teaching classrooms, and several more are being requested." Dr. Ott looks at Nate and says, "Okay."

Along with the highly advanced Artificial Intelligence system, each Bot-Teacher comes equipped with an ultrahigh-speed data processing system with an advanced quantum database. The database is unique in that it uses electrically charged object patterns, which is really cool. Instead of binary-coded data, the robot's database system goes beyond the ones & zeros of binary code. Its magnetically charged object patterns enhance solid-state memory circuits that store, recall, and process information with a capacity that goes way beyond that of a human brain. In fact, it processes faster than the speed of light.

Dr. Otts bot-teachers pass every teacher exam. The only challenge they had was those Common Core exams because it is completely constructed to falsify subject matter, thus, making no logical sense. Dr. Ott had to invent a twisted AI module to solve this issue. They call it the Zinn chip in honor of the late political activist; Howard Zinn, who was famous for his alternative American History trade books back in the 1980's. These are brilliant readings of twisted views that promote the Great American Shame; however, to create such twisted views takes twisted AI programming. Dr. Ott named this AI program technique "Twisted View Machine Learning," or TVML. Other subjects, such as math, science, English, and humanities, were easy to program. Once these highly educated bot-teachers were modified with Zinn chips programmed in TVML, and AI, they began to teach in the classroom. All were undetected by students as Dr. Ott was successful in creating them to be life-like teachers, programmed to take over all public-school teaching jobs. Best of all, no matter the industry vertical, Dr. Ott's bot-workers were placed quicker and more effectively than the wave of offshore outsourcing that had depleted American jobs a few decades ago.

Dr. Ott leaves the sales office building and gets back into his car. He drives back to the lab. While in the car, he turns on the radio and flips through every channel to find a good tune. He first stops at "I did it my way" (Frank Sinatra) for a few seconds, then flips the channel to "Money" (Pink Floyd). He sings a few lines of that tune, and then he turns off the radio. While driving, he looks at himself in the rear-view mirror and says to himself.

"Wow, I am a robot, man!"

He sings to himself, about himself. Suddenly, while Dr. Ott is still singing about himself, the voice of his mom comes through the 2-Way Radio in Dr. Ott's car. One can hear the feedback "screechHHHH" from here, to Mars, as his mom speaks through the intercom microphone.

"Otty."

"Breaker – Breaker."

"Breaker one-nine, good buddy."

"Otty, come home for dinner."

The music in his head stops. He gains his composure, clears his voice, and speaks.

"Okay, Mom, I'll be home in 5 minutes."

"Roger that, Otty, over and out."

Dr. Ott turns off the intercom and begins to hum softly beneath his breath while he makes up the words to sing. It goes like this:

"Looking at my photograph."

"Since I was young, I never laughed."

"Life for me was only math … But look what I've become."

Jazzy music hits the floor like a fog machine as Dr. Ott dances around the room in his skinny jeans. The song pauses for a moment as it builds momentum on stage. He looks out from the great theatrical as he sings to his imaginary audience, who are all fully attentive. Hanging on each and every word that resonates his tune.

"I'll take on the world ….

I Am a Robot Man!"

CHAPTER SEVEN
The Toasters Club Demos Product

THERE IS A CHARGE in the summer air. The sharply green colored trees tower in contrast to the deep blue sky. All the homes in the neighborhood have a rich coat of lushes vegetation as each front yard in the neighborhood is well-landscaped and well-manicured. Every home is ready to be featured in Sunset magazine as Californians take their home appearance seriously, especially in this neighborhood. Hamster climbs the steep street, taking short breaks as he nears the top. The humidity is very low; it feels electric. Not a cloud in the sky to be seen. It's a beautiful morning. The team assembles on the front porch at Annie and Peter's house. The team members high-five each other as they ride their bikes, scooters, and skateboards. It has become a new tradition for the team as they successfully complete so many sprints with much success. The excitement is high.

Today the Toasters will be demonstrating their completed Video Log product for the school. This is called the "Sprint Review" ceremony where in Agile Scrum, the team gets to demo their work. Annie and Peter's mom hands out the breakfast treats as always. Nina, Matt, Hamster, Lizzy, Annie, and Peter are all ecstatic as they gather around Peter and his laptop, viewing the finished website that is now displaying video blogs in the QA environment. It's totally cool.

Nina and Hamster's parents came to Wang's house to support the event and to be with the team as they went off to school to launch today's final sprint ceremonies. It's a big day. Mr. Wang, Annie & Peter's dad, is wearing his faded red MIT sweatshirt. He had taken the entire day off from work just to support his children. From forming to performing, he is proud of what The Toasters Club has become and what they are all doing with their successful team. It is not only a really special day for Mr. Wang but also special for all the team member's parents. They all support the Toasters Club. As mentioned, the Toasters Club just completed their final sprint. This means that the product they have been building is complete, tested, and ready to Show and Tell. They have been working on designing and building the Beachside High Wolf's Video Log platform. It is for the entire school, and it works great and looks great.

The Toasters finish breakfast, and now all have jumped on their bikes and started to roll. Bolt and Hamster followed on their skateboards down the hill to room 202. They all arrive. It's 7:15 a.m. and time for the Toasters Club's daily stand-up meeting, otherwise known as the daily scrum ceremony.

Here, they will go around the room. Each Toaster team member will answer these three questions:

1) What I Did Yesterday?

2) What I Will Do Today?

3) What Impediments Are There, If Any?

In other words, what has the team done since their last daily stand-up, what will they do before the next daily stand-up, and what blockers, "if any," are blocking the team from progressing and finishing the development of the final product? It's a short 15-minute ceremony, but it is highly effective as everyone on the core team meets and discusses its progress. One way to keep it short and effective is to avoid the 15-minute standup from becoming a status meeting, or a problem-solving meeting. If that happens, Annie, the Scrum Master, steps in and stops the conversation. She then places the discussion topic on the whiteboard as a parking lot issue for later discussion. Effective teams go through the daily stand-up in 15 minutes or less, and then they huddle to discuss issues after the stand-up meeting. The idea is to minimize and shorten meetings, so the team can get back to work designing and building stuff. There are only 4 meetings that a Scrum team attends during the sprint. We call these meetings ceremonies.

These ceremonies are:

- The Daily Scrum stand-up.

- The Sprint Review (with demo).

- The Retrospective.

- Sprint Planning.

The Toasters Club finished the daily standup. Next is the Sprint Review ceremony where the team can demonstrate the product that they develop. The retrospective ceremony is where the team asks two open questions:

- What went well?

- What can be improved?

Finally, the Sprint Planning ceremony is where the team plans for their next sprint. If it is a new product to be built, the team goes through Ideation to assure the ideas are feasible and meaningful before they sprint, so that they don't end up wasting time, or money producing a bad idea. The Ideation framework steps are of Design Thinking:

Empathize – Define – Ideate – Validate – Prototype – Produce – Grow

Ideation is the first step of the Toasters Club's approach, followed by Sprint and Growth, yet they have managed to keep imaginative inspiration at the center by not allowing the mechanics of these frameworks to strangle their creativity. It is this innovative perfection that sets them apart.

Once the sprint begins, the team plans up to 3 sprints ahead of time so that they only need to perform refinement planning of stories and make improvements as necessary. They even have a definition of done for the sprint, along with a Criteria of Acceptance for each story. This becomes a clear roadmap of what needs to be completed in the next sprint. The team stands side-by-side in a circle. Everyone is charged and excited. Matt passes the ball to Annie. A small ball is passed to each member who is to speak. It is a way to keep the team self-organized. Annie begins the 15-minute Sprint Stand-up meeting. "Yesterday, I completed the final stress test and acceptance test for Wolf-Blog. Looks great. The UI defects we had last week are resolved. Acceptance testing was signed off. Today I will copy and place all the completed test script artifacts in the repository. I will also include today's Product Owner and Stakeholder product approval from the demo as the official acceptance signoff of the Sprint Review is captured. That's all."

Annie starts to pass the ball to Hamster and stops sharply. Hamster holds out his hands to catch the ball. Annie sharply pulls the ball back. Holding the ball in her hand, she says. "Oh yes, no impediments."

Annie then passes the ball to Hamster. He gives the team his part. The ball gets passed to each team member and shortly, the ceremony ends. The Toasters Club will soon demo the product they built. A big milestone. They will be showing the new video log in the school hall, which seats over 700 people. The Talking Wolfs Streaming Video is named after their school mascot, The Wolfs.

For the demo, the Toasters Club members move into the assembly hall, where there is a big crowd that has already gathered, in fact, the entire school showed up to see their new video application. The assembly hall is filled. An overflow was created with monitors so that no one would miss this event. In the hall, there is not even a place to stand.

Nina walks on stage as the crowd begins to applaud. She motions for silence and begins to introduce the Toasters Club. She then narrates the demo; Peter clicks on its features. The assembly room is quiet as Nina provides a perfect presentation of the Wolf Video blog for the school. They love it. The silence is broken with excitement and applause as soon as Nina completes her presentation. Many hands go up with her invitation to ask questions at the end. The students are not only excited to have a new video log, but most questions also go toward how one can join the Toasters Club.

Hamster, Annie, Peter, Lizzy, and Matt walk out on stage. The Toasters Club? Wow – I didn't think anyone would want to join the Toasters Club. Matt says. "Let's keep the Toasters Club size small. Our number is seven. Let's keep this size and help others who are interested in establishing their own team with our help and collaboration." "Yah, good idea. Says Peter. "We can teach them how to start their own Scrum Team. Who knows, one day, we may need to scale with the help of a larger network of like-minded teams."

The morning bell rings – Morning Assembly adjourns. Time for class. Nina and Lizzy make their way to Music class. Dr. Roy welcomes the class as he has done for well over 25 years at Beachside High School.

Big Smiles, everyone, it's time to begin. It may seem unbelievable, but after graduating from Julliard, Dr. Roy went on to write many musical pieces. He even led a near-famous rock band in the 70s and had written many books on music theory where he mixes music with the science of frequency, time, matter, and Dr. Roy's good humor.

The entire class takes their seats. Suddenly, the classroom door swings abruptly open. It is Principal Spinner and some of her school board members. They came to Dr. Roy's classroom unannounced. It is a very large class located in the music auditorium. Principal Spinner and her School Board regime assembled in the back of the classroom and sat down in a row together. Dr. Roy says, "Welcome … Welcome to my Music class." He welcomes Principal Spinner and the board. He looks at the class and says, "We are so privileged to have our principal and her board attend this morning's session."

Dr. Roy warms up with a demonstration of how music responds. He takes his electric guitar and sets it in a guitar stand on the stage of the music class. He then goes over and cranks up the volume on the guitar amp until it is beginning to reverb. He backs down the volume slightly and takes his microphone. He hums in the musical key of A. The electric guitar responds by sounding in the key of A. He does it again. This time, he hums in the key of G, and the guitar responds in the key of G. The class finds this very interesting. Dr. Roy has always seen more in music, and he likes to relay this knowledge in class as he knows this is the normal that people long for.

He stands up clears his voice. "It's in frequency and time. It vibrates in low frequency, and as one understands the vibrations from Direct Current (DC) to Light, one can ponder its science and its spirituality. It is amazing. If one wants, one can see how close we are to the Creator in all of this. Music touches the very depths of our souls and causes us to feel a deeper sense. Is it possible to walk on or come into agreement with the molecules of mass and pass through walls? How does healing happen? Does the attitude of a man or woman matter here? Is it important what one thinks, what one speaks, and what music or vibrations one listens to? Could this have any influence on one's health and well-being, or is this pure conspiracy theory?"

Dr. Roy continues. "Is it possible to have the frequency of disorder come into alignment with the order, and reject disease like cancer, or heal broken bones as the frequency responds, disorder begins to obey, repair, and come into order? Is it not harder to have faith in the things of science or in physical things that so happen to be explained to us as random or chance? Can one be permitted to explore the possibility that there was a designer of order and see the face of God? If we equate the goodness of prosperity, production, and the power of positive thinking to the joys of life. Is it equally fair to equate disorder, destruction, death, and the catalyst of fear to the throne of evil?"

"Today, science and medicine reject God's joy, goodness, and love as fairytales and instead embrace fear as reality. Sure, fear sells, but it harms people who buy into it. Is earning money based on fear an honest thing to do? What if they were to reverse this attitude and embrace the frequency of life? Could this be a Heavenly Frequency, or does this all sound too cosmic? Perhaps so, but the idea is not too far-fetched for one who ponders the solid science of mass, frequency, and time."

Just then, Principal Spinner leans forward and walks out of the room, followed by the school board members. As the principal opens the door, she turns to Dr. Roy in front of the class in an agitated voice, obviously hating what she is hearing in her separation of church and state mindset, she says. "Dr Roy, please check your email. You must report to the admin office ASAP. Good day."

The principal is followed by the board members who also wear solemn faces, all except one who turns to Dr. Roy, then points his finger upward to the sky. Dr. Roy laughs and gives the board member a thumbs-up as he walks out of the room. Dr. Roy then turns to the class who by now are completely on the edge of their chair. He makes a quick announcement.

"Class, this is discussion time."

"As you all know by now, you all have a voice in my class, and so I invite you all to voice your opinion, as I especially welcome and value your views and arguments."

"I ask for us all to respect one another's opinions."

"Now, let's begin!"

The class jumps up with hands raised high as they are all excited by Dr. Roy's example and view on mass, frequency, and time. Dr. Roy looks around the room. He usually picks the most shy and quiet students first. That is … If they are raising their hands, which is rare. He looks around the room and sees Matt's hand. Matt is sitting in the back of the class. Dr. Roy calls on Matt.

"Yes, sir, give us your thoughts."

Matt stands up, "Are you saying that music connects us in a spiritual sense?" Dr. Roy answers Matt: "In my opinion, music reflects something that is beyond our body and our soul's existence, whether it's spiritual or not." The class continues with discussions and Dr. Roy completely forgets about the Principal Spinner and board member incident. But rest assured, Principal Spinner does not forget Dr. Roy's display in class. She types a crafty email and reports the incident as a perfect opportunity to replace Dr. Roy with the next teacher-bot. Her meeting will be Dr. Roy's dismissal.

After class, Lizzy meets with Dr. Roy and demos progress on her composition. It is a violin solo melody over an orchestration. It is her original music symphony. She shows her music sheets to Dr. Roy. He organizes the sheets and begins to play the piano. Lizzy picks up her violin and starts the melody. It is sweet; it is heavenly. She plays a few bars and stops. "That's all I have, Dr. Roy."

"Wow, Lizzy. Very nice piece… bravo, bravo," says Dr. Roy. He turns to Lizzy and continues by saying, "Lizzy, you have come a long way… you worked hard at it, and I am proud of you. Now get on out of here and go to lunch." Dr. Roy had a way of encouraging others to do their best. It is a special gift. A necessary gift. Lizzy packs her things and heads out to catch up with the other Toaster Club members for lunch. They had all decided to meet at TacO's. An off-campus fast food palace. It's Taco Tuesday's. This is not Lizzy's favorite food; she prefers PHO Fridays.

Incidentally, that afternoon Dr. Roy gets called into the office and gets fired. Today's music class was the last moment and the last time that Lizzy and all the other students were able to be with Dr. Roy on campus. The board replaced Dr. Roy with a bot-teacher named Myrrha Queue. No announcement, no goodbyes.

Just Bam … Gone!

CHAPTER EIGHT
Placing Bot-Teachers

I T'S LUNCH TIME, and the Toasters all decide to walk over and hang out at TacO's Cafe. They are approached by the waiter. She is short with permed curly blond hair, heavy make-up, and a thin-line tattoo outlining her lips, with no lipstick to fill in the deep, thin red O outlining her lips. She is focused on welcoming customers and oblivious to customer reaction when they notice the red O tattoo line that circles and outlines her natural lips.

"Welcome to TacO's Cafe."

Her lips form a perfect "O" each time she accents the letter "O". The idea of the lip tattoo is to outline lips with red ink so as to be filled in with lipstick later. For some reason, the "O" lady doesn't get it. Or perhaps she is starting a new trend with the red line O tattoo that surrounds her bare lips. Picture her lips as being the only place where make-up is completely absent on her face, and now you can see how she got the nickname… the "O" Lady. "Oh, you guys. You all must be hungry. Would you like to try our famous BurritO? It comes with your choice of freshly grilled barbacOa, or pol-lO. Do you like BARBACOA, or POL-LO?"

Everyone is looking elsewhere to avoid eye contact. Everyone except for Hamster! He is rather amused at the perfect formation of the letter O she forms with her lips. Annie bumps him on the shoulder and quietly whispers, "Stop staring at her Hamster."

The team receives their orders quickly and scarf down their food without saying a word. Nina breaks the silence. "Matt and I have a new assignment for The Toasters Club. It is a light community project, but the subject matter is very heavy. We will tell you all about it at the meeting tonight." "Okay, see you guys at the stand-up tonight." See ya Hamster. Matt and Nina head back to school, and the rest of the club finishes lunch and heads back to class.

Meanwhile, back at the High School, Dr. Ott's sales recruiters meet secretly with principal Spinner and the school board. The sales recruiters, Nate and Fetch, are going over their final roll-out plan to bring in bot-teachers and completely replace every human teacher at Beachside Park High School. Others present at the meeting are five administrators who make up the local school board, and Janitor Ed. Nate begins his presentation to promote the robot teacher idea to the school board. "This is what Dr. Ott is willing to offer to you. We will provide every classroom with subject matter bot-teacher experts so you can begin laying off your human teachers. After all, they get too many paid sick days off and often do not even back up your Saul Alinsky-type agenda. You see, our bot-teachers are loyal teachers. They will do anything we say."

Principal Spinner stands and faces the window. Her blue pantsuit drapes on her like an out-of-fashion bedroom curtain. She walks closer toward the window with the schoolboard behind her. She grins an evil grin. "I like it. This is perfect. The science and music bot-teacher are working out so very well so far. And they look so real. All my students are completely unsuspecting." Nate turns to her and says. "Yes, we have perfected HX/HI Principal Spinner."

The board turns to Nate with a puzzled look on their faces. Nate looks back at them and says. Oh. That is, Human Experience (HX) and Human Interaction (HI). Well, in fact, our educational robots are indeed human-like, minus the expensive pay role." Fetch jumps in. "Such freedom you now have, Principal Spinner… Ha, ha, ha, ha, ha. Freedom to spend all that hard-earned school budget of taxpayer dollars on other more important things like power and community prestige. Why waste it on teacher salaries? Ha-ha-ha, ha. Yes." Nate then begins to poorly recite an old Allice Cooper rock tune. "No more teachers, no more books, and no more dirty, ugly, discussing looks." Nate and Fetch give out an evil laugh in synchronization. "Ha-ha-ha-ha … Ah-ha-ha-Ugg."

The school board loves the idea. Pure greed and power glared in the eyes of Principal Spinner. It had long since been the desire of the board to decrease teacher salaries and increase school administrator job security and control. Principal Spinner put it together in her mind that the ultimate power was now shifting directly into her hands. Right into her two hands of twisted command and control backed by the School Administration. Principal Spinner stands up to ask a question so that she can secure her position. She says, "But this must remain a secret. Right? No parent should know about this… Ever! Furthermore, I must have full confidence from all of you. This plan depends on the Administrators of the School Board to withhold the truth in order to rise up to the greater good… total power and domination over the community! I must have your loyalty and your word, or you know where you will end up. Right?" Admin 1, 2, and 3 speak up in complete unison.

"You have our word, Principal Spinner."

But Admin 4 and 5 hesitate before giving in. Janitor Ed remained silent before Principal Spinner and the others. He is a man of deep convictions. He quickly whispers a silent prayer underneath his breath as Principal Spinner looks intently at Admin 4 and 5, completely ignoring the Janitor as if he was not there. Some self-aggrandizing people are blinded to ranking, casts, and professions of people that they perceive are unimportant people such as Janitors, Maintenance Workers, and Gardeners. Principal Spinner continues to give that stare to Admin 4 & 5 as if to kill. No white of her eyes can be seen. Her eyes are completely reptile black. So wicked in the moment as her eyes turn completely absent of the light.

"What about you two?"

"We need to know now … Are you in or out?"

She turns her back to them and speaks to them while facing the other board members. Speaking in a calm iniquitous voice she says, "We can make arrangements for your departure right away if you would like." Administrators 4 and 5 cry-out once in unison. "No Principal Spinner. We're in. We're in" As in any command-and-control organization, people will do anything to keep their job when they fear job loss. Just as the puppet and the puppet masters, Principal Spinner, the Schoolboard, and Dr. Ott know this all too well as they use it to their advantage. Janitor Ed continues to remain silent. He just takes it all in as he thinks to himself. "Oh, how easy it is to make people desperate. It's in the playbook of the dark side."

To manipulate with fear is the ultimate tool of any evil empire. That is because they are weak and need to resort to such things to avoid remaining small and ending up weak. During war time, evil phycologist had learned that people would do anything for a potato. Anything! Desperate people make great puppets. Incidentally, as it turns out, evil is completely outnumbered by goodness, but like hot air in a balloon, the balloon grows; however, once it is big, it only looks big. All it takes is a prick of a tiny sharp pin to pop it.

Principal Spinner turns to Janitor Ed. At first, his stomach turns, but then he chuckles to himself while he is waiting to be called on. I do need the work, but no matter what, I am not bowing to this nonsense. He thinks to himself, I have gone through a lot in this world. I will overcome this, too."

Janitor Ed is prepared to give his answer to Principal Spinner; he is ready to stand, which means that he is ready to get fired. He determined in his mind that he was not to go along with it. He is ready with his answer to Principal Spinner and the School Board. But she doesn't ask him. Ignoring Janitor Ed's significance, Principal Spinner instead barks out an order. She turns to Janitor Ed.

"Hey, Janitor, um." She snaps her fingers in the air.

"Um… what's his face?"

"His name is Janitor Ed," says Admin 2. "Okay, whatever." She then walks disrespectfully over to Janitor Ed and says, "Hey you." While she points to Janitor Ed. "You have 1 hour to turn a closet into a charging station for our new bot-teachers." Liking the moment … Her moment. She walks to the front of the door, stands, and pauses. "I'm ordering enough robots to teach all subjects at my school. No more human teachers."

"That is great news, Principal Spinner." Says Nate. "We will have that shipment in no time. Each Teacher comes with programmable subject matter expertise. You are getting quality bot-teachers with options to reprogram for any subject matter, be it math, science, or history. In other words, no more substitutes."

Principal Spinner cuts Nate off. "Enough sales guy." Why does she exert this meanness? Because she can. She opens the meeting room door, walks through, and slams the door behind her, exiting the meeting.

Nate turns to Fetch in the excitement of the $ multimillion dollar sales contract. "Get on the phone and call the order in right away. Be sure to get that charging room hardware over to the Janitor. Again, right away!" "Okay, got it." Says Fetch. "We will send over our charging station hardware to the janitor's office." Janitor Ed exits the room immediately again, speaking to himself. "Turn a closet into a charging station in one hour? Wow, our board is seriously wrong. I got to do something. Lord, give me wisdom."

Back with the Toasters Club, they are ready for their daily stand-up. The Toasters meet over the next project at Annie and Peters house. Mrs. Wang had baked delicious Manapua steamed veggibuns. She takes the tray and lays them out on the meeting table. Nina looks at Mrs. Wang. "Wow, thanks!" Matt joins in. "Yes, thank you Mrs. Wang; there is nothing like Dim-Sum at Toaster Club meetings." Mrs. Wang gives a big smile and says, "As they always say… feed your crew!" She walks out with a happily singing voice as she exits the room.

The Toaster club begins their meeting discussion by planning for Sprint 0. The process is already laid out in Scrum, so the team does not need to spend much time discussing the planning approach. Peter gets right to the point. The Toasters Club scrum team has listed products on their plate. In Agile Scrum, projects are called products. The next Product Vision is the Homework Processing System. Here's what we need to do, says Peter. "We need to empathy map our homework processing system by interviewing users of the system to understand how they would best interface with the system." Peter walks up to the white-board and with a stack of sticky notes, he proceeds to the design thinking sprint session by asking the team questions, saying, "If you had a Homework processing system, what would it do, and what would it look like. It would do all my homework for me?"

Everyone quickly replies as the room fills with noisy comments. Hamster stands up and speaks up. "I know what it would do. It will perform extra homework credit for me." Matt speaks out above the rest.

"I know. It would take out the trash and do all my chores for me." Nina looks at Matt. "Yes … I like that even better." The team responds in laughter. Peter turns and looks at the team with a bright smile. You can never tell what he is thinking. Is he happy or annoyed? Peter has always had a gift of leadership where he is able to bring the team back into focus without making a fuss.

Peter stands in front of the team, facing upward toward the ceiling, which quickly calms the team down. He continues to say, "Okay, okay, you guys. Sounds like a good idea. We might work on a system to process home chores later, but for now, let's get back on track with the homework processing system." Matt chimes in with a better title. "Let's call it the Homework Processor."

Peter goes to the board and writes down a vision statement to get the conversation started. These empathy mapping sessions are in 45-minute brainstorming sections generating questions to understand client users and other stakeholders. Surprisingly, a team can get a lot accomplished in 45 minutes once they are focused. Peter speaks as he is writing down the statements. "Here is the vision statement and purpose that we came out with for the Homework Kit product." Peter ignores him and continues writing the vision statement and the purpose of the product statement that was captured from their ideation sprint. He places this statement on the board to be applied as reference for Prioritization of tasks and extraction of the Minimal Viable Product, for the Product Backlog.

Vision Statement	Purpose Statement
To generate a process for an individual to perform homework in iterations and in time-boxed increments, with a Kaizen mindset of continual improvement and with a transparent sprint board that shows a prioritized homework backlog, homework in progress, and homework done, all in collaboration and cooperation between parents, students, and educators.	To provide students with a pathway to: ✓ Organize assignments per priority due dates. ✓ Increase weekly homework outputs through iterative time slices. ✓ Decrease mistakes in solving complex homework problems.

The teams quickly put together an outline to think-through how the product should look like and function once it is complete. A Design Thinking sprint will capture and map the product vision in terms of its functions, its purpose, its ease of use. What is it used for and how do we vision it will look when finished. The team also performs a minimal viable product exercise for its incremental prioritization.

The team now kicks into action to create the story map to capture all the functions of the Homework Processor. They complete Empathy Mapping in under 40 minutes. Tomorrow, they will pinpoint application features then prioritization and perform techniques to capture Minimum Viable Product (MVP) to make the product vision ready to create the Product Backlog and Sprint Backlogs. The meeting adjourns … mission accomplished.

Later that night, at the dinner table. It is late fall, and the sun is going down early these days as the night sky gives off a dark blue color. Some light clouds paint the sky, but the evening stars are bright in some areas of the town where streetlights are few and far between. It is a dry 65 degrees outside. This is cool for California. Nina rushes home from Toasters Club. As soon as she opens the front door, she can smell Mom's cauliflower casserole. "I'm home," says Nina. "Hi, Nina." Says her mom. "Oh, just in time. Can you get the buns out of the oven for me?" Her mom baked fresh dinner buns. So delicious! Nina's dad comes down the stairs in an old robe costume. He is headed to rehearsal for the church Christmas Nativity play. "Well, hello, Nina." Nina looks at her dad in the Joseph robe and says; "Wasn't Joseph a little younger than you when Jesus was born?" Dad grabs a dinner roll and sits at the table. "Well, yes, Nina, this play is different. It is a look at the birth of Jesus once Joseph and Mary are a bit older. They are looking back and discussing between themselves how wonderfully God had utilized their willingness to serve."

Nina and her mom sit at the dinner table with Dad. Her mom passes the casserole, and Nina serves herself a heaping spoonful. "Oh wow, I have never thought of Joseph and Mary that way. What sort of conversation are they having?" Her dad replies, "Well, let's just say that Mary was a little shocked when the Angel told her that she was going to experience a miracle of being pregnant with baby Jesus through the spirit of God, her knowing no man and all. This was before they were married. This was quite a controversy in the town where Mary and Joseph had lived. They had friends, family, and perfect people within a religious rumor mill that we all know. Yes, they too had those who live for this stuff, as if a drop of dopamine feeds the brain during the shaming of the lower ones, to get that good feeling of being of a higher spiritual status than others, as they lived in their perfect life. You see, it was particularly taboo during the early years of ancient Israel, BC, when it was nearly unheard of. When Mary and Joseph looked back at this time, they became more amazed at how God connected with man, bringing salvation through a means that shocked the entire religious world based on works. It was grace that kissed the world through true love."

Nina's mom chimed in. "Speaking of shock, did you hear that the school board is laying off 60 percent of the Teacher staff?" "That is interesting; my science teacher had abruptly retired a few days ago." Said Nina.

Nina's dad signaled to prepare for grace. When Nina was younger, her belief was in a simple, childlike way, but as she became older, things got in the way. School teachers completely left such things out. Friends of many views and cultures saying things that stretched and challenged her childlike faith. Does having faith require one to be shrewdly wise with a measure of genuine trust, to believe in something you cannot see?

Nina thinks to herself, "Dogs can smell something better than they can even hear or see. So, what if I have video Facetime with my dog? Would my dog believe that I am real? What if someone held the mobile phone to my dog's face for a video chat with me while I was remote. Because it is electronic communication, my voice would be different, and my dog would not be able to smell me like he can in person. To man, seeing is believing, but to dog, smelling is believing.

Although Nina often struggled with the idea of God and going to church. She knew that there were times when she did not feel God as it seemed her parents did. She does see her dad yell and cuss at home sometimes; in fact, the whole house shakes, especially when he forgets the password to his mobile phone. Her mom also gets a little nutty about her school and homework. Perfect parents? No way. Are they perfect people? Well, not at all; however, I see them struggle as they try to be genuine people who want to love God and love people the best they can.

Dad quickly gobbles up his food. He excuses himself to go to Christmas practice. Nina helps her mom with the dishes and quickly retires to her room.

Long day!

CHAPTER NINE
Deep Down in Dr. Ott's Lab

DR. OTT'S DEEP Underground Lab is in full force. His factory has been ramping up to meet the high demand for his robot recruits. His workers come to the main quad of the lab for an all-hands meeting with Dr. Ott. The workers are marked with a strange look in their eyes. The meeting begins with a quick report given by the sales recruiters Fetch and Nate. Fetch speaks out. "We have made great progress with placing the bot-teachers into the school system."

A major benefit to Dr. Ott was a large, heavy inflow of money into his bank account as 100 percent of the teacher-bot paychecks are deposited directly into the bank account of Dr. Ott's for-profit organization. Much of this is well-known to those secret government officials and school superintendents who had also sold out to the idea that greed is good.

They looked up to the Bureau of Land Management (BLM) during its American land grabs heyday. Putting those T-Party ranchers away in Oregon to protect the uranium rich land for the elite to launder through the enemy. These thugs chip away, one stroke at a time. It's part of the agenda. This was the beginning of what will be their finest hour. My, how money talks. It's way beyond the skies of Beachside Park and into a corrupt world where business monopolies are passed, media propaganda is paid for, and high-end fraud goes under the radar. To these twisted, evil ding-dongs turn out to smell like roses, even though they are completely ripping off the very taxpayers they claim to represent. You see, cutting out the human labor costs of teaching has a direct positive effect on lining up the pockets of the elite board members. Even local school administrators benefit. Most of all, it supports Dr. Ott's evil empire. It's a win-win.

Sales Recruiter Fetch quickly steps off the platform once Dr. Ott arrives. Dr. Ott steps onto the platform and right up to the microphone. He hits the mic to see if it is live, then he faces the row of workers. He looks intently at each evil gang member. Fetch whispers to the workers.

"Quiet everyone, he's about to speak." Dr. Ott looks at Fetch, then at the gang of thugs.

"What is everyone doing?"

"Get back to work… Now."

They all jump, surprised. Fetch is completely caught off guard but quickly gains his composure. He repeats after Dr. Ott.

"That is all, folks, so get back to work."

Directly above the factory floor is a delivery truck that is in the street. There are more and more trucks lined up to deliver robot parts. The delivery is made through large rectangle iron plates that cover the street. Drivers are alerted and given a code to enter on their mobile phones once they drive precisely over the street plates for the drop. The box trailers of each truck are equipped with a bottom delivery and receiver system that fastens to Dr. Ott's laboratory warehouse elevator. It moves up and locks in place providing supplies and picking up final robot charger room assemblies, but not the robots. Treated as live humans, robots are picked up by bus.

History class is about to begin. Nina runs to class. She is early but can't wait for history class to begin. Everyone loves Mr. Bryan's American history class. It is so interesting, so different, and so balanced. Most public schools are plagued with single-sided parochial viewpoints that disallow the taking in of any opposing view. The new "correct" standard of today is such that; all is well unless one voices a different view. Not so with Mr. Bryan. He says that it is important for students to be informed with researched facts of history and that public schools, as with public media, are meant to educate and inform, not to shape minds toward what is politically correct.

Mr. Bryan always showed pro-American insights, as opposed to mainstream American history classes of modern-day public schools, where the popular thought is to dig up trash on America so that American students become ashamed of their heritage. Not so in Mr. Bryan's class. He always managed to allow students to see it another way. Not clashing but inviting thought. Sure, there were bad things that Americans had done, but what nation is without error? There is a lot of good that America has in her history, too. What is wrong with students being proud of their nation, America?

Mr. Bryan was one of those special teachers who knew and loved the subject of American history well. He always had a way to convey American pride as he pointed out what is so good about a nation with virtuous-minded principles that stand out from the rest of the globe. To gain a true education comes from learning a truth and a fiction, then knowing how to decipher it by analyzing history through hermeneutics and topology, not with modern idealism that skews key information.

Nina gets to class. Although she is 10 minutes early, the class is nearly full. Mr. Bryan begins his American history lecture. Just then, Principal Spinner and 2 members of the school board pop into the classroom. "Don't mind us class. We are here to observe."

Word got out that Mr. Bryan was going to provide some historical insights into the topic of faith and America's founding leaders. Principal Spinner and the board sit in the back of the class, just as they did in Dr. Roy's Music class. Mr. Bryan was prepared for this day. By now, most of the teachers have been replaced by these new, strange, young, and perfect-looking teachers. He knew that his day was coming, so he was prepared to give his students the courage to research the truth and stand up for what was right.

Mr. Bryan starts by addressing the separation of Church and State. Class, the First Amendment guarantees freedom of religion. Mr. Bryan turns on the projector screen and then walks over to his lab top and reads the First Amendment of the United States." Congress shall make no law respecting an establishment of religion or prohibiting the free exercise thereof, or abridging the freedom of speech, or of the press; or the right of the people peaceably to assemble, and to petition the Government for a redress of grievances." (First Amendment)

He turns off the projector screen, walks over to the front of the class, and sits on the edge of the desk. Taking his glasses off to clean them. Mr. Bryan says. "Today, with the Ten Commandments being scraped off U.S. government walls and with prayer being thrashed from our schools and public arenas, this has equaled the campaign to eliminate faith and practice citing the Separation of Church and State.

The thing is, the Separation of Church and State was never intended to squelch religion and the freedom of speech. Instead, it was meant to keep the government completely out of these human affairs. It is nowhere to be found in our founding legislation. It cannot be found in the U.S. Constitution or any founding government documents. America's founding leaders would never have stomached such restrictions dictated on religion today."

Mr. Bryan walks back over to the projector and turns it back on. The title on the slide deck reads: Separation of Church and State. He walks over to his lab top, then looks up at the projection on the screen. "The meaning of the term Separation of Church and State came from a letter that was written in 1802 by Thomas Jefferson. It was in response to the Danbury Baptist Association of Connecticut to make sure that the First Amendment Right of Religious Freedom remains intact. You see, the early Europeans who came to America, did so to escape the horrible religious persecution that they had endured in their European homeland. Because of this, the founding principles were written to protect religious freedom. Even though early America was founded on Jewish & Christian biblical principles, the founders did not wish to force their religion, or any religion on others. The First Amendment for religious freedom was written so that the state would never force any type of religion, or any type of non-religion on the people. "Unfortunately, during our modern times this letter had been twisted and used as a source for Big Government to force its anti-Christian, anti-Semitic, and religious-based humanistic ideas on the people. Let's read the letter our self and see exactly what it says."

Mr. Bryan clicks the presentation to the next slide and projects the letter that Thomas Jefferson wrote on the screen. He proceeds to read it. "I contemplate with sovereign reverence that act of the whole American people which declared that their legislature should 'make no law respecting an establishment of religion, prohibiting the free exercise thereof; thus, building a wall of separation between church and State."

Mr. Bryan went on to say. "In this letter, Thomas Jefferson uses the term Wall of Separation Between Church and State to emphasize that the First Amendment constrains the U.S. government and not the American people. When writing the U.S. Constitution, our founding fathers had incredible foresight to write the First Amendment to protect citizens from an overpowering government in the future. Thomas Jefferson emphasized this fact. After all, the First Amendment gives tremendous religious freedom to the people; however, there is the big mouth of recent big government idealism that has latched on to the phrase; Separation of Church and State and twisted the words of Thomas Jefferson to reverse engineer our First Amendment rights. Today, so too often, we just turn over and hand in our First Amendment Religious Rights instead of taking a stand when a governing organization decides to take down a cross, a nativity scene, lifting up a prayer to God during school, or preventing the use of speech like saying Merry Christmas during the season."

Mr. Bryant concludes his lecture. "Class here, I leave you with the challenge to always investigate, research, and see that knowledge is the antidote to counter-twisted thinking as the canard of a modern idealism that has corrupted recent American history. Here is the quote that fits well here.

"There is a principle which is a bar against all information, which is proof against all argument, and which cannot fail to keep a man in everlasting ignorance! That principle is condemnation before investigation." William Paley (1794)

Principal Spinner stands up abruptly. Her angry manner is aimed at Mr. Bryant and his class. They watch her as she walks sternly to the door. She pauses and turns to face Mr. Bryan, then whispers in his ear in an eerie, agitated voice, with teeth clenched, she says.

"Enough of your historical mumbo jumbo. In front of this class, I take great pleasure in telling you that we are letting you go, so please follow me and do not make a scene. I'll have someone pack your classroom belongings and meet you at the office. Mr. Bryan, follow me immediately."

Oh, such cold, steel-hearted management on display. Today just happens to be Mr. Bryan's 15th anniversary as a history teacher at Beachside Park High School. Looks like there will be no celebration for him, just reprimanding a good teacher, where once a teacher's position meant something. It meant to be someone. Yes, times are changing rapidly. Freedom is in the crosshairs of this new ideology. Somehow, Mr. Bryan knew this day would happen soon. The class had 15 minutes to go, but he needed to keep his composure in front of the class as he followed Principal Spinner.

His head went numb. Although it is expected of this powerful principal and school board, there is a flash of injustice in the way this idealism is being applied. As the teacher and employee of the school district, it was his duty. Mr. Bryan turned to the class, and with strong confidence, he said.

"I'll see you guys later."

Everyone is shaken, and Nina slams her notebook down. The entire history class just witnessed the markings of tyranny, yet they are stunned. No one says a word. Perhaps this is all just an act put on by Mr. Bryan to get his message across. But it is not an act. True, it is an excellent first-hand lesson. It is even perhaps an awakening, but not an act.

Within 30 seconds after Mr. Bryan shuts the door, the door opens, and in walks the new history teacher to replace him. She has a similar look as the new science teacher. The same age, mid to late 20's, but this time with brown wavy hair, a fair complexion, and a perfect unblemished face.

"Hello, class."

"My Name is Miss Darpha."

"I will be your new History Teacher."

Her voice has a strange, canned tone. Something is strange about these new teachers, but it is hard to put one's finger on it. Miss Darpha moves to the front of the class and begins to introduce and enforce the alternative American History view of Howard Zinn, as programmed for the new history teacher. Mrs. Darpha says. "Now, class, please hand in your old history textbooks for this class. Please do it right now. Before you go, we will be passing out the best seller … A Peoples History of American Empire." by the world-renowned authority on how to change American history to fit the agenda in one generation, Mr. Howard Zinn."

While Miss Darpha, the new History Teacher, finishes the class, Mr. Bryan is sitting in the school office being out-processed. It so happened that Nina's mom was in the office at the same time. She volunteers in the school office twice a week to help with much-needed administrative paperwork. She overheard the firing of Mr. Bryan by the board. They spoke of his immediate replacement by a new special teacher. Nina's mom was clearly upset at the board for firing this history teacher. As Mr. Bryan walked by, she stopped him. Not wanting to let on what she overheard, she simply told Mr. Bryan how much Nina had enjoyed his history class. She said.

"Mr. Bryan, my daughter Nina always looks forward to your history class."

"Thank you so much, Mrs. Tanizaki." Said Mr. Bryant.

"I always enjoyed Nina's enthusiasm in class… please let her know that."

Carrying a cardboard box of his belongings, Mr. Bryan gives Nina's mom a warm smile, looks around the office room, and then walks out the door. Nina's Mom stands up, gives the office a dirty look, and sits back down to finish the administrative documents. She is clearly upset at what just took place, and the office knows it.

That night, the Toasters Club's 15-minute sprint stand-up ceremony happened. Next, they perform their Sprint-0 session beginning with the story map of the new product vision for the Homework Processor that Annie and Peter had come out with. This homework system is also based on Scrum, helping students stay organized and focused on their homework.

Annie is taking on the Product Owner role, so she is instrumental in hosting the design thinking product sprint, laying out the Story Map to capture its functionality, prioritizing, guiding the team toward value, using the Minimal Viable Product (MVP) techniques and then using this clear product vision to create the Product Backlog with Epics and User Stories. She gets help from the team, including Nina, whose role this time is acting as Scrum Master, with Peter as the Subject Matter Expert (SME).

One goal of this new Homework Processing learning system is to help students at Beachside Park High School organize their homework and practice the techniques of Agile Scrum, which will give them the edge once they go to college and then onward into the workplace already knowing how to perform in Agile and on a Scrum team. They meet for the Sprint-0 session. The session is very productive. They got a lot done and decided to break up and meet again tomorrow.

After the Toasters Club meeting, Nina and Lizzy walk home together. They take a shortcut across the High School Campus. Nina sees a blue glow coming from one of the windows.

"Hey, what's that?"

"Maybe it's a fish tank glowing in the dark." Says Lizzy.

"Yah, but this is coming from between the administration office and Mrs. Davidsons English class. Let's go check it out."

Nina runs up to the office window and looks through. The closet door happens to be open so that she can see inside. It is filled with multiple robots plugged in and charging. With further inspection Nina sees the new science teacher hanging from the row. She falls backward as if she has seen a ghost. "What's the matter, Nina?" Lizzy is afraid to look, afraid to find out, but her curiosity gets the best of her. She peeks through the office window.

"That's, that's…"

"I know, Lizzy. It's our new Science teacher, Mr. Ottkin."

"No way, that's our new Music teacher in the corner." Says Lizzy.

"I also see our new science teacher over there."

Nina and Lizzy get up and peak through the window to validate who is who? Or since they are bot-teacher machines… what is what?

"Oh wow – oh wow."

"What, Lizzy?"

"They all look very much alike."

Just then, Janitor Ed comes out from the utility closet. He hears a noise from outside and sees Nina and Lizzy looking back at him through the window. They begin running from the school into the darkness. He stoops down quickly but jumps back up so as not to look guilty. He squats back down. "Wait a minute, I'm Janitor Ed. I only work here; I'm not the one bringing these teacher-bots into the classroom." He stands back up and watches Nina and Lizzy run away. He yells toward Lizzy and Nina. "Run-away kids. Don't get messed up with this stuff that is happening right now." Janitor Ed whispers to himself. "Man, I got to do something, or these kids are going to be in danger when they come back. I know they will come back, so what shall I do?"

Nina and Lizzy run all the way home. "Not a word, Lizzy. Okay?" Hours later that night, while at home in bed, Nina had been in a deep sleep until the text from Lizzy startled her.

"Ding... I can't sleep, Nina, can you?

"Ding... Yes, Lizzy. You just woke me up. Why are you texting me?"

"Ding... how can you sleep in a time like this, Nina?"

"Ding... we got to tell someone. This is serious."

"Ding... I know Janitor Ed would never be in on this sort of thing."

"Ding... I think he is in danger."

"Ding... I think we all are in danger, Lizzy."

"Ding... go to sleep. We'll talk about it in the morning."

The next morning, Lizzy gets to the Toasters meeting first and tells Annie, Peter, Matt, and Hamster at the Toasters Club. She is not believed at first. As soon as Nina makes it to the meeting, they confront Nina. Okay, tell us your story. At first, Nina is shocked. She is still in a haze of what happened last night. She looks at Lizzy and speaks to the toasters club. "Oh, last night, Lizzy and I walked past the school office and saw a blue glow." Just then, Peter and Annie's dad and mom both took an interest and stepped in the room to listen. "We became curious, and so we peaked through the office window to see what it was. The closet door in the office was wide open, so we saw that the closet was converted into a robot charging room for the new teachers. You see, the new teachers are not real humans; they are life-like humanoids… robots."

Everybody in the entire room gasped. Just then, Mr and Mrs Wang speak up. "Tell us more then, what happened?" Said Mr. Wang. Nina responds. Nina says, "We saw Janitor Ed working in the charger room. He is a part of it." Again, all in the room gasped.

"Okay." Mrs. Wang coming to the defense of Janitor Ed.

"We know not to judge Janitor Ed."

"We need to confront him and allow him to explain."

"So many times, people get the wrong word or impression about a person, and they just accept the nasty gossip without challenging it."

"The bible says judge not, or you will be judged."

"It also says thou shalt not falsely accuse!!!!!"

Mrs. Wang continues. "I take this very seriously as we must take great care not to bear false witness. In other words, Toasters Club, do not draw any conclusions before knowing the truth."

Mrs. Wang was Nina's Sunday school teacher in the 4th grade. She recalls how Mrs. Wang had always something good and positive to say about others.

"What's the matter Nina?" Says Hamster. "Nothing," Nina responds. Becoming aloof and obtuse, as opposed to internalizing things, is exactly how Nina reacts to danger. It's a defense mechanism that Nina holds. She remembers how good she felt as a child in Mrs. Wang's Sunday school class. Nina thought to herself. "I am so grateful for the Wang's. My dad always says the Wangs are a fine example of those who live it and not just talk it."

Just then, Mr. Wang stood up and walked over to the center of the room. He stood there for a while, then turned around with a serious face. He says, "Toasters Club, it sounds like we all need to keep our eyes and ears open and our mouths shut. This has got to be bigger than we know now, and your life may be in danger. Okay? Again… okay, guys?"

The Toasters all respond in unison. All except Hamster. Hamster. He appeared like he was not paying attention, but in reality, Hamster was in deep thought. You know, he is beside himself in his curiosity. He needs to know more. Mr. Wang walks over to Hamster. "Okay, Hamster?" Stunted as if Hamster is awakened from a deep sleep. Hamster looks up at Mr. Wang. "Yes, sir, Mr. Wang. Okay."

The Toasters Club jumps on their bikes and skateboards as they do every morning before school day, but this day was different. Hamster is unusually quiet. It has Peter concerned. He speaks with Hamster as they ride bikes down the hill to school together. "Are you okay, Hamster? You know, my dad's just trying to protect you, me, and the Toasters Club. He did not mean to come down on you. You see, my dad and mom are dealing with some serious business issues. They had to lay off most of their full-time staff. People they valued as part of the workers who helped them build their business." Still riding bikes with the other toasters, Hamster looks at Peter.

"What did you just say, Peter?"

"I said my dad didn't mean to come down on you so hard."

"No, Peter, right after that, you said that your parents had to lay people off."

"Yes, new California state regulations have made it very difficult for small business owners to hire full-time workers."

"That's it. That's it!"

"That's what? Hamster, care to explain?"

"Guys. Toasters. Come here."

Hamster slams the brake on his bike and yells to the others riding. "Guys, gather around." Peter and the rest of the Toasters circle back around and ride toward Hamster. They all gather around together with their bikes and skateboards to listen to what Hamster has to say.

Hamster speaks up and says. "Guys, I figured it out. Listen up. My parents always said that when things don't match up, follow the money. Well, now, we see that those new teachers are really robots placed there by someone to deceive us. These people are replacing all the live human teachers in our school. Right? Well, this is brilliant. Someone is behind all this who is a mastermind. There is no way Janitor Ed is that masterminded person. He is just obeying orders, and I think that he is in danger." Matt speaks out. "What about Principal Spinner?" Hamster says. "No. Well, let me restate that. I think this is way too big for someone like Principal Spinner. Although we all know how power-hungry Principal Spinner is, this is likely a weakness that a mastermind has zoned in on to take advantage of her need for power by placing her in front. Principal spinner is likely in on it, but there is someone much bigger out there, pulling on the marionette puppet strings."

Nina looks at Hamster in amazement at how well Hamsters thought process fits the scenario. She says. "If this is the case, then they have gone rogue and underground. We have got to find out the root of this matter."

Onward to School!

CHAPTER TEN
Dr. Ott's Media War

THE TOASTERS ARIVE at school, and they start to notice something different at school. This is not just the power of suggestion when someone points out a black hat and soon you begin to see hats and chiefly black hats everywhere. Change is here and is becoming even more noticeable. There are a lot of new teachers, "Bot-Teachers" in class. Old teachers are gone … vanished.

Something strange is happening on campus. The power shift has begun. Yes, teachers are being replaced by humanoids. They are so lifelike. No one can really tell for sure that this is happening until they are fully engulfed in position and empowered. There is also a "new talk" happening in the news media. Dr. Ott did not need to purchase any media news airtime; all he needed to do was sell his bogus reporter-bots to the mainstream news media, and wham-o … Instant scrolling of fake news brought to you with digitized commentary bot-blotters for social media channels. This sneaky censorship not only squelched truth and common sense, but it also countered this just enough to confuse even the smartest of those who regularly watch it to the point that they would passionately defend its creed. Brainwashed to believe. Afterall, it's mainstream media, so it must be fair, balanced, peer-reviewed, and real. We can trust it … Right?

The philosophy of the underground news media is now mainstream among the people in town. It came before the invasion of education. Smear campaigns are in place to go against any opposition that may arise. To speak out, to call out Foul, for any senior jobs being replaced by new high-capacity younger bot-like persons, is considered hate speech. Even to complain that you lost your seniority over a bot worker is considered robotic intolerance.

The townspeople become paralyzed with fear. Meanwhile, thousands of robots invade the town and continue to replace key jobs in education, healthcare, financial institutions, security, media, transportation, and the government. Although most think they are real people. They have no idea that they are being replaced by robots, and for fear of being called a racist, the people say nothing. It's a perfect scenario for the enemy to successfully take over from within.

With the social media and mobile cellular outlets, the people of the town became accustomed to texting each other rather than assembling in one place face to face. But with social media now blocking and censoring all real news, most in town don't realize that they are being invaded. In fact, most town folks are hard-working citizens who want a better life for themselves and their children, but they do not see the change right away. Not until they receive a layoff notice and their job is gone.

During class, Hamster begins to pay close attention to the new teachers. He records their speech on his cell phone, and he secretly takes their pictures, but unbeknownst to Hamster, each bot-teacher comes equipped with cameras, audio recording, GPS, and real-time telemetric controllers so anyone can be monitored through their cell phone. With its Artificial Intelligence (AI), any CPU on the internet can be overridden, just like a drone that can be hijacked from a control room. That's exactly what happens.

Deep down in Dr. Ott's underground laboratory, Dr. Ott is on his elaborate personal computer counting money. He gets interrupted by Nate. "Boss, boss. You need to see this." Dr. Ott switches his control panel to see from the Bot-Teachers eyes.

"Who is this kid? Why is he taking pictures of unit 24609? Says Dr. Ott.

"I don't know boss, that is why we are letting you know."

"Follow him. Find out who he is, where he lives, his family, and internet IP address. At once."

"We tried already, and we can't get a face recognition of this kid, boss. He's not in any database."

"What? What kind of kid is this?" says Dr. Ott.

Dr. Ott continues. "Didn't he ever join a social network, take selfies with his mobile phone, or play Pokémon Go like all good citizen sheeple do?" Dr. Ott turns to face Hamster's image portrayed on the control screen wall panel.

"Who is this kid?"

Well, it happened to be that Hamster's great-grandparents, "both sets," were incarcerated in the German Nazi concentration camps. These horrific things happened when they were kids. They lost both their parents and were tossed into those horrible camps only because they were Jewish. They survived and were able to gain new hope and come to a new home in America. The one oddity his grandparents had. The one thing they always spoke about was for all their children to keep a low profile and to stay off the grid. They passed this wise idea to hamster parents, who made sure that the entire family took measures to stay off unnecessary internet usage. One can only imagine Hamster's life off-the-grid. Although he is a computer genius, it is not easy for one to stay away from social networking. Dr. Ott speaks to Nate and the team.

"We are going to have more and more conspiracy theorists like this kid."

"More to probe around as their tiny world changes."

"We need to bring out the countermeasure."

"It's time for The Fear Tactic."

Dr. Ott's workers now gather around his control panel. They began to come up with ideas to track down Hamster. One of Dr. Ott's evil gain members speaks to him. "Fear. That's right boss." Dr. Ott swivels his chair toward the worker. Beads of sweat appear on the worker's forehead as Dr. Ott stares intensely at him.

"What are all of you doing here?"

"Get back to work"

"Find out who that kid is. . . NOW."

His workers scramble. Dr. Ott's face shifts to calm as he goes back to count all his money. Each robot placed in work means a perpetual income for him, and that income is increasing as the business scales up exponentially. A salary of $36 per hour is not a whole lot for one to live on and care for their family these days, but as an outsourced bot rate, it undercuts the hard-working citizens in the town of Beachside Park, bringing down the worker's value. For Dr. Ott, it promotes business by 10X and beyond, laying off people and shifting wealth and power to him as bot owner. Just think, if you multiply the rate by 100, 500, 1,000, and 10,000 robot jobs per hour, times 8 hours a day, times 40 hours per week. That amount quickly grows into $millions per week. Money equals power, and power equals more control and more money. Of course, minus 10 percent for the big guy. It's a great way to spot corrupt politicians who go into politics on a poor government salary and come out filthy rich like Rock Stars, owning private jets and big multimillion-dollar homes. Go figure.

Dr. Ott begins to daydream about money and fame. He is standing on a pedestal next to his statue. All power is his, and the people are shouting Otty, Otty, Otty in his dream. "How strange," he says to himself. "How come all these people are calling me Otty and not Dr. Ott?" Just then, Dr. Ott wakes up from deep sleep to the voice of his mom calling him over the intercom.

"Otty. Otty. Otty."

"Otty? Are you there?

Breaker-Breaker."

"Otty, I just baked a dozen buttermilk biscuits."

"Come up and get them while they are still hot."

The whole crew looks back at Dr. Ott while he looks back at them with a sheepish smile. He shrugs his shoulders, presses the intercom microphone button, and quietly whispers so his crew can't hear.

"Um, okay, mom."

"Otty, I can't hear you. What did you say?" His mom says in a loud, scruffy voice. Dr. Ott speaks up as the crew looks away, pretending not to notice.

"I said that I would be right up, Mom."

"Okay, Otty. I read you loud and clear."

"Over and out."

The Toasters Club gets together for a chat on the athletic field after school. They share their stories of the new bot-teachers that are teaching class. Matt begins by saying. "It's not only the new bot-teachers. There is much more going on here in town." Peter chimes in. Saying, "I hear that they are hiring and bringing in these new bot workers at the local radio and T.V. news media." Bolt follows Peters remark by saying. "I heard today that many more parents are losing their jobs. In-fact; Jill, Andy, and Michael's parents were let go today." Bolt stands up to put his jacket on. Peter looked over at Bolt, oh and I forgot.

"The O-Lady at TacO's was let go."

"I was in there yesterday for lunch. They have a new bot-host."

More robots are being placed. Office workers, government employees, technical engineers, bankers, and even fast-food workers are being replaced by robots. Hamster stands up and addresses the team. "Tonight, we should go back and investigate that strange blue glow you guys encountered at school the other day. Guys let's all meet here tonight. Nina and Lizzy can show us where it is."

As they leave the field, two black crows fly right overhead and land next to them. They are on a mission to follow Hamster. They want to know where his home is. The crows are actually drones equipped with cameras and GPS tracking devices. They look and fly like real crows. Hamster makes it home while the crows track. Now Dr. Ott has his home address, name, phone number, email address, and Hamster's face tracked and recognized.

That night, the Toasters all meet. Together, they all walked over to the school, where Nina and Lizzy saw the closet full of bot-teachers. Nina points. "There it is. See the blue glow? It's coming from that closet." They get down on their knees to look into the office through the window, but this time, the closet door is closed, so they cannot see into the closet. Matt tries to open the office door, but it's locked. Just then, Janitor Ed happens by. "Well, hello, Kids." Says Janitor Ed. They are completely startled. Just then, Janitor Ed reaches into his pocket. Hamster yells out. "Take cover, he's got a gun."

They stand up to run, but Janitor Ed just smiles and holds up his hand, "why not use these?" In his hand is a set of keys. Janitor Ed was there to investigate, too, but he saw the Toasters Club all there in front of the school and knew that they were also out to investigate that closet. "I know why you are here. I saw you two, Lizzy and Nina, the other night. You were both ing out of here like two cottontail rabbits. I was working to change this closet into the robot charging room."

They all get into the office and open the door to see the closet full of bot-teachers all plugged-in and charging-up overnight. Nina turns to Janitor Ed. "What's going on?" Janitor Ed proceeds to tell them everything he knows about the sales recruiters, the school board, and even Principal Spinner. "There is someone evil behind all of this. I am not sure who this person is, but he is some sort of scientist. A mad scientist. He has an underground laboratory somewhere here in town. It is also a factory where they produce these robots. He is the one that we all need to be concerned about."

Nina looks at the team. "We have got to do something." Janitor Ed stops Nina. "Whoa, whoa, whoa! These are not good people, Nina. They hunger for power. You all need to be very careful here, as these robots are everywhere now. Try and be inconspicuous. Once you expose them, you will be in real danger."

The Toasters split up and run home. Some try and tell their parents, but they do not believe. Except for Mr. and Mrs. Wang, who believe, other parents find this all hard to believe. It sounds so much like a conspiracy theory that Nina decides to hold off on telling her parents until she thinks through what she is going to say. At the dinner table Nina's dad finishes prayer for their meal. Nina then decides to tell them, but her dad cuts her off. Nina starts to get angry.

"Why don't you guys listen to me?"

"Whoa, Nina," says Dad.

"Cool your jets here. We already know."

"What?" Said Nina.

"The Wangs told us. We were just waiting for you to tell us."

"So go on. Tell us everything you know about Janitor Ed and the bot-teachers."

Nina goes on to tell them what they discovered tonight. It is not Janitor Ed and the bot-teachers, someone else is pulling the puppet strings. With Nina's story, it was still hard to believe.

"Wow Nina. Couldn't the robots be like that automatic vacuum cleaner that you charge up, turn on, and release to clean the floors while you go about the day?"

"No Dad. These are life-like robots. They look like real people. Remember, over the last several weeks, my school has been firing teachers. These are the new History Teachers, Science Teachers, and Math Teachers at our school, except they are all robots that have replaced human teachers. They are now teaching the classes that I attend every day at school."

Nina's mom says, "Hey, that's right. That makes perfect sense. The other day, while I was in the high school office, I saw Mr. Bryan as he was getting fired from the school. I overheard Principal Spinner telling him to take his things and go. She was very mean to Mr. Bryan. In fact, I overheard Principal Spinner tell Mr. Bryan these exact mean words:"

"Get your catastrophic shoes off my office carpet; you are tracking failure all over it."

"That is so awful," said Nina.

"So true. I didn't want to tell you because I knew how much you admired him."

"It breaks my heart how mean people can be."

"It is at the point where some actually gain pleasure in trashing one's livelihood."

Nina's mom is now even more angry at Principal Spinner and the school board for what they are doing to the High School. These teachers were seasoned. No robot can replace that sort of experience and insight. Nina's Dad says.

"Okay, let me do some thinking. Right now, I have to run. I'm late for the Christmas practice."

"Oh, can I come along with you Dad?"

"Sure Nina, but we got to go right now."

Nina and her dad rush off to the church to practice for the Christmas play. While on the way, Nina discusses all the strange activities in town. She tells her dad how serious she is. Dad tells her. "I believe you, Nina, it's just that this is all so strange. You would think that the media would mention these strange things." Nina gives a quick reply. "Well, Dad, what if the media is in on all this, too? What if they are paid to spin the message, block the truth, and keep their mouths shut?"

They reach the church for practice. Nina sits and watches practice. Dad gets up on stage and sings. He is Joseph in the play. A bit old for the part, but no one else had volunteered. Nina thinks he is a cool dad. He still looks young sometimes. Well, from a distance on stage, that is. A very long distance.

In the Christmas play, Nina's Dad, sings a song about his love for Mary and their struggle in life together. God sanctions marriage. It is a beautiful thing, but there are evil forces that beat up God's meaning and purpose for marriage, too. It is difficult at times, but nothing of value is free from trouble. A kiss of grace. The savior of the world. A value so misunderstood and overlooked. Why God chose this way, and through this young, willing couple, is astonishing. The practice continues; meanwhile, Mrs. Wang is helping with setting up the stage for the Christmas play. As the actors start practicing on stage, she takes a break and sits down next to Nina.

"Hey, Nina, how's it going?" "I'm okay, Mrs. Wang."

"I know, Nina, it is hard to fathom. With your school and all the strange happenings."

"Yes, the whole school is now talking about this. These new teachers … I mean."

"You mean robots?" "Yes, Mrs. Wang, robots."

"You know, Nina, in a strange way, this is all starting to make a little sense."

"What do you mean?"

"You see, it is not only happening in your high school."

"Really? I thought this was all new."

"No, I am sorry to say that the corruption goes much deeper than high school."

"It's much bigger than we think."

"Oh, I didn't know that Mrs. Wang."

Nina did not want to probe any further out of respect. She knew that the Wangs had a very hard time with renewing their city business license this year. They had to let go of most of their full-time employees as a result. Nina wondered if this was related.

"Sorry, Nina. I did not mean to get into all that."

"That's alright."

"What I really wanted to speak with you about is the Toasters Club."

"I see it's going well. Way to go."

"Thanks, Mrs. Wang. You guys are a big influence on us."

"You know, Nina, I believe that you guys are much bigger than you think, too."

"Wow, you think so?"

Here's a little story. I married a not-so-perfect man, but he is smart and honest. Mr. Wang knows when to speak when to shut up, and when to fight. I know that he is a true leader of people because I see others like to follow his lead. What they don't see is that he also knows to turn to God for wisdom. I see that same leadership in you, Nina. Go to God daily if, it's small or big, no matter what. He values all who believe and want to know him. He will give you profitable, witty ideas that are most valuable. In hard times, he always comes through for those who…"

Truly Seek Him

CHAPTER ELEVEN
Snatched!

SHADOWS BEGIN TO APPEAR outside the classroom windows where Hamster is sitting. He is in the back row of calculus. At first, the shadows catch his eye, but he does not give it a second thought. It's only birds! Outside, the black crows are flying around, but these aren't normal crows; they are sophisticated flying bots disguised as large Black Crows, or perhaps Ravens, which are the larger of the two birds. They are spying on Hamster through the classroom window from the air. Dr. Ott and his workers took these measures since Hamsters family was off the grid. This is a way for Dr. Ott and his evil gang to keep an eye on Hamster today. If he speaks up, they want to censor and stamp him out.

At the school office, there are lines of new bot-teachers. The office workers and school staff do not know the new teachers are robots. The line of new teachers follows outside the office door from their delivery. There is a big unmarked white bus parked outside. The new bot-teacher candidates will be filling in positions for the various high school subjects such as math, science, history, and even Physical Ed. They will also be hired as attrition for teacher's aids and substitutes.

Most of the new teachers who are present are in the meeting room office, taking the exam. This is the teacher's exam for earning credentials to teach in class. Dr. Ott programmed each new teacher, enabling him to teach various subjects.

Each new bot-teacher passes the test in seconds, scoring 100 percent perfect test scores. This leaves the real human office school workers who are administering the exams, stunned with who they think are human teachers of such perfection.

One of the office workers even spoke up. These are smart candidates, but there is a certain coldness in their presence. These teachers lack warmth. Other school office workers begin to agree. Those who are evaluating the teachers decide to share their concerns and voice their opinions to the members of the School Board and to Principal

Spinner. Referring to the bot-teachers, the teaching certification office workers cite that, although all these teachers have the mechanics of teaching with perfect certification scores, these teachers all lack human interaction skills. Unfortunately, people skills are not tangible requirements; thus, they are not a big part of the hiring criteria. Besides, Principal Spinner quickly stamps out these concerns, stating. "Yes, the evaluation of people skills will remain absent from this test, as this is a standard teacher credential test. We will comply with this standard and so will you. We will not make a deal of it, so if you still want to collect a paycheck for your puny contributions to the school, you will not make anything of this as well."

Principal Spinner sure has a way with words. In her mind, she is a great leader. Her self-assessment is skewed by her tyrannical mindset. She is always so quick to point out a worker's insignificance under her rule of command. Nina's mom happens to be volunteering in the school office that day. She overhears Principal Spinner. This is a suspicious position to take, she says to herself. It's not just the new teachers, it's the entire attitude of the working environment. She does not know who to trust, so with the other office workers around her, she keeps this suspicion about them being robots to herself trying not to let-on that she knows anything about the influx of new teachers. She thinks the entire thing of firing the seasoned teachers and replacing them with new teachers is strange. Only Principal Spinner and the school board members know where the new teachers come from and how this action aligns with the true agenda.

The Toasters Club is meeting in the cafeteria. The cafeteria building and grounds are modern and highly functional. It would have made Frank Lloyed Wright proud of its achievement as its design was influenced by his amazing architectural talents from the West Architectural School in Scottsdale, Arizona. Lots of stone and glass windows give light indoors with nature and landscape both in and out. The Toasters Club meets to discuss what is happening in their town and at the school.

At the same time Dr. Ott positions two bot teachers to sit just in the outdoor space of the cafeteria. The tree blocks the view of these bot-teachers from the Toasters. These robots are equipped with special face recognition gear and special microphones to hone in on voices to capture what people are saying.

It is breakfast time in the morning at school, a few minutes before class time. The entire Toasters Club is present. They have positioned their chairs in a circle on the cafeteria floor. Bolt, Annie, and Lizzy on one end. Matt was sitting next to Nina. Hamster and Peter on Nina's right. They are all discussing the increased events of new teachers in the office. Matt speaks out first. "What can we do? We are being infiltrated by tyrannical-based gov-heads with robots. People are losing their jobs. From what I understand, it means that we are under siege."

Peter speaks up. "Hey, don't you think that you are overstating this, Matt? Everyone around me seems to be caring just fine in spite of the layoffs. If we are really under siege, then why so much apathy? "Peter, that's not apathy." Says Hamster. "That is ignorance," Peter replies. "Well then. What about mainstream TV and mainstream News? Nothing is said about this. You see, we rely on the Federal Communications Commission (FCC) board, and one of their six goals is Public Safety and Homeland Security. I'm not seeing them sounding off the alarm."

"I would argue that being under siege from within has a lot to do with a communications breach in security. The FCC doesn't at all seem to be bothered by the recent turn of events here in Beachside Park. Why should we?"

Back in Dr. Ott's underground control room. Dr. Ott and his entire staff are watching and listening to everything the Toasters Club members are saying through the camera eyes and microphone ears of the robots positioned in the cafeteria. "Hey, I'm starting to like that Peter guy." Says Dr. Ott. Way to go, Peter! Go ahead and plant that doubt. Twist those conspiracy ideas into foolish rubbish." "Yes, boss, we should recruit this guy," says Nate with a big smile. "Yes, Nate and I should replace you," says Dr. Ott, quickly wiping the smile off Nate's face.

Back in the school cafeteria, Hamster speaks up, "Think of it, Peter. Teachers at this school lost their jobs, and people in the town are losing their jobs, while certain officials in government are becoming empowered and rich. Look at Principal Spinner." Again, Peter argues. "Principal Spinner is not a government employee." Hamster and Matt quickly point out. "Oh yes, she is, Peter. She works for the public school system and its governing board."

Now, deep down in Dr. Ott's underground control room, Dr. Ott and all his workers are watching the entire conversation on the big screen. Dr. Ott controls the microphones from the robots. Again, the robots' eyes are mini-cameras, and the ears are highly sophisticated listening devices that can pick up sound and movement from a long distance. These robots are the ultimate spy asset. One of Dr. Ott's workers speaks out, referring to Hamster.

"Do you want us to snuff him out, boss?"

"No, leave Hamster alone."

"Let's see where this goes first."

Now, looking at the Toasters Club in the cafeteria through the robots' eyes, with live video data fed to Dr. Ott's underground control room and broadcast throughout all of Dr. Otts lab monitors. Dr. Ott and his gain all see Peter as he blurts out. "Oh, man! I did not think of it that way." Hamster Continues. "Follow the money. You see Peter. Just as the schools are funded by the government, it is possible that some high officials of the FCC can be in on this too. It can happen at all the major points of influence: Healthcare, Media, Transportation, Education, Government and even Security."

Lizzy speaks out. She had been quiet along with Annie and Bolt. "This all seems so unbelievable. Either we all had unraveled the biggest event that has hit our town in its 100-year history, or we all have gone completely bonkers… I mean psycho crazy!"

In Dr. Ott's underground control room, everyone is jumping for joy… Dr. Ott's workers speak out, referring to Hamster, "Man! That is exactly what we want, Right Boss? We want them dazed and confused." Dr. Ott doesn't respond. He continues to watch the Toasters Club in full discussion inside the school cafeteria. Bolt, sitting next to Annie in the cafeteria, raises a question.

"Hey guys, do you think it's about the money?"

"I mean, how is anyone getting rich off this sort of scheme?"

Even though Bolt's answer seems obvious, and a bit silly. The Toasters Club is a Scrum team, and in order for a scrum team to function well as a highly performing team, they must not put down another member's questions or ideas. This encourages one to speak freely. In essence, the Toasters Club disciplines themselves to treat others on the team with dignity just as they would like to be treated themselves. No Bad-Mouthing others. This environment gives way to continual improvement, transparency, and trust on the team. Annie gently answers Bolt. "Yes Bolt. On the outside it may seem that money has no part, as who can profit? But I assure you, some are getting richer outsourcing all those jobs, and some are getting poorer losing all those jobs."

"But it's not so much about the money as it is about the power that money brings. You see, money is a tool. In this case it is a weapon, a weapon for a rogue organization to take siege of our town from within. The more our local government regulates businesses, takes away jobs, and raises taxes that strip wealth from its townspeople, the more power and control they have over the town and its people. Fear is a power that bad managers and politicians can use to manipulate workers into submission. Climate control and pandemics being on the forefront of politically weaponized fear tactics." Hamster speaks out, "Yes, and who delivers these fear tactics?"

"The Media." Says Matt.

"Bingo." Says Hamster.

Annie continues. "Our parents are business owners and employ many, but they always teach Peter and me not to abuse that position. With power, one's evil philosophy, one's ruling agenda, one's command and control superiority can take over, no matter how disgusting and obvious."

"Guys, we are seeing a transfer of wealth taken from the good citizens of this town and given over to the robot builders and owners. Who are the owners? At this point, none of us know, but what we do know is this; these certain robot owners are a certain enemy who has taken up a position to kill, steal, and destroy people, not to give life a place to prosper, and leadership that builds them up; thus, we can conclude this as an indication that they are of the dark side." Annie stops and turns to the team. "We have got to put a stop to them now."

The team looks perplexed. Hamster whispers to Peter, "Wow, I have never heard Annie sound so, so." "Tough?" Peter responds. "Yes, tough Peter. For matters like this, you want people like Annie on your side. She is TNT, tough and tactful."

Now back in Dr. Ott's laboratory control room, Dr. Ott zooms his screen in on Annie as he spies on the Toasters Club meeting. He has never heard such words. It almost makes his tiny peanut-size heart grow. As he is watching, Nina stands up. "That's right, Annie. Let's put an end to this." Just then, the morning bell rings. Matt stands and leads the Toasters Club in a quick word before they dismiss. "In our fight against evil. Lord, make us accurate and true. Help us catch all the evil plots and actions against us." Matt places his fist out. With his fist extended, the team follows in a circle. "Go Team."

In the control room, Dr. Ott takes command. He begins to bark out orders.

"Get me the names, addresses, and all data on those school kids."

"Yes Boss."

"Keep robots #28363 and #42658 on Hamster."

"Yes Boss,"

"Bring-up Hamsters bot-teachers on screen 2 and 4."

"Yes Boss."

"Bring out the flying Black Crows to track Hamster and the kids. I want to know their every move today."

"Yes Boss."

Dr. Ott becomes agitated with his workers response. He pounds his desk. "Hey, look at me.

Quit calling me boss. Is that all you can say? How can I think for all of you when you all respond like that? I am intelligent. I am witty…

I am the Robot Man." Their faces reveal an empty head. With eyes slightly crossed and heads tilted to one side, they mutter their prescribed response in unison, as if they are part of the CIA-directed mainstream media in Operation Mockingbird. As we so often see these days. Dr. Ott barks an order, and they respond.

"Yes, boss."

A people who are incapable of thinking for themselves, Dr. Ott's evil gang members try to pay attention to Dr. Ott's commands. They tell him what they think he wishes for them to say. This is very common in command & control worker environments. Dr. Ott stares straight ahead as if in a trance. He then begins to rotate his head using his eyes to pan the laboratory, the factory, and the control room. His eyes pierce the dark underground lab with the intent to master-mind his organization and to ultimately control the town.

"I got it." Says Dr. Ott.

"I will call this part of my laboratory The War Room."

"Ah-Hahahaha." Dr. Ott laughs in a raspy voice.

Just then, Dr. Otts robot man's concentration is broken by a loud screech. It's mom. She struggles with the intercom.

"Otty, Otty, Otty?"

"Come in, Otty."

She proceeds to talk through the intercom as it echoes throughout the entire underground lab with a piercing, humbling sound that brings the powerful Robot Man to his knees.

"Yes, Mom."

"I went shopping today, Otty."

"Got you your favorite peanut butter, so I made some peanut butter sandwiches today."

"Time for lunch!"

"Okay, I'll be right up mom."

"Roger Willco. Over and out."

Dr. Ott gets off the intercom in his office. The control panel is lit up behind him. He looks down at the floor, shaking his head… humbled. Shaking it off, he now needs to shift gears and get back into his mad scientist character before walking out of his office in front of his workers. The thing is, he is in a glass office. Everyone in the lab can see it, and they have been listening, too. He looks up at the panel, thinking to himself… I am the Robot man. He decides to say it out loud.

"I am the Robot man!"

He turns around. Out through his laboratory office windows, he sees his entire crew looking back at him. "Hey. What are you guys looking at… get back to work."

"Yes Boss."

Throughout the day at school, Hamster gets that feeling that he is being followed. The two robots who are following Hamster manage to stay just out of sight, but during class, Hamster keeps seeing shadows of the black crows flying outside the classroom window, and the bot-teachers in each of Hamster's classes seem particularly interested in Hamster. As if they are queued to track him. Hamster has that funny feeling that he is also being watched by someone. Call it intuition.

After school, Hamster quickly darts out of the class. He looks over his right shoulder to see if he is being followed and runs into a female bot-teacher coming out of the office on the left. Both Hamster and the teacher fall to the ground. With Hamster still sitting on the floor in the crowded hallway, the teacher quickly gets back up without its wig, thus revealing its clear plastic crown full of electronics. Hamsters seize the opportunity to expose these bot teachers. He points to the robot in the crowded hallway and shouts.

"It's a robot."

"It's a robot."

Others come out of the office. Unfortunately, the bot-teacher gets escorted away by 5 other bot-teachers, so no one seems to have noticed anything. Hamster quickly realizes his situation and begins to shout again.'

"Hey, you. Yah, you, bot-breath. I'm talking to you."

Principal Spinner comes out of the office and walks up to Hamster. She calmly places her hand on Hamsters shoulder and whispers.

"Come with me, Hamster."

As she begins to walk back to her office with Hamster, he shakes away from her hands and starts to run. Meanwhile, back in the control room, Dr. Ott and the workers catch the entire thing on camera. Dr. Ott orders the team to snatch Hamster. "Go catch him."

Robots #28363 and #42658 are right on his tail. They lash-out and capture him by his backpack, but Hamster manages to break loose from his backpack, leaving it behind with the two robots. Seeing this on his control room screen, Dr. Ott roars out. "Get him."

Hamster runs out to the bike area, where his bike is parked and locked up. He tries to unlock his bike, but the keys are in the backpack that he left behind. He sees the robots searching for him, so he lies flat on the pavement. Another student sees Hamster lying on the ground. He comes up to Hamster. "Dude. Are you okay?"

This draws attention to Hamster. The robots spot him through the chain-linked fence and run toward him. Hamster is out of the bike area. The robots run around the fence and after him. Hamster turns and runs across the front of the school, past the flagpole. He sees Nina's mom in her car parked, waiting for Nina to get out of school. Hamster yells. "Mrs. Tanizaki, Mrs. Tanizaki." Hamster runs to Mrs. Tanizaki's car window. Startled, she jumps out of the car to greet Hamster.

"Hamster, what's the matter?"

"I'm being chased."

"Quick, please help me."

"Get in, Hamster."

Hamster jumps into the passenger side. Just then Nina is out of school, walking toward the parking lot. She sees her mom standing next to her car, and suddenly jumping in the car with Hamster jumping in on the other side. She then sees the robots catch up to the car, trying to surround it with her mom and Hamster inside. Hamster yells. "Go! Go!"

Nina's mom screeches out of the parking lot, chased by the two robots. Nina thinks to herself … Oh no, they are in trouble! The Robots cut across the front of the school to take a shortcut to catch up to Nina's Mom and Hamster. The robots are now running toward Nina. She quickly ducks away, not to be seen. The robots run right past Nina in hot pursuit. Meanwhile, in the control room, Dr. Ott directs his staff who is monitoring and controlling the robots. He barks an order.

"Quick. Get a close-up of her car."

"Capture the license plate."

Dr. Ott captures the car on camera; thus, the make, model, and license plate of Nina's mom's car. He proceeds to have them check the National Auto Database to see what kind of information exists in the database on her type of car, and then searches online on how to gain access to her car. Nina's mom and Hamster are driving further away. Nina sees her mom's car moving further up the street. Her mom is driving, and Hamster is sitting in the front passenger seat.

"Good … We are losing them."

"What happened, Hamster?"

"Why are those thugs chasing you?"

"No, Mrs. Tanizaki, those are not thugs. They are the teacher-bots we've been talking about."

Dr. Ott's team coordinates other robots to take a van and go help the robots with the chase, as he uses his DMV computer access to hone in on Nina's mom's car. Just then, Dr. Ott gains access to Tanizaki's car through the internet and shuts it down.

"Hamster, what is happening? Why is the car stopping?"

"Oh no Mrs. Tanizaki, they tapped into your car's system, overriding it electronically."

From the school parking lot down the street, Nina begins to run. From the distance, she can see everything going on. She sees the robots pull her mom and Hamster out of the car stopped in the middle of the street. A large white van pulls up and stops behind her mom's car. It is temporarily blocking Nina's view. In a flash, it drives away.

Nina stops running and stands in the middle of the street, waiting for the motorcycle traffic police to take chase. The police are always parked there on that corner, waiting for parents to break a traffic law so that they can give a ticket to parents who are picking up or dropping off their kids. This time. This one and only time, the police are not there to catch a more important crime act. Nina thinks to herself how some people complain about the police being present. But wait, when one needs their help and protection, that is when one realizes how so very necessary those brave men and women in blue really are.

Nina takes out her phone and sends an emergency text to her dad. She then runs up to her mom's car. They have regularly practiced emergency texting for family emergencies. Nina's dad calls it "A-LEI." It stands for Alarm, Location, Emergency, and Instructions. Here is how the emergency text goes. The one calling in the emergency types the letter "A" and sends it three separate times to get Attention (Ding, Ding, Ding). This is followed by "L" Location, "E" Emergency type, and "I" Instructions as time permits. The response to this message is a simple text: "Got It," followed by a phone call as soon as possible.

This text Alarm goes out to both mom and dad. Dad responds right away and calls back, but Nina's mom left her phone in the car. It's inside her bag. As Nina runs toward the car, she can hear her mom's phone ringing. It's still in the street with its two front doors wide open. Nina reaches into her mom's bag in the car. It's Dad calling. Nina answers. "Hurry, Dad. Mom and Hamster are gone. They had just been kidnapped by robots. I saw the whole thing. Mom and Hamster are gone. Dad, they were…"

Snatched!

CHAPTER TWELVE
Rise-Up!

NINA'S MOM AND HAMSTER are taken to the lab in the big white van. They reach the lab in minutes. Dr. Otts's lab is located close to the school. At the lab, Mrs. Tanizaki and Hamster are taken down to the third underground level, and they are both locked up.

Meanwhile, Nina investigates the scene of the car and then dials the police. Her dad arrives at the scene in minutes. Nina is still on the phone with 911 when he arrives. She drops the phone runs to her dad, and hugs him saying. "Dad." Nina's dad says, "Who were they, Nina? Who kidnapped Mom and Hamster?" "It was those robots. I saw the whole thing." Said Nina. "I couldn't do anything… They're gone." "No worries, Nina. We are going to find Mom and Hamster. We will find them indeed."

Nina's dad calls Hamster's parents and explains. He asks them to come to meet him and Nina at the scene. He tells them that the police will be there very shortly. He then calls his friend Mr. Wang, to come. Nina calls Matt to alert the Toasters Club. Matt calls together all the Toasters Club members to meet him and Nina at the scene.

The Toasters Club members waste no time to get to the scene where Hamster and Nina's mom are kidnapped by the robots. Of course, they were there to be with Nina and to help her find her mom and Hamster. The police arrive shortly after, but Dr. Ott and his evil men have put out a fake police report. Some trash about Nina's mom becoming delusional and kidnapping Hamster. Nina's dad becomes outraged at the notion of this fake news. He tries to talk sense with the police as they listen and evaluate the scene. Nina's dad addresses the police concerning this. "My wife is not a suspect. This just happened less than 10 minutes ago. Can't you tell from this scene? Why would my wife leave her car in the middle of the road with her phone in the car? Besides, my daughter witnessed the whole thing. She saw them being chased by the robots."

The police respectfully continue to speak with Nina's dad, but they are having a hard time grasping the idea. The first police officer says. "That's just what I mean, Mr. Tanizaki. Chased by robots? Sir, please understand that we need to file a report and check this complaint out; therefore, we need to do some investigation first." Nina's dad says. "Look, I know the story of the robots seems far-fetched. But my wife and Hamster are missing, and this is foul play, and time is not on our side. We need your help now."

Tell you what, Mr. Tanizaki," says the officer, "we will take your missing person's report about the… Um, robots. For now, we are going to have to ask you and Hamster's parents to go home and wait for 24 hours to see if your wife and Hamster come home. If they don't show in 24 hours, we will put out an All-Points Bulletin (APB). Until then, we cannot do anything, but for some reason, I do believe you. It's not about the crazy robot stuff but the other stuff. Call it police intuition. Anyway, I will tell my men to keep an eye out for anything suspicious tonight."

Immediately the Toasters Club went out looking for Nina's mom and Hamster, and so did Nina's dad and Mr. Wang. They spent hours looking. The Toasters came back to Nina's house a few hours earlier than Mr. Tanizaki and Mr. Wang. Upon hearing the news, neighbors, and friends begin to stop by Nina's house. Nina lives down the street from the Wang's, and just like the Wang's house, it is beautiful and quite large for a home in California. A lot of people have gathered at Nina's house including the Toasters, Nina, Matt, Peter, Annie, Bolt, and Lizzy. There are also Hamster's parents, Mr. and Mrs. Wang. Lizzy, Bolt, and Matt's parents also came to give support.

Mrs. Wang had made some hot tea and brought over some fresh fruit, mango, oranges, pineapple, lychee, Asian pears, cheese, some crackers, and a fresh berry tart cake. Aside from having the support of great friends, it is so refreshing to have such delicious snacks brought by Mrs. Wang during this uncertain time. She calls it food therapy.

Nina spoke out in front of everyone at their home. "Alright Toasters, it is time to switch. Let's apply our Toasters know-how and ideate a way to utilize our superpowers and organize our team toward

search & rescue. With all the parents present, and the neighbors available to help, the Toasters Club created am approach.

Meanwhile, deep in Dr. Ott's underground lab, Mrs. Tanizaki and Hamster are sitting on the ground together in the temporary cage that is located next to the wall between Dr. Ott's Laboratory control room office and the back exit door. From their cage, they can hear Dr. Ott and his gang in the control room, gathering data on the townspeople to later use it against them. In the cage, Hamster speaks. "Did you hear that Mrs. Tanizaki? They are planning something." "Shush, Hamster, they probably can hear you."

Dr. Ott and his gang discuss how they can manipulate bank data, job data, and police data on Beachside Park citizens. Dr. Ott's gang has also been accessing business data collected on its citizens, such as shopping habits, food purchase habits, travel habits, car types, church & synagogue membership data, club & organizational membership data, entertainment and informational site visits, and habits. Sites such as Truth Social, Prager U, Frank Speech, X, and Rumble air more alternative news sources for people who have lost trust in mainstream fake news.

All this data is being gathered to gain intel on the people of Beachside Park. The purpose was originally so that Dr. Ott's business could manipulate people into hiring his robots. But now, he can use it to rain down havoc on the people of the town. Because Dr. Ott recorded the Toasters cafeteria meeting last week, all of the Toasters Club members and their families are prime targets on Dr. Ott's hit list.

It's mid-Saturday morning. Nina wakes up in her bed. She fell asleep last night while friends and neighbors were all together in the living room. Her dad carried her to her room so that she could get a good night's sleep. As she awakens, Nina can hear people who are still at her house. She remembers yesterday's tragic event when her mom was kidnapped and taken along with Hamster.

She becomes anxious to find out any news, so she gets up and walks into the kitchen dining room, where everyone has been gathered all night long into the morning. "Hey guys, is anything new happening?" "Good morning, Nina." Said Mrs. Wang with a smile. "So far, no news, Nina, but a lot of people are searching for your mom and Hamster." Mrs. Wang stayed at Nina's house all night. She just steam-baked a Mango Manapua (Dim-sum) and placed it on the kitchen table. "Your dad and my husband went back out searching for your mom and Hamster."

Just then, the other Toasters Club members arrive. Matt busts in through the front door first. He forgets to take his shoes off, walks over to Nina, and puts his arm around her. "Good morning, sleepyhead," Nina replies. "Matt, take off your shoes, please." For traditional American Asian families and for Hapa-Haole families, like Nina's family, the home is clean and revered, so shoes come off and socks stay on. In fact, there is a pile of shoes on Nina's front porch at this very moment. Neighbors and friends have been stopping by since last night. There is a sign hanging on the door. It says, Take off Your Shoes and Stay Awhile… Mahalo! Nina and her family got the sign when they were visiting Hawaii on vacation.

Matt walks back out the front door to take his shoes off. Peter, Annie, Bolt, and Lizzy are on the front porch after taking their shoes off. They all walk in, excited and energetic; on the other hand, Nina is just waking up. Bolt blurts out. "Hi Nina, we got some news. Your mom and Hamster are still missing, and the town is under siege." Nina, clearly agitated with that news, says.

"Okay, guys, please tell me something new, we need to learn from our failures here, as so far, we have gotten nowhere."

Annie speaks up. "Alright, Nina. Here it is. The people who are behind this are overplaying their hand, and the regular news media is not covering anything on this. We think the news media is in on it. As Toasters, we need to counter their approach and create a News Team to get the word out. We need to take-on the evil media who have been successful at confusing the masses to sit down, stay down, and shut up."

"I like what I am hearing. It sounds more like an action plan." Says Nina. "Okay, guys, let's meet."

The Toasters go to the garage where Nina's dad has a Sprint Board over his workbench. They gather around and begin their Ideation sprint by applying the seven steps of Design Thinking. This gave them a feasible approach to begin Sprinting to build a mock-up of what their studio should look like and what they could do to differentiate their field work to look reputable to their target audience. They then came out with a strategy for Growth, by starting small, seeking outside sponsors who have taken an interest in their cause and then working forward to physically meet with everyone in town. This framework worked perfectly for the formation of a Toasters Club online news media. Nina directed the action.

"Okay, I will be Scrum Master. Annie, you take the Product Owner (PO) role." Annie goes to the board, "All alright, Toasters (Scrum Team), gather around the board. Here is what we need."

Annie maps the needs and functions of the online news media. She quickly inserts Epic's and high-level stories of all the things required to begin an online news media. Each of the Toasters contributes the initial Epics and User Stories for the Product Backlog. They created feature scenarios, staying focused on the feedback of spot surveys, and the necessary functions of an innovative interactive news media.

The Toasters Club quickly comes out with a Product Backlog and Sprint Backlog that captures the complete value of the need. They size up story points and estimate that it will take less than one day to complete. They each pair up and begin their sprint session. They decide to make each sprint for 2 hours. There are three sprints, so they plan to have the final News Studio ready in 6 hours. Nina, Lizzy, and Annie take the user stories to work on Creating Topics, Coordinate Events and Hosting the News. Matt, Peter, and Bolt work on the user stories to Capture Film, Capture Sound, and get their News Media word out through online distribution.

They begin their first two-hour sprint to begin building the first part of the news studio in sprint one. After two hours, the Toasters stopped building to demo the progress of the product to Annie who is the Product Owner. The sprint one demo is followed by the sprint one retrospective, which is conducted by Nina, the Scrum Master. In the retrospective the team discusses how they can improve in building the News Studio. The retrospective is followed by a quick Sprint 2 planning session and then on to Sprint 2, where the Toasters continue building the soundproof stage.

They build the soundproof room by collecting cardboard egg cartons and tacking the cartons on the walls of the garage at Nina's house as soundproof material. They then design custom lighting with homemade reflectors, boxes, and left-over lighting fixtures throughout the studio. Matt, Bolt, and Peter then gather camera equipment, microphones, sound mixers, and media editors from what they all had in their closet, and from friends in the neighborhood. Finally, they build a studio table and bring up some barstools for the news anchors to provide their coverage and shoot their stories on film. They begin registering and accessing online video channels to output their final edited news media stories while Annie, Lizzy, and Nina plan for their first news story event.

With the last sprint, Sprint Three, the Toasters Club is ready to film. Nina was voted to be the News Anchor. Nina, Lizzy, and Annie created a great 5-minute story to shoot as a tester film to see if they can reach their target audience. It is titled: "The Robots Living Among Us." Surprisingly, the tester picked up a big interest and response among viewers. Such a first-time success usually does not happen in their technical product development. The team is ready to start filming more.

It has been 4 hours, and the Toasters Club is making excellent progress. Nina goes to her room to change into more colorful clothes for the silver screen. While she gets ready, the Toasters get ready to film her breaking story. Matt sees an opportunity to take a little time off and decides to walk over to the kitchen to grab a slice of Mrs. Wang's berry tarts. Nina had finished changing and getting ready for filming. She comes out of her room in her news outfit and sees Matt eating in the kitchen. She follows after him. Matt grabs a slice of cake, turns around and heads back to the living room. He sits on the big chair, and chomps down the slice of cake. Nina walks up to Matt in the living room. "Matt, stop eating."

It is later in the day, Saturday evening. At the same time, the Toasters Club are filming their first live online news media to get the truth out, after releasing the film short of The Robots Among Us. At the same time Dr. Ott is launching a cyber-war data attack on the town of Beachside Park. The attack is meant to cut off Beachside Park from the rest of the planet. Dr. Ott will hold no quarter for any who are on his list as a potential threat to his robot operations.

It is not noticeable at first but soon people of Beachside Park feel the weight of Dr. Ott's cyber-attack. It first manifests as payment card cancelations, where Dr. Ott's team cancels hundreds of credit cards. Then Dr. Ott's gang hacked into the database of the local police, and they issued random warrants for the arrest of innocent citizens; the police started showing up at random people's homes with warrants for their arrests after a half dozen arrest families with the same last name, including 2-month-old babies and 97-year old's senior citizens. The police catch on that they have been hacked. They see that this is some sort of prank, so they shut it down. Next, the schools are hacked. Hard-working "A" students with 5.0 GPAs begin to receive 1.0 "F's," and those with "F's" get "A's". These new grade change notices are emailed to the student's parents, causing all sorts of turmoil between former A students and their parents. On the other hand, most "F" students who received an "A" remain completely unaware of their new upgrade, as many of their parents typically avoid evening emails from the school. They figure that it is just going to be more bad news anyway. It is not something one wants to come home to after working two jobs. In any case, Dr. Ott got the results that he wanted. For the most part, families in the community of Beachside Park are strapped with fear.

Back in Nina's garage, the Toasters finish their first live news story with Nina giving final information on the Toasters Club.

She says, "To join the resistance and help find my mom and Hamster, please subscribe to the official Toaster Club News Media by clicking on the subscribe button below. On behalf of the Toasters Club News Media, farewell till next time." "Cut… that is a wrap." Says Annie.

With Annie directing, Lizzy and Matt filmed with camera 1 and camera 2, Bolt handled the sound, and Peter quickly edited. The Toasters Club has its final news film product ready to upload its live feed, also the master film to release to all the major online outlets. Peter's dad has some friends in the online video channel industry who offered to help get the Toasters News story out. Peter gets the final cut edited and uploaded to all the major channels within 15 minutes. Annie stands on top of the news stage and says, "Nice job, Toasters Club … We got the word out. We also have 30 minutes to spare. Excellent Sprint." Matt, Bolt, and Peter begin to shout. "Alright, way to go! The Word is Out. The word is getting out."

Deep down in Dr. Ott's Laboratory, one of Dr. Ott's workers knocks on his office door window. With no response, his worker jumps up and down and waves his hands to get Dr. Ott's attention. The worker says. "Boss, boss." Dr. Ott looks up at him as he continues to wave his hands… "Get back to work, you insignificant slug." Says Dr. Ott. The worker continues waving his hands and replies, "But boss, those students launched a media war, and it's against you and your robots." Dr. Ott looks at him and says, "Dude, knock it off. You're acting like an octopus on crack." The worker persists. "But look, boss … Look." Dr. Ott switches channels to the ones labeled on his control panel as FAKE NEWS. These are all those alternative free online channels that he and others who are also just like Dr. Ott hate with passion.

"The Toasters Club News Media?" Says Dr. Ott. "Yes Boss." Replies the worker. Dr. Ott comments. "With such a catchy name. It can't be that bad." Dr. Ott clicks on the play button. He accidentally has his video screen set on broadcast, so the entire laboratory. The entire workforce gang, including Dr. Ott's satellite sales offices, can see the video. "NOOO. No." Dr. Ott blurts out. His voice is slightly heard over the speaker, but it is drowned out by the sound of the video. He is unaware and turns up the volume. It echoes even louder down in the chambers of his underground Laboratory. Hamster and Nina's mom listen to the Toasters broadcast coming over the intercom.

"Do you hear that, Mrs. Tanizaki … do you hear that?"

"Yes… It's Nina!" She begins to cry with joy!

"It won't be much longer, Mrs. Tanizaki."

"We're going to get rescued."

Dr. Ott stops the video and barks several commands to his gang. "Shut down the Internet and censor the Toasters Club News outlets."

"Okay, boss, but that is going to take a while." "SHUT IT DOWN." "Boss, we need to hack several internet sources that are feeding Beachside Park." "Then shut off the power grid first, hack into the internet, and shut it down." "You got it, boss."

Just then, bam… the power goes out. It is late in the evening, and the sun has just gone down, but it is still light enough to see outside. In the new studio, it is pitch black. Nina reaches for a flashlight while Mat opens the garage door for some light to come in. Suddenly, the power goes back on. The house is located on the hill, so Matt, Bolt, and Lizzy have a view of the homes in the valley below. They see the lights go on in a power wave across the valley. Peter looks at his PC screen and says the power may be on, but internet access is no longer working.

Nina's dad Mr. Tanizaki drives into the driveway with Mr. Wang and Hamster's dad Mr. Dorfman. They are back from searching for Nina's mom and Hamster. No Progress. It begins to weigh on Nina's dad, but he cannot let on. Yes, it is getting to him, but his good friends are so supportive. Hamster's dad also looks hopeful on the outside and manages to control his internal fears and doubts. These are men who grew up in a time when one stood their ground no matter what. Nina thinks to herself, "Standing strong and keeping one's faith in the solid rock is often mocked these days, but there is power to be found when keeping one's inner strength based on a God that moves mountains on behalf of those who do stand strong. Some battles may be lost, but the war is always won."

Nina's dad, Mr. Wang, and Mr. Dorfman all come inside. They look tired and beat. Nina's dad gains his composure and starts the conversation. "We looked for clues everywhere possible. The people of the town, and the police were so very helpful, and the search is continuing. However, on top of all this trouble, me and Mr. Wang got our credit cards hacked. Fortunately, Hamster's dad is ready for such occasions. He has some cash stashed away, otherwise we would not be able to pay for our fuel to drive around town."

As soon as Nina's dad finished his sentence, Bolt and Matt burst in the door. Again, Matt forgot to take off his sandals before entering the house. Matt started to speak, but Nina, at the end of her rope, yelled at him this time… "Matt, go back out and leave your sandals at the door. Now." Matt looked bewildered because Nina's jets were so heated. She was on edge, and understandably so. He went back out to take off his shoes. Bolt spoke up.

"Listen, guys, something totally crazy is happening. Matt and I, both our parents, had their bank accounts totally wiped out. No access to money, and all their credit cards are frozen." Matt goes to the front porch, flips off his sandals, and goes back inside right away. He hears Bolt speaking to everyone in the kitchen. Matt joins Bolt. "Yah, did you hear Bolt? Isn't that just absolutely radical happenings, guys?" Matt speaks in a strong California Surfer accent whenever he gets excited. He speaks the same when he talks about surfing 6-foot swells. Nina's dad walks over to Matt and Bolt.

"Guys, it makes sense. We are facing the same issue." Matt responds to Mr. Tanizaki, expressing his surprise in his most eloquent choice of words. . . "Whoa!"

Soon, more and more neighbors and friends began to quickly visit, including Lizzy, her parents, Bolt's parents, and Matt's parents. They gather in the house. There is much excitement happening and talk going around about the town being under siege. There is outright fear. Nina begins to speak out to calm the folks down. "Folks, it is obvious that the force behind the layoffs and outsourcing to robots at our school is the same force that has now launched a new phase of attack. That gang or person has seized bank accounts, cell phone access, and payment cards of good people in this town. They issued warrants for the arrest of innocent people in town, and they have also hacked and taken control of newer cars equipped with internet access."

Nina walks over to the center of the room. By then, people have moved from the kitchen to the living room. She continues to speak. "I believe they are also behind the recent power outage and the internet access that is now down. So, in essence, everyone in this town has been attacked, well, except for Hamster's parents, who we all know are off the grid. But they, too, are suffering a loss. These people have Hamster, and my mom, and we are angry at them; we are very angry at them for what they have done."

Nina stops speaking and remains quiet. She tries to hold her composure, but it's been a bit rough for her lately. She is tired, worried, and completely spent. No longer can she suppress her feelings. People come over to her to give her a hug and show her comfort. Nina slips out of the room and walks upstairs to her bedroom before hearing her dad speak. He speaks after Nina leaves. One important thing that he mentions is the fact that the force behind this madness has overplayed its hand.

Later that night, we see that most of the people who had gathered have now gone home. Nina had fallen asleep for a few hours but was awoken by the brightness of a full moon shining through her window and touching her forehead. She walks over to the window and thinks, where are you? Clearly troubled, she begins to talk to God in her own way. Half talking, half singing, and fully asking. If God is so good, why does He allow so much pain? Nina's prayer turns into a poetic tune.

"Where did you go? Or did I go?

You never told us that there'll be no pain.

Yet so quickly you get all our blame.

When evil plotters should be put to shame.

In all that I believe you for let your mighty kingdom reign…"

"Please Come Quickly in my Pain."

CHAPTER THIRTEEN
Nina Gets an idea!

EARLY SUNDAY MORNING. It has been over 36 hours since Hamster and Nina's mom has been missing. Nina's dad is up. She can hear him getting ready. Nina walks by her parent's room and yells in the room to her dad.

"Hi, Dad, morning!"

"What's going on?"

"I am getting ready for church."

Nina felt it was sort of odd that her dad was going to church at such a bad time in their life. Her mom was still missing, and the town was under siege by a mad scientist, and here her dad was getting ready for church. What? Nina felt this was a bit weird, but logically, it was really the best thing Dad could be doing right now. Be with like-minded believers, seek prayer, lean on the strength of its unity, and give back to others, as there is a lot of fear and unrest happening in the town of Beachside Park. Besides, it shouldn't seem strange, as going to church is what Nina's mom and dad had always done every Sunday morning since she could remember, instead of staying home, staying quiet, and thinking of himself. Dad was getting out, encouraging others, and giving of himself during his time of pain. Nina reflected on her prayer last night. Man, I don't really feel like it, but I know that I too, need to go.

"Hey, Dad, can I come with you?"

"Sure, Nina … But be ready in 30 minutes."

Nina and her dad finished getting ready. Dad opens the garage door. Unknown to them, the electric garage door activity activated the alarms in spy-bot's #28363 and #42658, located across the street. Dr. Ott had commissioned them to keep an eye on Nina. Both spy-bot #28363 and spy-bot #42658 are equipped with sound devices, visual trackers, heat and motion sensors. They are also outfitted to blend with

the crowd, but what is fashionable to one person may not necessarily be the norm.

Sitting in a bright red van parked across the street, the spy-bots think the van is inconspicuously positioned to spy on Nina. For some reason, commonsense and reasoning were not programmed into their little hard-drive-sized brains. If both spy-bots had reasoned that they could hide in a bright red van inconspicuously in the neighborhood, then it is obvious. Reasoning for robots is non-existent. Unlike human intelligence, robotic AI can copy-cat at best, but it is incapable of trumping any rational thinking of a human being.

Once again, the questions come... If man can reason, then only one of these three things is true: One: Robots are an evolutionary upgrade for man. Two: Robots are equal to man. Three: Man is not the same as Animals and Robots. May the rationale of your spirit cause you to listen to that still, small voice inside you, as this is the voice of wisdom.

Nina and her dad pull their SUV out of the driveway, turn toward the bright red van and pass it. "Hey, Dad, did you see that?" "Yes, Nina. That is sort of odd-looking." "Those are humanoids, aren't they Dad?" "Yes, Nina, they are indeed." The two spy-bots pull out in the bright red van and make a U-turn in the middle of the street. The spy-bots continued to drive in the bright red van inconspicuously, so they had determined in bot-logic. "Should we go back and confront them?" Says Nina. "No, let's see what they do while not letting them think that we know they are there."

The robots follow the Tanizaki SUV to the church. While driving, Nina's dad cranks up some radio tunes to scramble their conversation. They discuss plans about what to do. Nina tells her dad that she is really scared. Dad reassures her. "Look who we are dealing with, Nina. Two bubbleheads in a bright red van think that we did not see them. I mean, is that all they got? Think of who masterminded this all. Now think, just who is our Mastermind?" Dad sure had a way of meeting a crisis right to its face and deflate it.

Just then, Annie texts Nina. Nina had left her Mobile Phone at home, but she carried her larger mobile pad device with her, so that she could write some user stories. Suddenly, they hear a Ding coming from

Nina's mobile pad. "Whoa, Nina, you got a text message." "Yes, Dad." "Alright, the internet is back up." A stream of text comes from Annie.

Ding… hey Nina, where are you? Nina text back.

Ding… I'm with my dad on our way to church.

Ding… great.

Ding… we just got here.

Ding… meet me on the bench outside when you get here.

Mr. Tanizaki hears all the texting sounds back and forth from Nina's cell phone. "Who is that texting you so much Nina?" "It's Annie, she's at church." Says Nina. "Oh… okay." Nina and her dad pull the SUV into the church parking lot, followed by the spy-bots in the bright red van. "Hey, I think our every word can be picked up by those robots, so keep a tight lip in church and do not tell anyone yet. I have my eyes on them, but stay close. I don't think they will try anything, but just in case." Said Nina's dad. "Okay, Dad."

Before church, they meet up with the Wang family. Nina runs over to Annie, and they both sit on the bench near the lawn garden outside of the church. Nina takes out her Mobile Pad Device. She and Annie start to look at all the hits that they got last night on their Toasters Club News Media upload.

Peter is with his mom and dad, the Wangs. They speak with Nina's dad for a while before church. They are worried that nothing good has happened and that Nina's mom and Hamster are still missing. While Nina's dad was speaking with the Wang, he watched the two spy-bots walk into the church. Nina's dad thought to himself, now this can be interesting. You see, at this church; they have the best church greeters this side of the Mississippi River. They are energetic, they are huggers, and they love people. These robots do not stand a chance. This can be interesting!

Nina's dad wanted really bad to tell the Wangs that he was being followed by some robots now, but he felt that he would place them and others at the church in danger. Nina's dad calls for Nina and Annie.

"Come on Nina."

"Yes, you too Annie." says her dad.

Nina and Annie run over to go into church, but Nina accidently leaves her Mobile Pad Device outside on the bench. It's about to rain and she totally forgot it. As they pass through the front doors, Nina's dad sees the church greeters giving one of the robots a big hug. The robot tries to maintain its balance. Nina's dad starts to crack-up at how silly that looked.

"What is it, Dad?"

"Nothing. I'll tell you later."

Inside the church, the band starts to rock & roll with drums, electric guitars, and keyboards. The songs are excellent and upbeat. The Robots #28363 and #42658 both love the songs. They begin to dance. Nina sees the robots in the front row smiling and carrying on. "Hey, Dad, do you see that?" "Yes, get a load of it. Isn't that a total crack-up?" "Makes sense to me. You see, AI gathers inspiration from its environment. It is I/O based." "What is I/O based?" Says Nina. "Input/Output… It's like the expression; Garbage in/Garbage out." Says her dad. "You see, these robots gather intelligence from their surroundings, what they hear, what they see, and then reflect these influences for their output."

"I'm not following what you mean. Dad." Says Nina. "Okay, Nina, here is another way of looking at it. If the input is something of goodness, like these worship songs, then the robot's AI will reflect that goodness. On the other hand, if the input is of an evil source, an evil influence, or a troubled soul, then its output will reflect that evil. AI gathers information from its environment." Nina looks at her dad. "Oh, okay, I get it … GI-GO, Garbage In/Garbage Out."

Back in the deep underground Laboratory, Dr. Ott is looking through the camera eyes of the spy-bots. He, too, is caught in the moment and enjoying the songs. He catches himself singing along. "Hey, what am I doing?"

The song ends, and pastor CJ steps onto the platform to provide his message about the nature of God. He paraphrases the bible verses of 1 John. 4: 7-8 in his California Native accent. "Hey guys, let's all love one another. Because love is of God, everyone who loves is born of

God and knows God. Those who do not love do not know God because God is Love."

Just as Pastor CJ completes the verse, rain begins to fall. It hits loudly on the roof of the church building. Pastor CJ continues with his message; however, the rain hitting the rooftop is sounding so loud that it is hard to hear Pastor CJ. It rarely rains in California. Nina's mind starts to wander off. She is thinking how nice it is to finally have rain come and wash the dust off the streets. She snaps out of her daydream as Pastor CJ continues. "We all know the Ten Commandments of the law, right? Well, Jesus left us with two commandments. He said that if we truly, with all our heart, keep these two commandments, we will be keeping all ten commandments of the law. What are they, you ask? What are those two commandments? Love God – Love People."

It begins to rain even harder. The noise of the raindrops pounding on the rooftop gets so loud that it drowns out Pastor CJ's message. Nina goes back to her daydream about the rain outside. Suddenly, she remembered that she left her Mobile Pad Device outside in the rain. She stands to her feet. "Oh no. Dad. I left my Mobile Pad on the bench outside."

Meanwhile, Dr. Ott is sitting in the control room, displaying everything. Despite the noisy rain, he is picking up Pastor CJ's message loud and clear. His two spy-bots are sitting in the front row equipped with high resolution eye-cams and sophisticated sound devices with noise cancellation. Dr. Ott thinks to himself… "Time to go. I feel strange." He leaves the lab, goes up the elevator to his bedroom, and sits on his bed for a moment. He then gets up and heads outside to sit in his car. He starts the engine and drives off. "I need some air." He then turns on the radio to catch a new tune that just came out. The tune" Rain Falls Down," carries a deep American country tug to the heart. The words go like this:

"Some have lived a life with meaning.

Some can't look you in the eye.

Rain falls down on the good and the ugly.

Rain falls down on me."

After church, the spy-bots are called back to the lab by Dr. Ott. They pass by Nina and her dad, who are discussing Nina's Mobile Pad near the church bench where she left it in the rain. Nina picks up her mobile pad and tries to turn it on. It sparks with a puff of smoke. Dead. "It doesn't work, Dad." "We don't have time, Nina. The robots are getting into the van. We got to go. We'll deal with your mobile pad device later, okay? Now is our chance to follow them. I think they are going to lead us to Mom."

Nina jumps into the family SUV with her dad. They follow the red van with the robots to a business street near Nina's school. It circles in front of a hill. The red van then pulls into the strip mall and parks in front of a business. The two robots walk around the corner toward the hill in the back of the building. Nina's dad says. "Would you look at that?" The business happens to be a Personnel Sales Recruiter office. The business sign says Cambridge Cyber-Orders (CCO). "Bingo... we found them!"

There's a small sign in the window that says they offer cheap outsourced labor for any job, from fast-food burger flippers to executive managers. The sign also says that they can place sewage ditch diggers and T.V. news announcers in less than one hour. They claim that they have placed over 10,000 office workers, security officers, computer programmers, and teachers this year alone.

Nina's dad tries to keep his eye on the robots as they walk around to the back of the store and across the street behind the business. He drives past the business and turns the corner to track back to the street, past the store on the other side, and down the street where the robots were last seen.

They reach the point behind the business building and see nothing but the base of a hill with lots of trees and tall grass. There are also some large utility boxes near the sidewalk. They park the car. Mr. Tanizaki gets out, walks over to the sidewalk, and checks behind the utility boxes. He looks up the hill. "I don't see them. Nothing, we lost them." He walks past the utility boxes. "This is exactly where I saw them last. These boxes are likely city electrical panels."

Nina's dad walks across the street and looks up the hill. He walks over to Nina. She is still sitting on the passenger side of the SUV. She rolls down the window as her dad walks up to her window. On top of the hill is a large home. Pointing up the hills, Nina's dad says. "When I grew up, I knew the family who lived in that house on top of the hill. I was friends with their son. His name was Otty Watanabe. We rode bikes together. His dad was a test pilot. A tough, self-made man. All of us guys on the block looked up to him and felt very lucky to have his son Otty as our friend. You see, Otty was also some sort of a genius, just like his dad. Well, unfortunately, Otty's dad died in an air crash. He was testing some sort of an experimental hydrogen jet fuel system. They say his jet blew up in mid-air. It was only Otty, and his mom left to continue life's journey. I don't recall there ever was a funeral held for Mr. Watanabe. I'm not sure what ever happened to Otty Watanabe and his mom. Some face tragedy like this and internalize it as a family curse, followed by shame and isolation. I doubt that they still live there anymore." Nina's dad gets back into the SUV and drives off. While they rode past the red van parked in front of the business. Nina's dad speaks enthusiastically. "This is great, Nina; I know we found the place. Let's go get the search party and bring them back to this area and search for Mom and Hamster."

While driving back to the house, Nina was quiet. She had been thinking about her Mobile Pad Device being destroyed in the rain. Nina processes things like that at times. It's like a puzzle, she felt that God was trying to tell her something. A question that was stirring inside her, suddenly clicked. She decides to ask dad.

"Dad, does electronics and water mix?"

"What was that Nina?"

"I was wondering if electronics and water mix."

"No Nina. If it is powered up, electronics will short-circuit once it encounters water."

"You see, water is a good conductor and once it crosses between power VCC (voltage) and ground… it will burn it up."

Nina picks up her lifeless Mobile Pad Device and begins to see if she can get it to work. No success. "Dad, aren't robots electronic?" "Wait …" He pulls over and slams the brakes. "That is brilliant."

Are you thinking what I am thinking?

CHAPTER FOURTEEN
The Rescue Mission

IT'S NOW SUNDAY evening and it's getting dark outside. As opposed to the long bright summer days of California, daylight time in December is short. Particularly during Christmas time in California where the days are short, warm, and dry.

Nina contacts the toasters to assemble them at her house. They are going to form a search party once again. Nina explains how she and her dad had narrowed the spot to where they had last seen the two spy-bots, near the hill adjacent to Beachside Park High School.

The doorbell rings. Mr. Wang and Mr. Dorfman, Hamster's dad, came to join in the search party. The Toasters Club got right to business, developing an approach and coordinating the search. Nina drew out a map of the area they were targeting. They huddle. Nina stands next to the whiteboard and speaks the plan. "The Toasters will ride their bikes to the top of the hill on the other side of our school. Dad, you drive Mr. Wang and Mr. Dorfman. Park in the area next to the red van and walk to the back of the stores and across the street toward the base of the hill where we last saw the spy-bots. Me and the Toasters will ride our bikes to the top of the hill where we will spread out and form a search line and walk down the hill toward you at the base of the hill. You guys do the same. Spread out and form a search line from the back of the store and walk across the street to the base of the hill where we will meet. Look for clues. Note anything that can be used as a potential portal entry point."

Nina draws an arrow showing the direction of the search for each party. After the search party huddle, Matt steps up and asks the team to form a tight circle and join hands. Nina's dad, Mr. Tanizaki and Mr. Wang join in. Mr. Dorfman grabs Matt and Nina's hand in the circle. Matt says. "Let's bow our hearts. Dad, Father, we all agree that your goodness shall rule, and we will see your miracle. In so doing, make us swift and true in our aim to fight and defend. Give us wisdom on our part to accomplish the mission to break the power of the enemy. In your mighty name. Amen.”

Mr. Dorfman looked frazzled. He addresses Matt in front of the group. “You spoke with God directly as if He is a loving, friendly God, but I don’t get how He allows such evil in the world. They have my Hamster. It makes me want to cut through the religious crap and trust His word. Starting with Psalms 106. Hearing you speak with God, Matt. Well… I needed that.”

The Toasters ride their bikes over to the hill above the school. It’s a steep ride up a long driveway to reach the base of the large home on the top of the hill. Arriving just outside the house, they jump off their bikes, ditch them in the brush at the main gate of the home, and walk over to form a large line across the crest of the hill. As they begin walking downhill in a line, Matt thinks to himself.

“Man, for once, I wish I could do something really cool in front of Nina and the club.”

“What if I was the one who found the missing puzzle that led to Hamster and Nina’s Mom?”

“How cool would that be? I want to be cool.”

The team continues walking downhill side-by-side, searching every inch as they head down toward the base of the hill, searching the area for any clues as they go. Nina’s Dad, Mr. Tanizaki, Mr. Wang, and Mr. Dorfman had already parked and walked to the back of the store where Nina and her dad had last saw the spy-bots this morning. It was when they parked the red van in front of the storefront. The back of the store faces the street. It is empty and quiet. There is a door to the store and windows, but one can look through the store from the back windows and clearly see that it is completely empty. Besides, Nina and her dad saw the spy-bots cross the street just before losing track of them.

Across the street is the hill with the street curb, a sidewalk, some utility boxes, pine trees, and a mix of tall grass and other types of scrubs and bushes. Mr. Tanizaki motions to Mr. Wang and Mr. Dorfman.

“Okay, let’s stay quiet.”

"I feel we are in the right place."

"Something has got to be on the other side of the street at the base of the hill."

Just then, Nina spots the large utility boxes at the bottom of the hill. She is curious about that spot as she and her dad had last seen the spy-bots at that very spot this afternoon before they lost track.

The utility boxes are located near the sidewalk at the bottom of the hill. Nina's dad, Mr. Wang and Mr. Dorfman are across the street and about to approach that area. They cannot see any of the Toasters coming toward them from the top of the hill. Nina and the Toasters begin to break through the bushes and shrubs, making quite a noise. Hearing all that commotion from the hill, Nina's dad yells. "Get down. Shut up."

Mr. Wang and Mr. Dorfman stop and squat in position. Not knowing that they made good time, Nina's Dad, Mr. Wang, and Mr. Dorfman all thought that Nina and the Toasters Club were still on their bikes riding to the top of the hill. Nina and the Toasters all hear Nina's dad tell them to get down. Thinking that her dad was also commanding them to get down, they all stop and take cover. Enraged and seeing the brush move, Mr. Wang, who is a 2nd degree black belt, stands back up. "No way, guys. I had it. Let's grease these guys."

He charges up the hill unknowingly towards the Toasters Club members. Nina's dad and Mr. Dorfman jump up and follow Mr. Wang. Mr. Wang sees the shadow outline of someone in the brush and takes aim. He makes a maneuver up the hill past the spot and then comes back down the hill so that he can use the force of gravity to make his punch. Charging downhill, Mr. Wang takes formation to throw a kick. He yells in Karate language, "Hai-yah" as he flies 4 feet off the ground right over Nina's head, not seeing her. His foot fully extended forward in the strike position. Just then, Matt stands up with a blank stare on his face. "Dude!"

It's his last word. Nina catches a glimpse of Mr. Wang's right foot as it connects squarely with Matt's jaw. Matt falls backward right on top of Annie and Peter… OUT COLD. It's what one would call friendly fire in battle.

Mr. Wang felt awful. Bolt, Lizzy, and Hamster's dad help to lift Matt's limp body off Annie and Peter. Nina's dad, being a volunteer fireman, looked over Matt to assess his condition. Matt's tongue sticks out slightly in his comatose position. He's okay, but we need to get him off the hill and into a more comfortable position. Using the fireman's carry, Nina's dad takes Matt down to a grassy place at the base of the hill. Everyone follows.

With Matt being out cold, there is nothing more one can do. Nina's dad tends to Matt and contacts the paramedics. Nina walks over to the utility boxes. She has a feeling. She looks for any type of clue that would lead to an entryway. A place that perhaps could lead to the whereabouts of Nina's mom and Hamster. She goes over to the first utility box and starts tapping the doors. There are three utility boxes lined up in a row. They are large stainless-steel boxes with double doors that open up on the panel. The box appears to be large enough to fit a person. She thinks to herself. "I wonder if there is something to these boxes?"

Annie sees Nina walking around the utility boxes, so she joins Nina. She goes to the other utility box located a few steps away and taps the 2nd box and then the third. "Hum. This one seems hollow." Says Annie.

Nina goes over to the third utility box and begins to look all over the box. There is an inlaid lock that requires a key. It is located on the right panel door. Nina pushes the middle of the lock with her finger and out pops a tiny pad with four tiny buttons. She looks intently at the four buttons and sees a code pattern. The two buttons in the middle look untouched; however, the two buttons on each side look worn. She takes a wild guess and presses the two side buttons at the same time. There is a slight delay and then … Pop! The double doors open. "Whoa Nina, you found it." Inside the box is an opening stairway that leads down to a lobby room with an elevator. The opening is large enough to fit one person at a time. Nina goes first, followed by Annie.

Meanwhile, Peter is getting treated as Matt's fall had injured Peters shoulder. Lizzy and Bolt are with Matt and Peter while Hamster's dad and Mr. Wang are out ready to flag down the paramedics and direct them to Matt. Nina and Annie don't tell anyone as they descend through the Utility box to the lobby area where it opens-up to a normal size room with an elevator on the right side. Nina says. "I'm going to take the elevator down and check it out." "I'll be right behind you Nina." Says Annie.

Nina presses the elevator button, and the doors open immediately. The elevator is large enough for a small group of people. They enter. Inside, the elevator panel has 3 choices: Lab-1, Lab-2, and Shop Floor. Annie selects the Shop Floor. The elevator door closes and immediately lowers. It reaches the shop floor, and the door opens. As soon as it does, they hear Hamsters voice over the factory noise as the robotic machines assemble more bots. He's talking in a half whisper, half loud voice. No response can be heard, but it is obvious that Hamster is speaking to someone. Nina and Annie follow Hamster's voice. It leads them to a cage. They see Hamster and Nina's mom sitting on the bottom of the cage. They can also see Dr. Ott, just beyond the cage. Nina turns to Annie. "There's the face. The face behind the evil bots." "Yes indeed!" says Annie.

Dr. Ott is looking at his video monitors. Nina and Annie are just out of his view. He gets up and walks over to the cage, holding Hamster and Nina's mom. Nina and Annie duck behind a wooden crate and see Dr. Ott as he taps on the cage. "Hey, boy!" It scares Nina's mom. Dr. Ott puts his index finger over his mouth and motions for Hamster and Nina's mom to be silent. Nina peaks from behind the crate and spots a 3-inch size red button. It is a quick latch for the cage located in the middle of the wall just above Dr. Ott's head. Just then, Hamster sees Nina peak from behind the crate. Hamster suddenly shuts up. Unfortunately, that was not a good move, as it caught Dr. Ott's attention.

"What's the matter, Hamster?"

"Why are you suddenly so quiet?"

"This is the first time you obeyed my order."

"You have not been silent for days… Hum, I wonder what's going on?"

Dr. Ott turns his head and catches Nina's eyes. Trying not to look surprised, he says. "And who are you?" "Oh no… were busted, Annie.

Run." Nina quickly jumps up and slaps the cage latch button. It opens the cage door and releases her mom and Hamster. They get up and run with Nina and Annie. Dr. Ott yells. "Hey, hey, hey!"

Dr. Ott starts to run toward them, then stops and goes the other way toward the control room to alert the crew and release his robots into action. He quickly types on his keyboard to give commands to his robots as Nina, Annie, Hamster and Mom all run toward the elevator. They all jump in and press the elevator button. The door hesitates to close. They all say in unison.

"Come on (softly)."

"Come On! (Slightly louder)."

"COME ON! (Very loudly)."

As the door closes slowly, they see through the crack in the elevator door, two vicious looking attack bots running quickly, full speed toward them. The elevator doors finally close and it begins to lift. They hear the robots bang loudly on the doors as they go up to ground level.

The elevator reaches the top, and the doors open to the foyer. They all head out of the elevator and down the hall toward the short, narrow stairway where the entry shaft is covered by the utility cabinet. They squeeze through the utility door, one at a time, and then … Out. Annie exits first, followed by Hamster and Nina's mom. Nina exits last as Annie yells across the street for help.

Nina's dad is still with Matt, who is out cold. He is also with Peter, Bolt, and Lizzy. Mr. Dorfman and Mr. Wang are sitting on the curb across the parking lot in front of the store, still waiting for the paramedics. They can all hear Annie yelling out loud. "We found them."

Nina's dad runs over to embrace Nina and Nina's Mom as Mr. Wang and Mr. Dorfman comes running from across the parking lot. Just then, Mrs. Wang drives up in her large SUV. She parks and jumps out. "Guys, guys… oh, thank God." Suddenly, Nina looks up to see two robots, bot #28363 and bot #42658 appear 100 yards up the hill. They took a shortcut to the supply elevator located in the middle of the street. "Hurry, hurry… they're on our tail."

Nina's Dad helps Matt into the Wang's SUV. Mr. and Mrs. Wang, Annie, Peter, Hamster, Hamster's dad, Bolt, and Lizzy also jump into Wang's car, while Nina and her mom and dad all run across the parking lot to their SUV. Mr. Wang sees the robots give chase, so he hangs a U-turn, jumps over the curve, and drives across the parking lot to shield Nina and her family as they make their way to the SUV. Being locked up in a cage since Friday, Nina's mom has trouble running. Nina's dad helps Mom, but her legs begin to slow down. Nina yells to her dad. "Give me the keys – give me the keys!"

Nina's dad reaches into his pocket and performs a lateral pass of the car keys to Nina. She catches them mid-air and runs ahead to unlock the car. Nina gets into the driver's seat and starts the car just as Mrs. Wang drives up, shielding Nina's family from the robots that had shot out to get past them and attack Nina. They now head right for Nina's parents. Nina clicks into reverse with wheels screeching and smoking; she speeds backward toward her parents and pops open the side door. "Quick, get in."

Nina stays at the wheel, and when she sees her parents jump into the SUV, she shifts forward and floors it. With wheels screeching and smoking. They bug out of there. Nina has no license; however, she and her dad have practiced driving doing circles in the parking lot for months. Besides, Nina is also an ace with Formula one video racing games.

They Get Away!

CHAPTER FIFTEEN
Facing The Enemy

"MERRY CHRISTMAS! I SAID… it's Merry Christmas, not that Wimpy Wuss-Mas "Happy Holidays" greetings I see. You city-gov freaks," mumbles a middle aged, bearded man with long dark-hair as he rides, wobbling on his bike past the large billboard sign that triggered him. It reads: "The City of Beachside Park Wishes You a Happy Holiday." Having a hard time with the change toward an overing reaching social censorship. The bearded man continues to pedal past the sign, mumbling. "Holiday? Happy Holiday? Oh man, how weak, how feeble, how pathetic. How politically correct. They cover their ears. They don't want to hear the word Christmas, and the power that tiny baby, of whom we celebrate, gave to the world. Well, there is good, and there is evil. Who is the force that overcame evil on Christmas day?"

The bearded man takes his bike, jumps the curb, and crosses the empty street. He continues past a pool of plastic deflated Christmas ornaments on the lawn of a home near the edge of Beachside Park. He laughs out loud as he rides straight toward downtown. Due to Dr. Ott's town siege, he had lost everything. First his job, then his bank account, his family, his house, and then his dog. There is nothing left except his mind, and he is doing his best to keep from losing it, too.

They say that laughter is the best medicine. It can also be a sign of mental instability. In this case it is an "In your face" attitude toward the spirit of the compromise that pulled him under. At this point, there is really nothing left for him to fear at all. Like military veterans who had faced death in battle and had come home to talk about it. A severe financial loss can have a "Fight, or Flight" effect too. They say that after facing death, there is a point you reach where things really don't matter anymore, compared to life itself. From here, it can go well for him, or it can stay sour. Well, the bearded man is determined to start his own venture to get through and build an even better life. It's as if he is a man on a mission.

It's Monday, 24 hours since Nina's mom and Hamster had been rescued. With the town under siege, the school was closed today. They had sent the police over to find Dr. Ott's Lab, but the police could find no evidence. No point of entry. The utility boxes are missing, and there is no shop nearby. Just a "for lease" sign in the window. "Wow!" Says Bolt. "There must have been a clean-up, man."

It's disappointing that nothing can be traced back to Dr. Ott's Lab. You got to hand it to them, the police hear a lot of wacky stories, but it seems they believe this story about the underground lab, the chasing robots, and the mad scientist Dr. Ott. Unfortunately, the police had to give up the search. Due to the recent blue state "defund the police" mandates, there is a lack of officers available to investigate what social elites call a conspiracy theory. Nina stands up in front of the Toasters Club. "Hey, Toasters, it's time to take matters into our own hands." "Got any ideas?" Says Lizzy. "Yes, Lizzy … you are my idea." "What?" "Lizzy, your talent is our secret weapon. You see, we are going to put on a performance, and you are going to play your songs."

"What?"

"You heard me Lizzy!"

"WHAT????" Says Lizzy in her Jewish mom's tone.

The Toasters Club meets at Peter and Annie's house. Mrs. Wang, their mom, AKA "the snack lady" had prepared some delicious snacks, tea's, juices, and fruit, including lychee, sliced juicy oranges, mango, pineapple, and assorted berries that she got directly from the farmers market nearby. She also picked up the best of all mocha cakes, this side of the Pacific, from JJ's Taiwan Bakery. "Wow, thank you, Mrs. Wang." Others join in. "Yes, thank you, Mrs. Wang!"

Nina notes to herself how Matt always seems quick to be thankful. Especially when it comes to free food. But this time, he's not eating. Hey Matt, is everything alright? Just then, Mrs. Wang walks in the room and looks at Matt's face. "Hey, that's quite a shiner, Matt. How do you feel?" Matt yielded two black eyes from Mr. Wang's kick that knocked him out cold. Matt was out for two hours after that kick. Now, his face resembles that of Rocky after the boxing match. But it does not feel nearly as bad as being knocked out and having to be carried out in front of his friends, including Nina. Being a teenage guy is hard sometimes. You want so badly to be the hero, but activities turn up that make you the wimp. To say the least, Matt is embarrassed. He is also disappointed after saying that prayer to be seen as a cool dude. Matt responds to Mrs. Wang. "Um, I'm fine." "Oh, you are fine?" says Mrs. Wang. "Well, actually, I'm a little sore." Mrs. Wang hands Matt a mango and whispers to him. "Ah, toughen up, Matt, you'll live."

Nina takes position next to the whiteboard. Matt excuses himself. He puts the Mango back in the fruit bowl and says. "Hey guys, I need to sit this one out. I'll catch up with you all later." Nina says, "Okay, no problem, Matt. See you later." As Matt walks out of the room, he overhears them talking. Lizzy says, "Matt must be in pain." Hamster barks out, "Oh man, he needs rest after that shiner Peter and Annie's dad gave him. Bolt, you were there, did you see Mr. Wang's incredible kick?" Hamster and Peter laugh. "Ha, ha, ha, ha. Dude, that was awesome. Bolt immediately responds. "Guys, that probably is not how Matt feels," Annie speaks up. "Thanks for that, Bolt. I agree."

Nina breaks the awkward silence that followed in the aftermath of their conversation. "Okay, Toasters Club. Let's gather around in a circle. And get this done." They are going to Ideate and develop an evening event that is designed to gather all the people of Beachside Park and get them to move by taking a stand. This is a movement by the people, against Dr. Ott and his bot advancement. She takes a 3 x 5 sticky note and writes the first epic item of what they want to do. It says: The event to Get Our Town Back.

Soon, the Toasters are brainstorming on 3 x 5 sticky notes:

- ✓ What we want to do?
- ✓ How we want the event to go?
- ✓ What is its purpose?
- ✓ What will each performance look like?
- ✓ Who will sponsor?
- ✓ Who will attend?
- ✓ How will the word get out?

Each sticky note is stuck to the board representing a certain value needed in the event. Either it is a must have, a should have, or a nice to have. "Let's prioritize the story map by first identifying the priority." Nina writes the priority list on the white board in this fashion:

- Priority 1 > Must Have

- Priority 2 > Should Have

- Priority 3 > Nice to Have

Next, the team goes through each item to decipher its Minimal Viable Product (MVP). This will place it in a ready state to become User Stories, so that the Toasters can begin Sprint 0 Planning for the Product Backlog. The Toasters Club continues to develop the plan. They move right into Sprint 0. Everyone on the Toasters Club scrum team is chipping in. There is a lot of excitement in the room. Nina speaks out.

"Are you guys alright to keep going?"

"Let's finish Sprint 0." Says Annie. Hamster is determined to make this work.

"We got to get the word out; therefore, I'm in all the way. Whatever time it takes."

Nina calculates how much they must do. They still have the Product Backlog to complete for the big event, and they need to create the Sprint Backlogs for how many sprints it's going to take to produce the stage production. The Toasters Club sprint iteration goal is to hold a town event on stage with a music concert featuring Lizzy, a dance performance featuring Nina, and the rally to inspire the townspeople of Beachside Park to take a stand and stop the siege against their town. The town needs to realize that they no longer need to live in fear. Anyone can be empowered to do something. Soon, this overwhelming corruption of Beachside Park will be dealt with.

Meanwhile, in town, it is almost Christmas day, and nobody in town is celebrating. Dr. Ott and his gang had been laying low. Today, Dr. Ott is going into town disguised as Santa Claus. He wants to get a first-hand look at what the people were up to and what they were saying about his takeover. He sadistically wanted to get a close-up view and see the townspeople crying, oh boo-hoo, acting in fear, and ready for submission.

He drives to the town park, where he parks his car and gets out dressed as Santa Claus. He then walks over to the park bench where some have gathered so that he can get a closer look. From the park bench, he watches the bearded man ride his bike past him. Dr. Ott was immediately surprised as he was expecting a fearful man, but that man was acting joyfully and triumphant. Humming a Christmas song as he passed by.

In an instance, almost as if it were a script from The Grinch Who Stole Christmas, as Dr. Ott thinks to himself. "Do I detect a happy voice? How can this be? One would think that if I stole everything from these people, fear and despair would grip the voices of the men who have lost everything. How could it be? This man is literally jumping for joy. Is this what is happening across the entire town?"

Dr. Ott further observes. It is the tone of a man who was speaking about a friend he knew that found hope in the middle of despair. Dr. Ott couldn't believe his ears. The man continued.

"Sure, he had lost material things, and sure, he had lost financial security and even friends and family, but at least he still had his wit, his mind, and his faith."

Dressed in his Santa costume, Dr. Ott gets up from the park bench. A crowd had gathered at Sam's Café, so he walked across the street, entered Sam's Café, and sits down to observe more. He can overhear one man with an untucked green plaid shirt and faded Levi jeans speaking with a group of others around the table. "For a while I was just rolling over and going along with what was happening to our town. I did not want to be politically incorrect. It is frustrating to be falsely accused as a racist. I love all people – I love robots."

Dr. Ott begins to chuckle. Again, he speaks to himself. "Hey, I like this guy already." Just then, a curly-haired waitress taps Dr. Ott on the shoulder. It's the O- lady from TacO's. "Sorry, Santa but you got to order something or let someone else sit here." Dr. Ott realizes that he has left his wallet at home. He turns to the O-Lady and says. "But I'm

Santa." The O-lady responds, "SOOO you are sweety. Dr. Ott looks up and sees her O shaped lip tattoo. He immediately thinks to himself. Wow, that is really strange. Just then, the O- Lady forms a perfect "O" with her lips. "OO Oh… oh well now. Ho-Ho to you, my little Ho-Ho-Biscuit."

Completely startled by the O-lady, Dr. Ott jumps to his feet and starts to walk back toward the sidewalk. By now, Dr. Ott is looking untidy. His Santa outfit is a bit out of position and his fake beard is catawampus. Again, he overhears the group at the table talking. He decides to slow down and act like he is texting on his cell phone so that he can listen in on their conversation. He stands and listens. Again, this is to gain intel from the townspeople.

At the table are five men, including the one with the untucked green plaid shirt. They all had worked together at T-Bone-Tech for quite some time. They were recently let go in a mass layoff last month. They were all between 40 and 60 years old. In other words, extinct dinosaurs now living as misfits in the land of corporate America.

Dr. Ott observed the man who was getting ready to respond. He had a grey beard, a red t-shirt and shorts which made him look relaxed and casual; however, he is the loudest of the five. Responding to the man who sat next to him, with the untucked green plaid shirt. "Robots? Well, they are fine, but these bot-teachers are so life-like it is scary. They had me fooled."

Across the table from him was a soft-spoken tall, clean-shaven man playing with his paper straw cover. He peers through his glasses. "I like robots too, but if they are programmed by an evil idea to kill, steal, destroy, and take over with their evil non-progressive ideas. I draw the line there. It has gone too far."

Suddenly, the man next to him speaks out. He is leaning back in his chair, wearing a bright yellow t-shirt, blue jeans, and a well-groomed pitch-black mustache. His hair is slicked back, as it is balding a bit with strands of what hair he had left. He has been listening intensely to the others while playing with his coffee drink. He has not yet taken a sip. He wanted to continue remaining silent and just listen to the others, but this time, he couldn't help but reply. He stands from his chair. "Well. What can you do about it? For that matter, what can anyone do about it? These robots had taken advantage of the very nature of a people with a good heart. Our city government and school superintendents welcomed them in with no thought of how it would affect and endanger the lives of everyone. Well, I for one, would like to know... is this financial greed or political power & control?"

He picks up his coffee drink and takes a deep sip. It's a "Fat-A-Chino" mocha ice-cee drink with whip-cream squirted in a cone shape on top. He looks at everyone around the table and continues to speak. Others at the table notice that he is now wearing a nice milky-white whip-cream mustache. The healthy white whip-cream is lumped up underneath his nose. It completely cancels out his black mustache. It is slightly dripping and seems to highlight his bright yellow polo-shirt as he speaks. He is unaware as the white creampuff bobs up and down underneath his mustache nose. He continues to speak. "Well guys, as in the quote by that most famous corrupt politician. What difference at this point does it make? In context, I ask you all, was her remark pure frustration, or arrogance?"

Thinking that he had made quite the speech, his temporary illusions of grandeur are squelched when he realizes that no one responds. Instead, everyone at the table remains silent. No one was listening. They were distracted by that whipped drip on his mustache. Was it going to drop? He decides to pipe down, still unaware that the whipped cream on his face is almost ready to drip. It hangs like a large cave-like stalactite of whip cream protruding from his mustache. He sits back down in his chair and remains silent.

Just then the man in the untucked green plaid shirt and faded Levi jeans breaks the silence and the concentration of those waiting to see the whip-cream drop. "You know what guys? While this siege was taking place, in one way or another, we all were apathetic toward what our corrupt politicians were doing to our town. We even bought into all the lies that mainstream media was feeding us as they covered up for those twisted politicians. Even when, in our hearts, we knew that they were all a bunch of pathetic liars. Am I right, or am I right?"

Looking discussed and shamed, no one at the table responded. The man in the green plaid shirt continues. "Now, because we allowed these robotic circuit-card pogo-sticks to infiltrate our town, we have lost everything. Lesson learned. I am dumping all my politically correct mumbo-jumbo, and I'm taking a stand. We are all going to take back our town. Right?"

The entire table breaks out in a roar... "RIGHT!" Caught off-guard and startled, Dr. Ott fumbles his phone. It does a double-back flip in the air as he tries to catch it in mid-air. His hand tips it like a downward volleyball slam, thus putting it into a spinning, flat-face trajectory with the floor. The mobile phone screen faces downward, and at a very high velocity, it remains in a floor collision pathway. The phone crash lands with the screen face down, flat on the concrete floor. Bam... shattered!

Dr. Ott bends down and picks it up just as the black-bearded man parks his bike and walks up to the café' to meet his friends at the table. He walks by Dr. Ott. "Woah... Bummer, Dude!" Dr. Ott scoops up his cracked mobile phone device from the floor and quickly exits the café. He walks across the street toward his car in the parking lot at the park and opens the car door to hear his mom speaking loudly. Her voice breaks in over the car intercom. Standing there, he shuts his door, but he doesn't get his door quite shut in time. People in the park can hear Dr. Ott's mom speak loudly over the car intercom speaker.

"Breaker one nine, breaker one nine."

"Otty. Otty? Come in, Otty."

Still standing at the car door, Dr. Ott grabs the microphone and tries to reply in a discrete manner. In the process, his glasses slip off and into the car. They land underneath the seat. Now, he is almost blind. Dr. Ott feels around the floor seat mat for the glasses as he speaks to his mom. "Yes, Mom, I read you loud and clear." He now has the attention of multiple people, sitting in the park, jogging, passing by, and playing basketball. They all stop and stare at the strange man, Dr. Ott. The fact that he is still in his shabby red Santa Claus outfit doesn't help.

His mom, still loudly coming across over the intercom, continues. "Otty, your friends are here. They are wondering where you are. They told me to tell you. Oh, wait a minute. I wrote it down."

"Hold on, Mom. I need to find my glasses." Just then, Dr. Ott scrambles to jump into the car and turn down the speaker, but instead, in his fumble to decrease the volume, he turns up the base speakers. His mom begins to speak again. This time, the car vibrates loudly amplified with the low-pitched boom-box speakers blasting across the park.

"OKAY OTTY – I FOUND IT!"

"THEY SAID TO MEET THEM IN THE SECRET UNDERGROUND LABORATORY!"

"NEXT TO THE ROBOT STAGING AREA"

Just then the people in the park start to walk toward Dr. Ott, taking out their mobile phone cameras and catching him on film. They all begin to videotape Dr. Ott. At least 20 people approached Dr. Ott's car with their cell cameras on. They captured him jumping into his car and screeching out of the parking lot as some dialed 911.

The Toasters gather around for their daily sprint standup meeting to create the Awareness Concert. They have orchestrated an advancement plan, they call it;" The Standup Concert." They were given the green light to use the Beachside Park Amphitheater this weekend, but there is not much time. Just a few days to get people to attend and to get everything in order. Matt begins the 15-minute daily standup. "Yesterday, I closed the user story to confirm the usage of the sound equipment and lighting stage at the Amphitheater. We were able to get a top sound engineer, a stage lighting pro, and a stage manager to volunteer and help. Today, I will attend our first dry rehearsal. No Blockers"

The Toasters Club goes around the room with each member, discussing what they did yesterday toward putting the Standup Concert together and what they will be doing today in their scrum session. Hamster, Annie, Peter, and Bolt spoke of the advertising story for passing out flyers, erecting signs and billboards, and getting people in each block and division to sign-up to get the word out for the meet.

Annie and Peter posted the message on their own video channels because Dr. Ott and the rogue town government was able to convince social media to censor all Toasters Club messages.

Nina and Lizzy were the last to speak at the stand-up. They worked together on two stories that have the two songs that Lizzy composed. Nina choreographed a beautiful ballerina dance to her violin song called "Shining Dance of Hope." The last song involves the Toasters Club. They are all going to sing this last song together. She is undecided what to name it. So far, the big event is coming together like clockwork. The Toasters will be practicing it for the first time tonight. The team ends their 15-minute stand up meeting with a cheer.

"Toasted!"

Charged, they all go to pass out flyers to their Standup Concert rally event and to spread the word. They ride their bikes to the park in the town center and they see many people had gathered at the center. They get up closer and jump off their bikes to listen. Nina had fortunately brought her backpack with her video camera and equipment. She quickly gets her camera out and walks up to some people standing nearby. "Hey, what's going on?"

A woman with a blond ponytail was standing next to Nina. She is in a tight gray jogging outfit that resembles a star-track uniform. While Nina points her camera at the woman in the crowd, she politely asks if it is okay if she captures her statement on film. The woman agrees. Nina asks her to tell us what is happening; The woman says. "Sure. From what I understand, the people over there at the park saw Dr. Ott, the mad robot Scientist. He was parked in his car, cloaked in a Santa Outfit. He got away when they approached him. But they still got it all on video." Nina replies. "Wow, thanks for speaking with us and letting us know."

Nina signals to the Toasters Club. They gather around Nina. "See that outdoor stage platform behind the row of grass? Help me get these people over there." Matt looks over to see the platform. He notices that it's in front of Beachside Parks Amphitheater. "Hey, that is perfect, Nina. It's near the Amphitheater where we will be having our Stand-Up concert tomorrow." Nina responds. "Wow, this is a perfect opportunity to get the word out."

She turns to Hamster. "Hamster, you and Peter quickly ride back to Peter's house and bring back the Microphone, Speaker, and battery-powered amplifier. I need this on stage." Peter and Hamster bug out of there and quickly get to Peter's house. Matt and Bolt jump on stage. They are followed by Annie, Lizzy, and Nina. Matt speaks out. "People! We have something very important to ask you. We are going to make an announcement soon. It's about joining together and getting our town back."

Nina jumps in; "Hey guys. Please text or call your family, friends, co-workers everyone you can think of. Tell them to come immediately and gather around here. We are going to begin in 20 minutes." The small crowd of 20 soon grows to 100, 300, 500, and more. People are so tired of the siege with Dr. Ott and the bots colluding for power with the elite corrupt government that they are willing to stand against those who are sold out and supporting Dr. Ott's movement.

While Hamster and Peter were gathering the equipment, Peter's dad recommended his powerful 100-watt mini sound system and a few microphones. Mr. Wang, Peter's dad, says. "You guys need to be heard. Now hurry and toss it in the back of the car." Mr. Wang drives them back. They make it back just in time to set up the mini-sound equipment. Now, the size of the crowd is approaching 13,700 people. They are all taking a great risk but don't care. It reflects a people who are fed up. So many people are disrupted and unsettled. Annie takes the camera and continues to film.

Nina turns to Hamster and Peter. "Guys, before we make our announcement, help me interview some of the people. I want to hear what they have to say." Peter and Hamster each grab a microphone and stand on either side of the stage. Peter is on stage left and Hamster stage right. As soon as they get into position, Nina speaks out. "People, please let me have your attention. Let's gather around closer." Nina pauses for it to get quiet. "We have an announcement to make. It's about getting our town back. But first, we want to hear back from you. Please tell us your story. What has been happening with you since the siege?"

Immediately a man in a green jacket jumps up. "I have something to say." Peter quickly runs up to the man and holds the microphone for him. The man in the green jacket begins to speak. "During this time, I have been reduced to a pile of rubble. Today, my life is like a country song. I lost my job. I lost my pick-up truck. I am bankrupt. I…" He begins to choke up. He pauses to regain his composure. "I can't even afford a Christmas gift for my wife and children."

On the other side of the stage, Hamster holds the microphone for another man wearing a smoked grey suit. "The police came to my front door at 6 am with guns drawn to serve a warrant for my arrest. It was in front of my family. They put me in handcuffs and took me downtown to jail. They said that I was accused of robbing a bank. ROBBING A BANK? Come on! I have online banking and an ATM card. I have never been arrested before… I'm not a robber. In fact, I have not set foot inside a bank for years. The police let me go, but my criminal record cannot be erased, so there goes my life's career down the drain. It's so strange. I can no longer find decent work, and I can no longer vote. I thought I was going crazy until I learned about the plot to destroy our town and people like me. I have been falsely accused. If online data and information is so easy to manipulate, then people and the authorities should be more willing to exercise the benefit of the doubt. There should be some safeguards of common sense."

A woman carrying a Hermes Jane Birkin bag, also wearing huge black Chanel sunglasses with a makeup face to match, steps toward Peter and grabs the microphone from his hand. "I'll have you all know… I was at my favorite exclusive department store that I frequent. They told me that my payment card was denied. The bank canceled all my cards. What? No shopping? I was paralyzed as the realization set in that I could no longer shop. It's in my life's blood, you know. The thought came to me that my life was completely over. So harsh… so cruel. I can't go shopping until I get my new credit cards. That can take weeks." She cries. "Why me? I want my life back."

Nina moves forward to address the crowd. "People, we are here to get our town back and our life back." The crowd of people begin to cheer. Matt speaks out as she points to the Amphitheater.

"You see the Amphitheater over there? We are here to announce that tomorrow at 7:00 PM. We, The Toasters Club, will be presenting a plan to get our town back. It's called the Standup Concert and there will be music composed by our very own team member Lizzy and dancing by truly yours… Me. Our Agenda is to show you our plan and rally up to fight off these robot invaders."

Again, the crowd cheers as Matt continues. "People … We can do this. Together, with God's help, we are unstoppable."

Unstoppable!

CHAPTER SIXTEEN
Standup Concert!

THE TOASTERS CLUB walks on stage. The Amphitheater is packed. Everyone is rallied up. The excitement in the air overpowers the once depressing mode that the people of Beachside Park once had. Anticipation is in the air. Hamster is in the lighting control room manning the lights. Bolt is positioned in the sound room. Annie is on camera one, filming front stage. Matt has taken his camera into the crowd to catch their reaction. He is located way up in the top seats.

The lights go off, and the crowd begins to clap loudly as the Beachside Park Youth Orchestra begins a moment to tune their instruments in the orchestra bay. A spotlight shines at a point on stage… The stage is empty.

The conductor walks out, and the tuning of instruments subsides. It is quiet for a few seconds as the spotlight focuses on the conductor. Soon, the crowd begins to clap and cheer for the conductor. He takes a bow. It's Dr. Roy, the former music teacher at Beachside High School. Many are pleasantly surprised. He jesters for Lizzy (first violin) to stand. She is dressed in a long black concert dress.

The audience applauds as Lizzy quickly stands to her feet. Her appearance is surprisingly resilient and confident. It's risky to compose a song or create any sort of art, and give it to the world. What if no one likes it? This is an uneasiness entertained by any artist who creates art; however, there comes a point in time when a composer must stand and say, "I like it; therefore, it is good."

Lizzy had been composing and perfecting this song for over a year, practicing it for months. She stands confident, holding her head high. With her violin in hand, she takes a bow and quickly takes her seat. Lightly sitting down, she adjusts her position and begins her song.

The spotlight goes out for a few seconds and then back on center stage. It is now focused on Nina who has taken center stage. She is in a white ballet dress, her arms raised high with her fine fingers pointed to the sky. The audience applauds once more. She pauses, head held high.

Dr. Roy motions to Lizzy and conducts the orchestra. Lizzy's violin fills the air, giving the sweetest sound known to man. The deep drums, percussions and strings, bass, cello, viola, and violin respond in a rhythmic background, complementing Lizzy's solo. Nina takes a bow and slides to her toes, stepping in concert to the tune; her choreography reflects Lizzy's interpretation of her Sheer Steps of Hope. Lizzy's music and Nina's dance glide in concert revealing the beauty of one's imagination as what it is meant for the inspiration of mankind. That is to tap deep down into their own imaginative being and pull out the talents that God has sanctioned for true artists to share, giving it as gifts to all, to everyone in the world.

As the world holds value in its deep culture and deep reverence, the highly dedicated worship of something. Some music, not all tunes, but some certain tunes that man creates, whether purposed in reverence or captured as profane works, its sound is such that it permeates the soul of man as if God had kissed the world with His grace. After all, where does music come from? Ask any honest musician as they hear a tune in their head.

Of course, there is Garbage. In Garbage Out (GI/GO), but for the tunes that touch one's soul, it is a music that transcends language, culture, and localized knowledge to point out and remind man that there is a deep love of the true Composer who is never mad at us, but instead "crazy mad about us." As His masterpiece, he had created man to freely choose good or evil. To know Him and love him back, or not. If we as man were forced to love God, then we would not be human; we would be robots. It's our choice to freely love that makes that love so astonishing.

Lizzy strokes her last note as Nina lifts her arms and takes a gracious bow to the floor. The audience breaks into a loud cheer as the lights go on. Conductor Dr. Roy jesters to Lizzy and Nina. He applauds them and turns to the crowd to motion them to quiet. Dr. Roy begins to speak. "Folks, that song Lizzy and Nina performed is about hope. I know the world today is full of uncertainty, but songs like this remind us that there does exist a way of substance. In that, there is hope, and in this hope, we can stand-up and go through life with our heads held high. Our next Toaster has a story that I'm sure you all can relate to. Please welcome Hamster Dorfman."

The audience applauds as Hamster walks briskly on stage. He is wearing a wireless microphone headset on the right side of his face. Hamster begins to speak as he walks to the center of the stage. "Well, hello there. Hello, hello, hello, Beachside Park." Hamster begins to shout. "I'm here to proclaim. THIS TOWN IS UNDER SIEGE NO MORE" The audience immediately breaks out in loud applause. They are ready to fight and take their town back.

Hamster proceeds. "I'm sure you all heard by now. Last week, I was in a cage with Mrs. Tanizaki, Nina's mom. We were both abducted by Dr. Ott's gang of humans and hemorrhoids… um, I mean humanoids. We spent 48 hours in captivity. What I witnessed is a man who we need not fear. True, we should be cautious; he has a deep dark underground laboratory full of robots and a big control room. He also has people such as his goofy sales recruiters and technicians who help him create and maintain these robots. They have all positioned themselves against us."

"True, he has been successful in bringing our town and her people down by means of the online grid. This means that he is serious and will stop at nothing to keep is agenda going forward.

It is also true that he has the media on his side, but keep in mind that fake News has no moral compass; thus, they can be bought out. Oh, and let's not forget the band of dirty politicians, including school superintendents who have fired good teachers like Dr. Roy and replaced with their purchase of Dr. Ott's Bot-Teacher product … Well, they all crossed the line of the law. This according to my dad, who is also an attorney. Guess what he says? THEY ARE ALL GOING TO JAIL."

"From the time Dr. Ott has taken our jobs away, our security away, and even our confidence in a governing system away. We have lived in fear. Yes, this all was super crazy! But folks, even though we are dealing with a mad scientist, a robot man, one whom, for some reason, had traded in his brilliance for his thirst for power and evil. We will stand up, we will succeed, and we will be stronger than we ever were before!" The crowd applauds.

"As I close, I want to say, wasn't Lizzy's song and Nina's dance a moving piece of art?" The audience applauds and stands to their feet. It lasts for nearly a minute. Hamster motions to the audience to take their seat. As they begin to quiet down, he says. "Okay, we have one more song for you, but first, we are going to reveal our plan. I am going to invite Matt, our fellow Toaster. Please welcome Matt."

Matt takes the stage. He uses a projector to project a simple Kanban board with a handful of user stories to go over with the crowd. He points to the board and speaks.

"Okay guys, here is our Toasters Club plan: 1) Water. 2) Barricade. 3) Attitude. It's easy to remember. 1-2-3, you see? We have three things to cover so pay attention.

1) Water: We discovered that Robots have a weakness. It's called Water! Sure, you can waterproof a watch, but not a sophisticated ambient fan-cooled nonmilitary-speck robot. At some point, water will seep in and cause their power circuitry to fail."

a) Our solution is to ask you all to bring your water guns, your heavy-duty soakers, your water balloons and your water hoses and buckets. Bring them to the barricade tomorrow morning at 7 AM. Sharp."

2) Barricade: We need to secure a place and hold a position to protect our people. Dr. Ott's robots are not capable of scaling walls."

a) Our solution is to build a wall to keep out these creatures and protect the good people of Beachside Park. It will be built near this Amphitheater at the end of the park, across the dry creek bed. We need you all to bring materials such as old tires, cardboard boxes, and wooden carts. Again, bring them to the barricade tomorrow morning at 7 AM. Sharp."

3) Attitude: Don't forget your attitude. You and I have been attacked and hurt. No evil one on the other side wants to give you a peace-loving hug. These evil rulers and bots want to harm you, kill you, and completely obliterate you off the planet. I need you all to agree with this plan."

Matt continues. "As certain that bad news sells, the same is true with the gospel of despair. Yes, it is a twisted play on words, as gospel means good news, and despair means lost hope. Here's the thing. Bad news, prophecies of the world ending, and gloom and doom all cause people to despair. What happens when people entertain these thoughts? They become paralyzed by their spirit of fear. Folks, where does this type of fear come from. Good or evil? Well, who is the force? You cannot build, and you cannot fight if you lose your sound mind of judgment over to the spirit of fear. Fear is a great tactic that the enemy uses to reduce one's faith. Sure, gloom and doom attract more people and sell more books, audio, and video material."

"The bottom line is this: Choose the Force. He has attitude… in your face attitude. WE NEED ATTITUDE. And speaking about attitude, our next speaker was the head history teacher at Beachside High School until he was replaced with… you guessed it, one of Ott's Teacher-Bots.

We welcome Mr. Bryan for this short timely historical insight. Mr. Bryan, everyone…" The audience stands and cheers as Mr. Bryan makes it to the stage. He is carrying a folded white flag with him as he makes his way to the microphone. He stands and looks at the audience as they quiet down.

He begins to speak. "There comes such a time when we need to act on our intuition. For some, it is a gift of intellect; for others, it is but common sense. A sense that the risk of certain harm and destruction is at hand. Well, this is such a time. It is time to pull together and strategize. It is a time to seek wisdom."

"There was also a time in our American history when the tyrannical stronghold of King George III was unbearable. His policy of oppressive taxation was to force all Americans into absolute obedience along with the early Europeans who were persecuted in their European homeland.

They came to America in the 1620s to seek freedom of worship as separate from the political state-run religions of that time in Europe. You see, the Pilgrims came to America to escape religious persecution and build a new home of freedom. Thirty-one had gathered to make a covenant with God. It's called the Mayflower Compact. For the last 150-plus years up until the 1770's, they had tasted freedom. Now, with the threat of King George, the Americans had seen enough. With battle lines drawn, there was so much at stake.

"Revolutionists such as John Hancock cited 2 Chronicles 7:14 from the bible in a quest to urge the American revolutionaries not only to pray, but to act by repenting, humble themselves toward God, and to turn from their wicked ways, which is every man's struggle. To pray and to act.

There were also strong philosophers of the time, like the writings of John Locke in 1609, who influenced American revolutionaries like John Hancock, Thomas Jefferson, John Adams, and Benjamin Franklin. During the Revolutionary War period of 1775, paraphrased to capture its meaning today, John Locke's words went something like this: "If a group of people, or an individual, is denied their God-given freedom on earth by an overreaching government power, and they have done everything possible, yet still have no appeal on earth, they still have one thing they can do. That is to give An Appeal to heaven."

That expression took off with popularity with the American Revolutionists. Its popularity grew with lightning speed." Mr. Bryan paused for a moment and, took out the white flag and unfolded it. He then held it up for the audience to see. As he held up the flag, he concluded by saying. "I urge us all to pray, to act, and to give An Appeal to Heaven!" Mr. Bryan walks off the stage as the crowd cheers.

Matt then walks over to get his guitar as the cheering subsides. People take their seats. The other Toasters all come out on stage. Matt begins to strum his guitar while Lizzy brings her violin and begins to play the lead melody; Peter goes to the drums and joins, Hamster picks up the bass guitar and starts his riff, Bolt hits the keyboard, Nina and Annie stand in front and clap their hands. The audience responds with clapping and chanting. Nina goes to the microphone.

"This is another one that Lizzy wrote. It's a prayer song for …"

"An Appeal To Heaven!"

CHAPTER SEVENTEEN
Charge!

BUSY-BUSY BUSYNESS rocks the town of Beachside Park as the Toasters Club's idea planning takes off like a rocket. It is early the next day, before 7:00 am, and the people have already started to gather at the barricade. They are ready … Everyone is united! The excitement in the air has overpowered the stench of despair that the town once had.

Meanwhile Dr. Ott is also busy preparing for the attack. Drunk with power, he feels empowered by the support of the underground elite town government and their media, who are also high on power. They are a faceless secret society with an evil agenda to control the town and enslave its people by corralling them to a life of impoverished government dependency. Let the government be your sugar daddy! The return on this high-cost investment … Guaranteed votes!

Dr. Ott directs his gang of humans and robotic humanoids to dismantle each warehouse entry from supply drop-off to the factory floor and turn his underground laboratory into an underground fortress … a bunker.

Once complete, there will remain only two access points: One is the stealthy utility elevator access that is in the middle of the street next to the hill. It is accessed by supply trucks driving over the solid iron doors in the street. The access here has a large vertical/horizontal elevator that runs from the street level down to the shop floor. The other access is Dr. Ott's unknown personal access. It comes through the mini elevator he has in his bedroom closet. It descends from his bedroom closet into his laboratory office on the first floor, where he has access through a trap door that is activated from his command chair. In an emergency, his chair becomes a pod-like capsule and lowers into the elevator chambers from right under his desk.

Dr. Ott is now the face of evil for the people of Beachside Park, yet they also know for certain that he has been getting support. City officials, the school board, the high school principal, and the media are all suspected to have taken part in it, too. They will all be exposed soon. Now that the people know, the tide is quickly turning.

The Toasters begin to organize different groups of the townspeople into teams of teams; they are strategically positioning themselves to assemble water-weapons that destroy robots and to construct the barricade. There are community groups and businesses alike, all joining the fight. In the crowd, one can recognize some of the people. There's the "O-Lady from TacO's, Greg & Nancy from the T.V. Real Estate commercial. They had lost their dog Wolfy a while back. There is also the Wang's, Peter and Annie's mom & dad. They invited their dojo teacher and his Tie-Quan-Do Karate studio to fight. Of course, there is all the parents of the Toasters Club, including Nina's, the Tanizaki's, Hamster's parents, the Dorfman's, Bolt's mom, Matt's parents, and Lizzie's parents. They are all there to support. Janitor Ed runs up to Nina.

"Hello, Nina; where do I report?"

"Janitor Ed… you're here."

"What, after a concert like last night? You guys are the best."

"I loved Lizzy's music and Nina, your dance was out of this world."

Seeing Janitor Ed speaking with Nina, the other Toasters Club members ran over to welcome him. They give him high-fives. Annie and Lizzy give him a hug. "Well." Janitor Ed said, "what would you like for me to do?" Janitor Ed had always been very private about his past, but Nina knew something about him that not so many others in town knew about Janitor Ed's history. In Janitor Ed's former military service as U.S. Army. He came home decorated but was paralyzed from neck down after his helicopter was forced down on the very day that he was to return home to his nice Minnesota town in the U.S.

Rumors say that Janitor Ed had a nice, beautiful blond Minnesota fiancé whom he was to marry when he returned, but despite of her Minnesota niceness, she dropped him like a hot potato when she learned of his predicament. He was alone in a German hospital recovering when he got the word. It came in a package with her engagement ring. The note read. "I signed up for marriage but not to be a nurse's maid."

As a gunnery sergeant, to say that Janitor Ed was rough and tough around the edges would have been an understatement, but with this loss, being discharged from the Army, and facing a lifetime crippled. Well, let's just say that it got to him. One night in the process of his loss. While lying on his bed, he looked up in a complete moment of despair, mixed with surrender and a tiny flash of belief. "God, if you are real, then somehow show me. I'm not asking to get anything good out of the deal; I just simply need to know." Why did he ask the most dangerous and disruptive prayer one can ask? Even Janitor Ed himself couldn't explain it. The next day, he began seeing people in his hospital unit who were hurting, too, so he decided to reach out to them. First with just a smile, then with a few kind words. He never thought it was much help or any sort of big deal, but soon in his true heart, he did not feel so alone in that hospital. There were no sparks, and his legs were not better, but the next day something was different. In his own voice. His own rough, cussing but genuine military voice he says. "Whew-hew… this is Beep-N Great. YAH! This is @#%#@% so Beep-N, Beep-N, Beep-N great! Well, %$*Beep-N God… if what you say is Beep-N true, then I'm going to Beep-N enjoy my crippled, sorry little Bleep-N life. You know? It that Beep-N King of hearts? If the bible is true in all it says, then you and I are going to get to know each other. Right? You @#*&^% bet we are! Ha, ha… thank you. Hey God, did I ever tell you that you are BEEP-N-GREAT?"

Okay, okay. Nothing religious about his language. It is rough around the edges, but somewhere in his imperfection was a heart that truly cried out for mercy. Does God really see the heart of man? Doctors said Janitor Ed would never walk again, but he still wanted to believe. Where did that belief come from? In 6 months, he was not only walking, but he was also running. In 8 months, he checked out and fully recovered. Was it a miracle or just a coincidence? It depends on who you ask. Nina turned to Janitor Ed and addressed him by his former military rank. "Master Sergeant Ed… grab a heavy-duty squirt gun and report to the barricade on the eastside."

Janitor Ed took a stand at attention and saluted the Toasters Club. Whoa, Nina and the Toasters were totally blown away by the weight and honor of what Master Sergeant Ed, a true hero, had just done. He took off for the east side and caught up with the others on the barricade, ready for battle.

More people showed up, including Beachside Dance, the Community Center, Beachside Chamber of Commerce, Beachside Park Youth Orchestra, Beachside High School Theater Glee Club, Beachside Swim Team, The Fire Department, Western Car Wash, and Beachside Agile Coffee Chapter, to name a few.

Each team worked together in collaboration and cooperation. Some constructed the barricade across the dry creek bed with tires and wooden crates. Others use water hoses to fill up water guns, heavy-duty soakers, and buckets of water balloons and to distribute the supplies across the line. The logistics are astounding. It resembles military operations. The Toasters Club formed various teams and showed them how to work together as self-organized, cross-functional teams. With each team working brilliantly in unison, they set out to complete the task with agility, following battlefield logistics by producing water-filling stations and positioning water weapons and supplies across the barricade. Nina, Annie, Peter, and Hamster begin documenting this big day. Annie and Peter begin filming while Nina narrates. "Today is a day of independence. Just like in 1776' when a tyrannical kingdom tried to over-tax and oppress its people. Here, too, an underground evil empire armed with robotic job warriors, these evil elites used a strategy to use state-controlled education, media propaganda, and massive job loss as a tool to weaken the people."

Nina points out how these perpetrators and evil-doers took advantage of a good economic crisis.

The lie was simple to sell with the media never mentioning true job statistics or any of the evil doings that the dark side was committing, such as punishing businesses for growing and hiring and rewarding institutions for laying off people and hiring robots. Individuals were confused to think that their job loss and inability to find decent professional work was their own fault. It happened as more and more decent jobs went to the robots, and the economic power of the people weakened. This is the perfect status of the people according to the dark mindset of the evil Scientist, Dr. Ott, and his rogue elite government officials. "But the one thing Dr. Ott and his evil-doers were not anticipating", Nina cites. "Was the strong will of the people. A people who eventually found the strength to stand and say: We will not be slaves again!"

Yes, Dr. Ott and his evil gang miscalculated the will of the people, which they cannot take away. With that, the people will rise up, so they must keep the people down. Panning across the barricade, Annie captures the look of people's faces as they all work together to get their lives back. Annie focuses the camera back on Nina as she continues to narrate. "People of the town have gone through a lot" says Nina. "They now just want something to go right for once. Looking into their faces, you know they believe. What you see is a people who will not give up. The town's people are ready to fight."

As smoke fills the sky, the teams of people, residents of Beachside Park, all join in on the battle line to fight. On the opposite side of the barricade, Dr. Ott, sitting in his control room, sets command for his robots to assemble. They move through the shop floor and ascend through the elevator to the street exit where multiple buses are all parked in a row waiting to transport them. Rows of robots' step into the large white busses and are taken to the barricade, where they take-up position in a straight line as the battlefield builds up. Dr. Ott views the barricade through the eye-cams of his robots. "What are these people doing?" Says Dr Ott as he views the screen in his lab. He pounds the desk with his fist. "Do these so-called weekend warriors in business suits really think they can protect their town and outsmart me?"

Dr. Ott, in his moment of madness, stands from his chair. "They will never succeed! With their toy guns in one hand and their balloons in the other, these schoolboys & girls will all rot in hell. They will never succeed … Aha-ha, ha, ha. Aha-ha, ha-ha, ha, ha!"

It is 12 noon. People on the barricade are prepared to fight. Matt says,

"Hey, let's get our 30 caliber semi-automatic rifles and ammo to position them nearby."

Nina cuts Matt off. "No. Keep them hidden instead. We don't need them anymore."

"You mean to use our toy water pistols instead?" Matt, Bolt, Peter, and Hamster look puzzled.

"Matt, everyone… Trust me on this. I don't have time to explain."

"Let's go."

The Toasters Club crew grab their portable film equipment and ride their bikes to a position for the film shoot. Nina gets out her drone camera and catches footage of the barricade as they go. Bolt and Lizzy find a spot to edit. Things are getting active along the barricade. Although they have never fought before, they all sense the time for battle is near. The Toasters Park, their bikes, quickly stand and form a circle to huddle.

"Okay, let's put this film together and send it out live." Says Nina.

"Hamster, stay here and monitor the feed once I post it live."

"Roger that, Nina."

Matt speaks out. "Hey, Bolt and Peter, come with me."

"Let's go to that bolder over there and stand watch."

Meanwhile, on the barricade in the face of a certain battle, the people of the town spread out side-by-side along the barricade with courage on their faces and uncertainty in their stomachs; they build up their voices as the moment to charge nears. Mr. Brian is passing out the white flags, stating, "An Appeal to Heaven." On the other side stands Dr. Ott on the field in a safe position to command the battle. He is with Nate and his group of political thugs. He pans the battlefield with his Binoculars.

"Looky, Looky, Looky" says Dr. Ott. "Those fools are waving white flags to surrender. Are you surrendering so soon, you dupes? Guy's, take no prisoners. Crush them. Ah-ha-ha. Nate, looking through binoculars, says, "those aren't flags of surrender, boss." Dr. Ott, still looking through his binoculars, says, "Oh, now what is this? What is that stupid Christmas tree doing on the flag? Who are these guys on the frontline? Santa's little special elves? Nate says. "They are not positioned to surrender, sir." Dr. Ott pounds his fist; "HEY. I WANT A REAL FIGHT. Game over. We will perform the three C's on these goody two shoes." "The three C's Boss?" Says Nate. "Capture, Cook, and Consume. I am so looking forward to crushing these low-brain-e-acts. Advance… ADVANCE!

Dr. Ott escapes off the battlefield and heads to his deep underground laboratory office in what is now his bunker to continue the fight at the command center of controls. On the good side of the barricade, the people begin to see a formation of drones appearing on the horizon. Dr. Ott's voice can be heard over his hovercraft drone speakers that he placed across the sky just shy of the barricade. As his drones fly past, Dr. Ott uses his megaphone over the drones that are carrying his voice, amplified over each of the drones' loudspeakers.

"We're going to rain down terror on you. Stop what you are doing now, or you will be toast." The recording annoyingly repeats itself. "We're going to rain down terror on you. Stop what you are doing now, or you will be toast." In the distance, one can hear Dr. Otts muffled voice as it echoes the same message over and over again. And again.

Not shaken in the slightest but instead fed-up, a man on the border raises his high-powered soaker squirt gun to the sky and takes aim. He points it in the air toward one of Dr. Ott's loudspeaker drones hovering over them on the barricade and shoots. Out comes a highly charged stream of water directly toward the drone. The secret water weapon hits the drone dead center and knocks it completely out of the sky. The drone falls lifelessly to the ground. Everything gets quiet for a moment. What just happened? Matt stands up and walks over to the broken drone. He picks it up and then looks over at Nina. "I see what you mean, Nina." In spontaneous unison, a loud cheer bursts from the crowd. "Hey. Did you see that?" Said a voice in the crowd. "Hooray!"

Excitement is in the atmosphere. The noise is very loud as the crowd of voices on the barricade yelling and clapping for joy. Soon, the others begin to fill their secret high-powered soakers and shoot at the drones. One by one, they knock them all out of the sky. The noise of the people cheering on the barricade gets louder and louder and louder as they rally in unison.

Matt jumps up. "Let's film this live for our online audience."

"Yes, we got to go. It's happening. We got to go now." Says Nina.

"Help me get the cameras and film equipment."

The Toasters Club members get to position and begin documenting the battle just in time. They take a position as suddenly, like clockwork, a line of robots begin to advance toward the barricade in attack mode. The people begin to take positions at the barricade to fight. The noise gets louder as the people rally in unison. Together, they shout in one strong, united voice. "... CHARGE!!!"

In a flash, buckets of ice water are hoisted up and dumped on the advancing robots. Jets of water rain down as the front line of high-power water gun sharp shooters turn their attention to the advancing robots. Right away the robots take casualties as "fizz-bam, fizz-bam, fizz-bam-bang." The water shorts out their electronic power units and a puff of white electrical smoke sparks out of a robot's head as it falls limp to the ground. Decommissioned. Some robots fall right away, and others retreat, unaffected by the missed attempts to squirt them down.

The Toasters Club members are positioned in different areas with cameras to document the fight. Annie films Nina as she reports the battle. They catch the first exchange, all on camera with robots falling to the ground. Nina looks at the camera and screams. "It works … Yah!" The Toaster's cheer and excitement grows among the people on the barricade; however, down on one side, the robots find a weak area in the barricade. They begin to dismantle it as Dr. Ott directs more robots to go to that weak area in the wall and help. Janitor Ed sees the robots rushing over to dismantle the barricade. "Break out the Water Balloons." He shouts.

Lizzy runs. She gets to the scene to rebuild the wall just as the robots successfully break through. The barricade collapses on her as she screams. Bolt, Matt, Peter, and Hamster drop their cameras and run to help Lizzy. The robots begin to grab Lizzy as they block the attempt to rescue her. Bolt jumps over them and runs directly toward Lizzy without hesitation. He dips over to the box of water balloons and scoops up 4 balloons without stopping. One water balloon flips out of his hand and fly's up over the heads of the crowd of people who had come to help. It spins out of control as in slow motion and lands right on top of the O-Lady's head. Friendly Fire! She screams and falls to the ground as her makeup runs off her face. All except the big "O" tattoo around her lips. She rolls and jumps right back up … Laughing! The O-Lady shouts, "O, O, Oooo, it's Cold."

At the same time, Bolt reaches Lizzy as she struggles to break free from the robots. He jumps high in the air and douses the Robots with the 3 remaining water balloons. "Direct hit … Splash 1, splash 2, and splash 3." Yells Bolt. Two robots spin-off Lizzy. Their heads immediately explode in an electrical fire. The third robot is still trying to hang on to Lizzy. It got wet, but for some reason, it managed to escape the water from saturating its vital components. That is until it turns its head to the left while attacking Lizzy. This caused the water to flood directly into its right ear canal. The robot experiences a flash of light as the water shorts out its circuitry between voltage (VCC) and ground (GND).

Again, as in slow motion, with its mechanical arms still loosely around Lizzy, she gets a good look at the robot's eyes as its head illuminates like a Christmas tree. Kaboom! With a binary brain, there is no real life. It's either one or zero… on or off. Its eyes show no emotion. Lizzy notes that the bot had no fear of its impending death, no understanding of its state of being. Its legs just collapse under the weight of its limp, powerless body. It falls straight down to the ground, now with its arms in a circle around Lizzy's feet. She steps over the robot's arms and gives a hard backward kick to the bot's head as she breaks free. Nina and Annie caught the whole thing on film. They reach Lizzy to help. Lizzy runs over to Bolt and gives him a big hug.

"Wow. That was great."

"You nailed those buggers."

"Thank you so much, Bolt."

Still embraced, Bolt begins to feel dizzy. She smiles as Bolt raises his shoulders and shrugs it off as if it was no big deal.

"Man, I thought you were a goner little Dude. I mean Dudette."

"Lizzy. I mean little Lizzy Dudette."

Bolt pats Lizzy on the head, which she really hates. She starts to say something about it, but just then, Hamster yells out to the Toasters.

"Guys, look, look over there."

Hamster points across the field to where Dr. Ott had commissioned a new wave of robots to assemble and charge. Dr. Ott had positioned hundreds more of his robots to line the field. As he is looking at the battle taking place in the comfort of his plush office chair, he studies the positions of the people through the bot-cam displayed on his large screen TV in the control room of his deep underground bunker. Dr. Ott sees a perfect opening in the broken-down wall where the Toasters are and where he now has access to defeat the Toasters Club and the Townspeople. The time is now to end the battle and crush the town for good. "Oh, this is perfect." Dr. Ott says out loud. "It is perfect. I got them now … Ahh, ha, ha, ha."

Dr. Ott stands up to give his command, and suddenly, he sees his mom driving her car near the barricade. It's a very large car. One can barely see the top of her curly, permed grey head of hair, her arms spread wide grasping the steering wheel like a biker reaching for the handlebars of his chopper. Her eyes peeking over the huge steering wheel. She is driving a large late-model American sedan.

It is grocery shopping day at Otty's house, and because of the barricade, Dr. Otts mom had to go around to find a place to park. She stops her car, gets out and goes to the back of the car to pull out her roller portable shopping cart. She unfolds it and with the portable roller cart trailing behind her, she beelines past the squads of robots toward the town's grocery store. Completely in her own world. The battle goes on hold as Dr. Ott's mom, an old woman, walks with her grocery cart across the battle line. Dr. Ott stops, his robots stop, the towns people stop, the Toasters Club and everyone on the battle line stops.

Dr. Ott's mom walks by with her shopping cart, completely unaware of the battle. Completely unmindful of all the people lined-up on the barricade. Completely oblivious to the hundreds of robots in line ready to advance, and the multitudes of towns people in battle ready to take their town back from the robots. She slowly walks by, as everyone admires her determination to go grocery shopping at this time.

Unfortunately for her, all the stores, including the grocery store that she is headed for, are closed for the battle today. Matt, not knowing that this is Dr. Ott's mom, thinks instead that she is in great danger, so he makes a quick decision to jump through the weak part of the barricade and go rescue her. He runs swiftly through the creak on the enemy side just as Dr. Ott's mom gets to the Beachside Food Market and tugs on the locked doors. She looks through the windows and then looks at her watch. She taps and plays with her watch for a while and then walks up to the store door again and knocks on it. Dr. Ott's mom peaks through the store windows to see if anyone is around. It is dark inside. Matt finally makes it to her at the storefront. Hello mam. Mam? She looks up at Matt. "Yes, sunny boy." "Mam, the store is closed today." What. Closed?" "Yes mam, in fact all the stores are closed today, mam." "Why? New Year's Day is not for another week." "Yes, mam. Let me help you back to the car." Matt carries her folded shopping cart. Dr. Ott's mom turns around and heads back to her car with Matt's help. Everyone on the barricade watches as she crosses the battlefield and gets back to her car with Matt's help. He places the portable shopping cart in the trunk for her and waves her off. Dr. Ott's mom drives away as Matt makes his way back crossing the battlefield, then crawling through the opening in the broken point of the weakened barricade.

As he makes it back through, Matt looks at the blocks of wooden boxes crumbled at the barricade and says, "Hurry, hurry. Help me repair the wall." The Toasters desperately try and rebuild the wall as Dr. Ott's robot's advance. They quickly call attention to the townspeople fighting along the wall. Many come over to join them in rebuilding the wall. Dr. Ott sees this weak point of the barricade now fixed. His window of opportunity is gone. He decides to target that very area, anyway, systematically sending waves of warbots and war-dogbots to that very spot. Dr. Ott gives the command. "Advance to the barricade and get those people."

The robots march to the barricade and ram into it. Mr. Wang looks down at the barricade and sees the predicament. He quickly organizes his fellow karate group to grab a supply of water balloons and toss them to the advancing robots. They lob the water balloons at the charging robots. Suddenly a metallic colored fiber cylinder rises vertically from the right hand of each charging robot. The balloons arch downward for a direct hit; however, the robots place their thumb over a small button on the cylinder and out flips an umbrella, just in time to meet the balloons. Splash!

Only a small group of robots on the back row get hit as a flash of water ricochets off the last row of umbrellas and slides right in-between the umbrellas in a 30-degree downward angle. Water forcefully splashes directly into the faces of the last row of robots. The force drenches them. They immediately fall to the ground and explode in an electrical parade of sparks and smoke. Mr. Wang yells out.

"I love the smell of burnt electric circuits in the afternoon."

The Toasters Club and others at that part of the barricade immediately retreat as the robots forcefully break through the barricade. Mr. Wang's karate group grabs another supply of water balloons and launches them at the robots, but as the robots bust through, they begin chasing the Toasters and the others. Hamster thinks to himself, how clever of Dr. Ott to quickly adapt his robots right on the battlefield and fend off the oncoming water weapons. Hamster yells out to the team. "Exercise Plan B. Exercise Plan B. Plan B"

Just then, the swim team runs over to the pool in the park. They open-up the pool area. Nina's dad drives the firetruck forward to give chase to the robots. The entire town comes in on both sides of the firetruck, lobbing water balloons and shooting heavy-duty water guns. They manage to corral the robots, now totaling two dozen, toward the pool area. The firemen begin to spray their large firehose alongside the robots to channel them into the pool area. The firehose is attached to the top of the fire truck. This action of the towns people leaves the robots no choice but to march directly into the pool area. It's the last wave of robots. The robots give pause as the entire town points their water weapons at them.

Dr. Ott, still in the control room, sees his predicament. He's Lost! Surrounding the robots, everyone in the battle converges toward the pool, shooting water guns and dumping boxes of water balloons on them. They push Dr. Ott's last standing robots into the pool. "We did it!" Says Nina.

People begin to dive into the pool and with the robot carcass descending to the bottom of the pool, they begin jumping in. Splashing and performing cannon balls of victory! The entire town comes out and celebrates their Independence. The Independence of Beachside Park.

The Toasters Club gathers to do their high-five group hug. Alright Team. Toasted! Matt is smiling ear to ear. Hamster jumps up and down for joy. Annie, all smiles and completely drenched takes out a small handkerchief to dry off her glasses. Peter borrows Annie's handkerchief, so he too can dry-off his glasses and see. He takes Bolt's hand and shakes it. Bolt in turn shakes his wet-head and gets Peters glasses all wet again. Lizzy keeps mummering. "I can't believe it. I can't believe it. You guys … We did it!' Nina, gains her composure and says, "Alright Toasters Club … What's next?"

Matt, Peter, Hamster, Annie, Bolt, Lizzy, and Nina all look at each other with excitement. Peter says. "You know what is on our plate.? The Homework Processor App." The Toasters Club says in unison.

"It's our next cash box."

"Cool, let's do it!"

"You guys are crazy." says Nina.

Nina looked over at Matt. Not wanting to reveal what she was really feeling, she said.

"Hey Matt. I saw you helping that old woman… Cool!"

Outwardly Matt stayed cool by replying. "Thanks."

But inwardly, it was "Oh wow, she saw that? Wah Hoo, big smiles everyone!"

What Nina really felt, she kept inside. It went something like this… "Now, that's my Hero."

Meanwhile deep in the dark underground laboratory bunker. Dr. Ott, turns off the big Screen T.V. in his control room, defeated. He directs his gang in the lab to drop what they are doing and get out! Dr. Ott then takes his hand and slams the RED KILL BUTTON. His gang knows that as soon as he hits the red kill button, they have 15 minutes to clear the lab and get out. Dr. Ott's evil gang-members all quickly head for the elevator that ascends to the street. There are only five evil gang members left. The others had ditched Dr. Ott days ago when they saw that the people were beginning to fight back.

Dr. Ott's gang members all get out to the street level. An orange dump truck pulls up to the spot where the heavy iron doors are still open on the street. The dump truck has a mysterious orange paint texture with tented glass so that no one can look in and see who is driving. Cleanup Man? It dumps several tons of smelting asphalt into the elevator shaft and drives away just as another truck pulls up. Again, with heavy tented glass. It's equipped with an open trailer carrying a heavy street roller.

The evil gang watches the heavy roller as its automatically controlled rollers pack the asphalt to street level. It takes just seconds for such as small hole. It bumps the iron doors on street level, and they close over the newly patched hole … Sealed. Within seconds, an unmarked white bus drives up to the newly patched spot and picks up the entire evil gang including Nate, Fetch, and Principal Spinner standing on the curb. They all escape. Their white bus joins up with the other white buses that are all lined up and driving out of town. The buses slip out of town while the people of Beachside Park are distracted by their victory.

Deep in the underground lab, Dr. Ott takes one last look at his crumbling empire. He sits down in his office chair and begins to reflect on how he lost the Town of Beachside Park. "Why, why, why?" Suddenly Dr. Ott is shaken by the lab alarm. Time is up! He jumps in, buckles up, and presses the button on the office chair to activate his escape. The chair immediately turns into a capsule pod. His desk slides open, and off he goes. His capsule glides through and is thrusted upward above the lab toward his bedroom closet and stops. He unbuckles and walks out and into his bedroom unharmed. Just then a large explosion takes place in the lab underneath. The earth shakes, but the explosion is muffled by the earths underground buffer; after all, the explosion charge is measured to only be enough to cut off all the power generators. It is also to sever and cut all internet connections, thus, isolating and sealing the lab completely off. It feels like a small earthquake, a California tremor.

Dr. Ott's mom is back in the kitchen. "Otty, did you feel that? Otty?" Dr. Ott opens his bedroom door and walks into the kitchen, where his mom is sitting at the table speaking through the intercom loudspeaker. "No need to be speaking through the intercom Mom. Look, I'm right here." "I think it was a 4.0," says Dr. Ott's mom. Just then, a white bus drives up Dr. Ott's long driveway and up to his front door. It parks, making an airbrake sound and opens its door.

"Hey mom, what do you think about taking a vacation in Mexico?"

"Wonderful idea Otty, I'll pack my bag."

"That's already taken care-of mom. Come with me. Let's go."

With the automated bot-bus parked in Dr. Ott's driveway, an assistant steps out of the bus to escort Dr. Ott and his mom onto the big white unmarked bus. It closes its doors and shifts gears to back out of Dr. Otts driveway, then onto the main road to disappear. Just like in the past with those white government buses as they traveled from the Mexican border to disappear across the nation. Except, in this case, Dr. Otts white buses are headed south on I5, toward the Mexican border. It is fascinating and clever how Dr. Otts white busses also vanish. First, they activate automated automobiles to drive in front of all the freely flowing traffic headed southbound along the coast on the San Diego freeway. This causes a major traffic jam for no reason. Very common in California. As the traffic is closed off, the white buses drive onto a southbound freeway ramp located just a few miles down the road. Once the white buses had cleared 10 miles down the San Diego freeway, the automatic automobiles were channeled off a ramp so that the traffic could flow once again. Like the lines at Disneyland, it's called crowd control. Totalitarian States like California have lots of crowd control systems.

Dr. Ott's white buses have all crossed the border. They were the last bus seen by border patrol on the freeway south of a huge border wall that was recently completed. They are now headed further south into Mexico....

Vanished!

Aftermath . . .

That evening, victory was celebrated in an incredible way. Right after victory was established, they cheered and, in unison, began cleaning up the town. It was Christmas Eve. An amazing sight as everyone sang Christmas songs, no matter their core ethos. It was in the spirit of praise to the living God that they all experienced a great miracle. A new beginning! Joining together, they worked. They picked up and tossed out the debris of war. They broke down the barricade and hung up Christmas lights. Pools of plastic Christmas ordainments came to life. The town's Christmas tree was raised, and the nativity scene was reconstructed near the main road.

One would think that Christmas gifts after a war would be slim. They were, but this was neither the focus of the parents nor the children of Beachside Park. Instead, gifts of thankfulness toward what God has done. A restoration of faith and meaning of the celebration of the birth of Jesus. The children of Beachside Park woke up to a Christmas that will always be remembered.

Later in the new year, the local TV station was set to broadcast The Toasters Club's pre-recorded documentary on the battle of the bots. The entire town has been waiting for it to air. With his widescreen on, Janitor Ed sits and adjusts his lazy chair in the living room to extend its footstool. He picks up his bowl of popcorn from the side table with his eyes fixed on the TV screen. The Toasters Club documentary of the "Battle of Beachside Park" begins. The film starts off with Nina in focus.

Sitting in his easy chair, Janitor Ed says to himself. "Hey … I know that girl." His dog looks up at him and wags his tail, then turns back to watch TV. Janitor Ed found him while walking along the beach over 100 miles from town. He calls him "Wolf" as he could only make out the first 3 letters of his broken, chewed-up, dog tag … W-O-L. Janitor Ed assumed the "F" was missing from his broken dog tag. The Toasters Club's documentary begins to air as Janitor Ed pops a fist full of popcorn into his mouth. He picks up his remote and turns up the sound.

The Toasters Club documentary shows clips of the Beachside Parks battle scene. It fades to how Beachside Park looks today. Nina starts by announcing the Toasters Club program. "Hello, this is Nina, and we are the Toasters Club. It has been three months since the battle and disappearance of Dr. Ott and his Bots. I thought that you would like to know how the town of Beachside Park has been doing since that day. I also thought that you would like to find out what the Toasters Club is up to these days.

"After the battle, the people of Beachside Park pulled together. They are highly involved with draining the swamp of local corruption. No more will they allow a Mad Scientist and his AI bots to sneak in and exploit this town or another town in America. The US Military stepped in, and trials were set. Principal Spinner, multiple school board members, and many city officials are facing jail time for treason." Janitor Ed stands at attention with popcorn flying out of the bowl. Standing, he says, "I salute you, Nina, and the Toasters Club."

Wolf looks at him and wags his tail. Wolf thinks to himself… I'm so glad to have a joyful home. Janitor Ed reaches down and pets Wolf on the head. He then sits back down in his chair. Nina continues her narration. She speaks about the cleaning that happened within the news media. Two local T.V. stations went out of business today. Some say the blame was due to the shift in online media that caused the lost ratings, but we all know that these TV networks had washed out content.

Here, instead of informing the public, they set out to influence the public. With lies and evil narrations,' they skipped research and the true validation of their own sources. Finally, the media was top-heavy with managers who had absolutely no imagination or desire to build a workplace environment that inspired workers to be creative and the best that they could be at their craft. People simply stopped watching! Instead, they turned on to the new wave of high-quality online internet T.V. stations with creative homegrown studios. They have been popping up across the country to fill the void. These studios maintain the responsibility to show content that carries fresh and tasteful-oriented entertainment as the TV and motion picture industry reinvented itself with a technique of real-time customer feedback and self-regulated sponsorship, ratified against the corruption of censorship. Here, the news was held responsible by independent feedback. This is still in play; however, it's discovery is looking progressive. And it is this quality that we bring to you today on our Toasters Club channel.

Nina takes her microphone and walks over to introduce her parents and the other parents of the Toasters Club, who have gathered to watch live. Sitting in the first row are Nina's parents. Her dad looks awkward as he sits in his chair. Next to them are the Wangs, the Dorfmans, Lizzy's parents, Bolt's mom, and Matt's parents. Camera one follows Nina as she thanks them for supporting the Toasters Club. The Toasters Club breaks out in loud applause.

Mr. Wang stands up. "I have something to say." Nina passes the microphone to Mr. Wang. "Folks, every parent has a dream to see their children grow up and do much better than we have. Yet, in these recent days this dream was under threat. Crushed by the lust for power perpetrated by a mad scientist and his cronies. I am so glad to see that this evil had met a major blocker in our Children, the Toasters Club! It was their bravery, ingenuity, and enterprising spirit, together with God's hand, that put this madness to end. They say that generational wealth is passed on to the children. Well, the measure of wealth witnessed today included innovation, creativity, wisdom, and bravery. This measure our kids hold is indeed a measure of wealth that will last a lifetime."

Again, Janitor Ed stands at attention. With popcorn now all over the floor, we can hear it crush beneath his feet and through his toes as he says, "Right on Mr. Wang… right on!" The Toasters Club channel reads 5,197,947,112 viewers now watching this streaming documentary as it airs. It has gained much worldwide interest since the struggle! Yes, the entire town of Beachside Park, across America, and even around the world, is watching Nina and the Toasters documentary. The title of this documentary is: Real or Robot? How Beachside caught on and stood up to evil.

The video feed cuts to a commercial on the latest Toasters Club product … It's the Toasters Club Homework App. It went viral, right after the Toasters Club produced it and launched it to market. They were able to get some investors to help boost the product. Nina finishes her narration with this word. " The conclusion of Real or Robot? How did

Beachside catch on and stand up to Dr. Ott? It has only been three months, but so much in the town has come alive. The great people of Beachside are feeling empowered. School clubs of action are popping up all around. People in general, want to know how to do stuff. Many are inspired to form clubs of their own. Clubs for Music, Dance, History, Software Code, Structure Architecture, Web App Development, Filming, Writing, and Creative Design Thinking are gaining in popularity across the nation."

It is happening across the nation; people are starting their own Action Clubs with mission-minded Small Groups, business builders focused on generating local jobs, and organizations hosting sessions on Family Core Values, thus repurposing their outreaches with the power of framework; Ideate – Sprint – Growth coupled with the power of teamwork. People from all over are coming to visit Beachside Park, reviving its tour industry where this was once dead. This great victory has placed them on the map as a worldwide destination. Jobs have also come back to the town.

Best of all, Beachside Park High School is back to normal. All the former teachers have come back, including Dr. Roy, Mr. Bryan and even Mr. Dunn where science class is as usual; however, there seems to be an openness to discuss scientific views outside the theory of Darwinism. In fact, his new slogan is. "Keep closed minds outside the door, Science is for open minds that want to explore."

The Toasters Club documentary concludes. Moments later, the TV screen in Janitor Ed's living room fades to black. Janitor Ed had fallen asleep in his easy chair during the commercial. The room gets quiet. It's a small, cozy room with one wall displaying a clock and the other wall showcasing his military decorations. Unknown to Janitor Ed, his dog Wolf, formerly known as Wolfy, gets up. He uses his teeth to pick up the TV channel control from the armrest of Janitor Ed's easy chair. And sets the channel changer down on the floor. He then lifts-up his paw and presses down on the button…

OFF!

The End

www.ingramcontent.com/pod-product-compliance
Lightning Source LLC
Chambersburg PA
CBHW040138160726
48006CB00014B/1540